KAHLESS TURNED TO PICARD AND WORF. "THERE IS TREACHERY AFOOT," HE SNARLED.

"Treachery which will tear apart the Klingon™ Empire, if left to run its course."

"From what quarter?" Picard inquired.

"The Klingon Defense Force is undertaking a military coup designed to unseat Gowron and the rest of the council." The emperor grunted. "I know because I overheard two of the conspirators whispering in a dining hall in Tolar'tu, during the festival of Maur'tek."

Picard looked at him skeptically. "But the leaders of the Defense Force were handpicked by Gowron. They have sworn to defend him with their very lives."

Kahless's eyes blazed. "That," he told the human, his voice thick with revulsion, "is why they call it treachery."

KAHLESS

MICHAEL JAN FRIEDMAN

POCKET BOOKS

New York   London   Toronto   Sydney   Tokyo   Singapore

POCKET BOOKS, a division of Simon & Schuster Inc.
1230 Avenue of the Americas, New York, NY 10020

A VIACOM COMPANY

STAR TREK is a Registered Trademark of Paramount Pictures.

This book is published by Pocket Books, a division of Simon & Schuster Inc., under exclusive license from Paramount Pictures.

ISBN: 0-671-00887-0

First Pocket Books paperback printing March 1997

10 9 8 7 6 5 4 3 2 1

POCKET and colophon are registered trademarks of Simon & Schuster Inc.

Printed in the U.S.A.

For Valerie Elyse, who was worth the wait

Acknowledgments

In some ways *Kahless* is a homecoming for me. You see, before I began writing *Star Trek* novels almost ten years ago, I broke into the field with a bunch of heroic fantasy books.

Most of them were based on Norse mythology, my personal favorite. They were tales of romance and high adventure set against a backdrop of cosmic significance. And I don't feel the least bit guilty plugging them, because they're all out of print.

What's more, I hadn't written anything even vaguely like them since. Until I got the idea for *Kahless,* that is.

Wouldn't it be fun, I wondered, to tell a heroic fantasy story in the *Star Trek* universe? And what better place to do that than on Qo'noS (yup, that's an uppercase "S" on the end), home of those grim and bloodthirsty Klingons?

Mind you, it wasn't the first time I'd dug into the Klingon mythos. A couple of years ago, I wrote a four-issue set for DC Comics called "Shadowheart," which dealt with the tension between Worf's Klingon heritage and his upbringing among humans. And even before that, I took aim at Klingon treachery and ambition in the original-series book *Faces of Fire*.

In other words, I wasn't completely new to this. Still, I have to admit, I wasn't quite prepared for the magnitude of the undertaking.

The thing is, I wasn't the first person to be fascinated by those fun-loving guys with the bumps on their heads. Certainly, Ronald D. Moore and Rene Echevarria vastly expanded our knowledge of Klingon lore as writers for the *Next Generation* TV show—and they were hardly the only ones.

So much had been written about Klingons on TV and in the movies, doing my preproposal research made me feel like I was working toward a doctorate. So much triumph and tragedy, so little time.

Anyway, I managed to get it all in here, or just about all—the myriad little tidbits that shaped our understanding of Worf's race. There were a few things that just didn't seem to fit, like the time Kahless plowed his father's field with his *bat'telh*, or that business about the wind at Quin'lat. But you'll find just about everything else.

So now comes the part where I thank everyone who helped me on my way to *Sto-Vo-Kor* (or was it *Gre'thor?*). Like a gumshoe in a classic mystery novel, I find myself lining up all the usual suspects.

Kevin Ryan, editor nonpareil, had the brilliance to buy this book. That alone would have earned him a place on this page. But on top of that, he stretched me on the rack of editorial privilege until I creaked and groaned and invoked the Geneva Accord . . . and finally turned out something he wasn't entirely embarrassed to publish.

John Ordover, Kevin's right-hand man, is a font of Klingon information. If I could write one-hundredth as fast as John can read, oh how prolific I'd be then!

As usual, Bob Greenberger did his best to distract me from my writing with every manner of diversion known to man. But that was important too. One needs to keep a perspective on one's work. Just ask the Jack Nicholson character in *The Shining*.

Paula Block of Paramount's licensing department doesn't get nearly as much recognition as she deserves— at least, from the average reader. Of course, we writers recognize her. A bright and personable woman, she works hard behind the scenes to make sure what we turn out has the ring of authenticity to it. And in all the time I've worked with her, I've never seen her quash an idea for continuity reasons if there was even half a chance of salvaging it.

I should also thank my friend Phillip Alder and my brother-in-law Keith Ditkowsky for their technical support vis-a-vis my computer programs. No computer, no writing; no writing, no books. So thanks, guys. And remember, a mention in the acknowledgment section is always a lot nicer than actual remuneration.

My mom and dad . . . what can I say? It was nice being raised by you, but it's kind of nice being an adult too. Now I can tell you about all the things I put over on you all those years. Like those stomachaches I used to get on Tuesdays and Thursdays when it was time for Hebrew School? Faked 'em. Every last one of 'em. Sorry about that.

And while we're on the subject of child rearing . . .

everyone should have kids like mine. At an early age, both Brett and Drew learned that when Daddy's working, he's to be left alone. Of course, they ignore that rule every chance they get. But I find some small consolation in the fact that they at least know which rule they're breaking.

Finally, there's my wife Joan. When I'm up against a horrific deadline, often of my own making, I turn to her and beg for pity. And invariably, I get it. Joan picks up the slack, taking care of everything else in our lives, while I chain myself to my desk. And when the book is done and people are marveling at my dedication, only Joan and I know who really deserves the credit. (Though I guess you know it now, too.)

So there we have it. But before I go, I'll leave you with one last bit of Klingon advice. *"qaStaHvIS wa' ram loS SaD Hugh SIjlaH qetbogh Ilod."* Translation: "Four thousand throats may be cut in one night by a running man."

Don't look at me. I don't know what it means either.

Michael Jan Friedman
Port Washington, New York
February 1996

HISTORIAN'S NOTE

This story takes place in the eighth year of Jean-Luc Picard's command of the *Enterprise*-D—after the events chronicled in *All Good Things* . . . and prior to those described in *Star Trek Generations*.

PROLOGUE

In ancient times, there was a road here.

But that was more than a thousand years ago, long after the end of the so-called heroic age. The rolling terrain had long since been claimed by flowering brush and snaking vines and a dense forest of gray-and-yellow-streaked *micayah* trees.

Which made it all the more difficult to excavate, thought Olahg, as he watched a half-dozen workmen finish clearing a stand of *micayah* with their hand tools. They could have used disruptors, but this forest was prized by those Klingons who lived in the vicinity, and it wouldn't be a good idea to cut down any more of it than they absolutely had to.

The clerics of Boreth, of whom Olahg counted himself a member, had plied the High Council for years to obtain permission to dig here. If they hoped to excavate other sacred sites, other locations where Emperor Kahless had walked, it was critical that they treat *this* place with respect.

By the time the work crew was done with Olahg's appointed, twelve-meter-square plot, the *micayah* were gone. So were the mosses and shrubs and flowering plants that had grown in the spaces between them. All that was left was the pungent smell of *micayah* sap, unraveling in the wakening breeze to the shrill protest of distant treehens.

The foreman of the crew stood up straight. Turning to Olahg, he grinned through his sweat and his long black beard. A Klingon's Klingon, he had a brow heavy with thick hornlike ridges.

"How's that, Brother? Clean enough for you? Or shall I cut the rest away with a *dagger?*"

The initiate swallowed, dismayed by the foreman's gravelly voice and broad shoulders. "It is clean enough," he confirmed, and watched the crew move to the next designated section, where another cleric awaited them.

Olahg sighed. He had never been one for confrontation. Nor was he built for it, with his skinny limbs and his slight, fragile frame.

Certainly, that quality had not made his life easy. It had caused him to fall from favor with his father rather early in his youth, and all but ensured him a desk job in some deadly-dull Klingon bureaucracy.

Then, several months ago, Olahg had heard the Call. He had hearkened to the small, insistent voice within, which had urged him toward the teachings of the legendary emperor Kahless.

It was the Call that had brought him to the planet Boreth and its shadowy mountain monastery, and placed him in the company of the other clerics. And it was the

Call that had convinced him to spurn worldly things, embracing a life of pious contemplation instead.

Olahg had fully expected to spend the remainder of his worldly existence that way—sitting around a smoking firepit with his brethren, seeking visions in the scented fumes. He had grown comfortable with the prospect. He had even convinced himself that he was happy.

However, only a few weeks after his arrival on Boreth, the wisdom of Kahless began to lose its appeal. Or perhaps not the wisdom itself, but the rather austere way in which it was handed down to Kahless's disciples.

He came to long for a more personal relationship with the object of his admiration. He yearned for an audience with the great, glorious Kahless himself—or, failing that, the being made from Kahless's genetic material who had been named the Empire's ceremonial emperor a few years earlier.

But petition as he might, Olahg could not seem to win such an audience. He was told time and again that Emperor Kahless was too busy, that his duties kept him away from Boreth—though when that changed, he would surely visit the monastery.

When he could find the time.

Even though it was in that monastery that the clone had been created. Even though it was the community of clerics on Boreth to whom the emperor owed his very existence.

The idea was a festering wound in Olahg's soul. He couldn't sleep for the ingratitude of it, the injustice—the need he couldn't seem to fill.

And the spiritual Kahless was no more accessible. Though Olahg sat before the prayer pit until his face grew raw with its heat, no visions came to him. It was as if he had been abandoned, spurned by the icon of his faith as surely as he had been spurned by everyone else in his life.

Koroth, chief guardian of the monastery, had told him that Kahless was testing him, that the emperor had something special in mind for him. But as much as Olahg honored and respected Koroth for his insight, that was difficult for him to believe.

More and more, he felt alone, apart. And he came to resent the very personage he was supposed to worship.

Shaking his head, the initiate surveyed the patch of earth that had been cleared for him. The severed ends of stray *micayah* roots still stung his nostrils with their pungency. Later, the excavation teams would move in— not only here, but in all those other places the ground had been cleared.

Then the digging would begin in earnest. For, according to the clerics' best guess, this was the area where the historical Kahless made camp on the long trek from his fortress to *Sto-Vo-Kor*.

Sto-Vo-Kor, of course, was the Klingon afterlife, to which Kahless disappeared after his death. It was a leap of faith to believe in such a place, but Olahg had done so wholeheartedly. At least, in the beginning.

The initiate knelt and picked up a handful of earth. It was rife with tiny bits of rock.

Was it possible that Kahless had really stopped at this spot and laid down his burden? That he had stretched out beneath the heavens here? Perhaps even spent his last night on Qo'noS in this place, breathing the fragrant air and taking in the sight of all the stars?

Allowing the loose earth to sift through his fingers, Olahg stood and brushed off his palms. It would be difficult to find conclusive proof that Kahless had been in this spot. After all, nearly seventy-five generations had come and gone since. Even if such evidence had existed once, he doubted that it would have survived intact.

That was not the way a cleric was supposed to think. It was not the way of faith. But it was the way he felt right now.

The initiate was about to look for his colleague Divok, to see if it was time for the midday meal yet, when he saw something glint in the rising sunlight. He smiled at the irony. Here he had just been thinking about what they might unearth, and an artifact had already presented itself.

No doubt, it would turn out to be a sign from Kahless that Olahg's faith had been well-placed, and that the universe's cosmic plan would now be revealed to him. He grunted derisively. Yes—and after that, spotted *targs* would sing Klingon opera from the rooftops.

More likely, it was some piece of junk cast aside as someone strolled through these woods. Or maybe it was the tip of some bigger piece of garbage, discarded some years ago, when this forest wasn't quite so large.

At any rate, Olahg wasn't going to get his hopes up. Not by a long shot. He had done too much of that already.

Crossing the small, squared-off clearing, he saw that it was indeed a piece of metal that had caught the light. As he had suspected, it seemed to be the corner of something larger.

Olahg kicked at it, expecting the thing to dislodge itself from the ground. It didn't. It was too firmly anchored.

His curiosity aroused, he knelt again and dug around it with his fingers. It was hard work and it made his fingers hurt, but in time he exposed a bit more of the object. It looked like part of an oblong metal box.

Getting a grip on the box with both hands, he tried a second time to move it, but it still wouldn't budge. So he dug some more. And some more again, as the morning light grew hotter and more intense.

Little by little, making his hands raw and worn in the process, he came that much closer to unearthing it. Bit by bit, it revealed itself to him.

He could see there were symbols carved into it. Ancient symbols, he thought, though he didn't have the knowledge to confirm that. But they certainly *looked* ancient.

Or was it just that he *wanted* them to look that way? That he wanted this box to be of some significance?

As his fingers were cramping, he collected sticks and rocks from outside the clearing to use as tools. Then he set to work again. It took a while, but he finally scooped out a big enough hole to wrest the thing from the ground.

With an effort that made his back ache and strained the muscles in his neck, he heaved and heaved and eventually pulled it free. More curious than ever, he laid the thing on its side and inspected it.

It was about a half-meter long, made of an alloy he had never seen before, and covered with the markings he had noticed earlier. The metal was discolored in some spots and badly rusted in others, but all in all it was remarkably well preserved.

That is, if it was anywhere near as old as it looked. And, the initiate reminded himself, there was no guarantee of that.

He picked it up and shook it. It sounded hollow. Yet there was something inside, something that thumped about.

Turning it over, Olahg saw what might once have been a latch. Unfortunately, over time it had rusted into an amorphous glob. He tried to pry it open with his fingers, but without success. Finally, he picked up one of the rocks he had gathered—the biggest and heaviest of them—and brought it down sharply on the latch.

It crumpled. The box opened a crack.

Only then did it occur to the initiate that he might be overstepping his bounds. After all, this excavation was to have been an organized effort.

But he had come too far to stop now. With tired, trembling fingers, he opened the box the rest of the way.

There was a scroll inside. Like the box, it was not in the best condition. It was brown and brittle at the edges, fading to a dark yellow near the middle. And the thong that had held it together was broken, little more than a few wisps of dried black leather now.

Olahg licked his lips, which had suddenly become dry. A scroll was mentioned in the myth cycle, was it not? It was said that Kahless had left his fortress with such a thing in his possession.

But for it to have survived the long, invasive ages since? The seeping rainwater, the corrosive acids in the soil? Was such a thing possible?

Then he remembered—the work crew had torn apart the surface of the forest floor, along with the *micayah*. There might have been something—some rock, perhaps—protecting the box and its contents from the elements. Still, he didn't know if that could be an explanation or not. He was not a scientist. He was a cleric.

Carefully, ever so carefully, Olahg picked up the scroll and unrolled it. Fortunately, it didn't go to pieces in his hands. It was still supple enough to reveal its secrets to him.

The thing was written in a bold, flowing hand. However, it was upside down. Turning it around, he held it close and read the words inscribed in it.

The first few words gave him an indication of what the rest would be like—but he couldn't stop there. He felt compelled to read more of it, and even more than that, stuck like a fish on a particularly cruel and vicious spear.

For what words they were! What terrible words indeed!

The initiate's heart began to pound as he realized what he had stumbled on. His eyes began to hurt, as if pierced by what they had seen.

For if it was true—if the scroll was indeed what it purported to be—this was the work of Kahless the Unforgettable. Yet at the same time, it was the greatest blasphemy Olahg could imagine. He looked around, to make sure no one had seen him reading it.

No one had. The other clerics were all tending to their own sections. He could barely see them in their robes through the intervening forest.

He had to put the scroll back in the box. He had to make sure it was never seen. Not by anyone, ever.

Or . . . did he? The initiate swallowed, allowing his eyes to feast again on the scroll and its contents.

Certainly, one could call it blasphemy to let this get out. But it might be a greater blasphemy *not* to.

If this was the authentic word of Kahless, should it not be given a voice? Should it not be heeded, as the emperor no doubt intended—for why else would he have written it?

Olahg hesitated for a moment, his head feeling as if it would burst like a *caw'va* melon left in the sun. He had never in his life had to make this kind of decision. Nor was he likely to again.

Peace? Or truth? His hands clenched into fists. He pounded the ground on either side of the open scroll, hoping for an answer, wishing one would be handed down to him.

And then he realized . . . it already had been. He had been allowed to find the thing. He had been given a gift. And a gift, he had been taught, should never be wasted.

Rolling up the scroll, he secreted it in the folds of his robes. Then he walked away from the cleared patch of earth, through the still-dense forest of *micayah* trees.

None of the other clerics noticed. No one stopped him.

A sign that he was doing the right thing, Olahg inferred. If he travelled quickly, without rest, he could make it to the city by morning.

CHAPTER 1

The Modern Age

The volcano shot glorious red streamers of molten rock high into the ponderous gray heavens. But that was just the first sign of its intentions, the first indication of its fury.

A moment later, in an angry spasm of disdain for the yellow and green plant life that grew along its black, fissured flanks, a tide of hissing, red lava came bubbling over the rim of the volcano's crater. The tide separated into rivers, the rivers into a webwork of narrow streams—each one radiating a horrible heat, each one intensely eager to consume all in its path.

In the distance, thunder rumbled. At least, it appeared to be thunder. In fact, it was the volcano itself, preparing to heave another load of lava out of the scorched and tormented earth.

The name of this severe and lonely place was Kri'stak.

It was the first time the volcano had erupted in nearly a hundred years.

A Klingon warrior was making his way up the volcano's northern slope, down where the rivers of spitting, bubbling lava were still few and far between.

The warrior wore a dark leather tunic, belted at the waist and embossed with sigils of Klingon virtues. The shoulders of the garment were decorated with bright silver circlets. On his feet, he wore heavy leather boots that reached to midthigh; on his hands, leather gloves reinforced with an iron alloy.

The warrior's enterprise seemed insane, suicidal. This was a volcano in full eruption, with death streaming from its every fissure. But that didn't seem to dissuade him in the least.

Picking his way carefully over the pitted slope, remaining faithful to the higher ridges the lava couldn't reach, he continued his progress. When he reached a dead end, he simply leaped over the molten rock to find a more promising route elsewhere.

At times, the figure vanished behind a curtain of smoke and cinders, or lost his footing and slipped behind some outcropping. Yet, over and over, he emerged from the setback unscathed, a look of renewed determination on his face. Sweat pouring from his bright red brow, he pushed himself from path to treacherous path, undaunted.

Unfortunately, his choices were narrowing radically as he approached the lip of the crater. There was only one ridge that looked to give him a chance of making it to the top—and that was guarded by a hellishly wide channel.

It wasn't impossible for him to make the leap across.

However, as drained as he must have been by this point, and as burdened by his heavy leather tunic, it was highly unlikely he'd survive the attempt.

Spreading his feet apart to steady himself, the warrior raised his arms above his head and unfastened the straps that held his tunic in place. Then he tore it from him and flung it into the river of lava below, as if tendering a sacrifice to some dark and ravenous demon.

In moments, the tunic was consumed, leaving little more than a thin, greasy trail of smoke. Nor would the Klingon leave the world much more than that, if he failed.

But he hadn't come this far to be turned away now. Taking a few steps back until his back was to yet another brink, the warrior put his head down and got his legs churning beneath him: It was difficult for his boots to find purchase on the slick, steamy rock, but the Klingon worked up more speed than appeared possible.

At the last possible moment, he planted his right foot and launched himself out over the channel. There was a point in time, the size and span of a long, deep, breath, when the warrior seemed to hover over the crackling lava flow, his legs bicycling beneath him.

Until he completed his flight by smashing into the sharp, craggy surface of the opposite ridge. For a moment, it looked as if he had safely avoided the lava, as if he had come away with the victory.

Then he began sliding backward into the river of fire. Desperately, frantically, the warrior dug for purchase with fingers and knees and whatever else he could bring to bear—even his cheek. Yet still he slid.

The rocky surface tore at the warrior's chest and his

face, but he wouldn't give into it. Slowly, inexorably, by dint of blood and bone, he stopped himself. Then he began to pull himself up from the edge of death's domain.

Finally, when he felt he was past the danger, he lay on the ground—gulping down breath after breath, until he found the strength to go on. Dragging himself to his feet, too drained even to sweat, he stumbled the rest of the way up the ridge like a man drunk with too much bloodwine.

At the brink of the crater, the Klingon fell to his knees, paused, and pulled a knife from the inside of his boot. It was a *d'k tahg*, a ceremonial dagger. Lifting a thick lock of hair from his head, he held it out taut and brought the edge of his blade across it. Strand by severed strand, it came free in his hand.

For a long moment, he stared at the lock of hair. Then he dropped it into the molten chaos inside the volcano, where it vanished instantly.

But only for a moment or two. Then it shot up again on a geyser of hot, sulfurous air. Except now it was coated with molten, flaming rock, an object of unearthly beauty, no longer recognizable as a part of him.

Mesmerized, the warrior extended his hand, as if to grasp the thing. Incredibly, it tumbled toward him, end over end. And as if by magic, it fell right into the palm of his gauntleted hand.

Bringing it closer to him, the Klingon gazed at it with narrowed eyes, as if unable to believe what had happened. Then, his glove smoking as it cradled the lava-dipped lock, he smiled a hollow-cheeked smile—and started his journey down the mountain.

Worf, son of Mogh, hung in the sky high above it all, a spectator swathed in moist, dark cloud-vapors, his eyes and nose stinging from the hot flakes of ash that swirled like tiny twisters through the air.

He hovered like some ancient god, defying gravity, hair streaming in the wind like a banner. But no god ever felt so troubled, so unsettled—so pierced to the heart.

For a moment, all too brief, he had been drawn to the spectacle, to its mysticism and its majesty. Then the moment passed, and he was left as troubled as before.

"Mister Worf?"

The Klingon turned—and found himself facing Captain Picard, who was walking toward him through the clouds as if there were an invisible floor beneath him.

The captain had come from the corridor outside the holodeck, which was still partially visible as the oddly shaped doors of the facility slid shut behind him. It wasn't until they were completely closed that Picard became subject to the same winds that buffeted Worf.

The captain smiled politely and tilted his head toward the volcano. "I hope I'm not interrupting anything important," he said.

Inwardly, the Klingon winced at the suggestion. Certainly, it had *seemed* important when he entered the holodeck half an hour ago. There had been the possibility of solace, of affirmation. But the experience had fallen far short of his expectations.

"No," he lied. "Nothing important. I am merely reenacting the myth of Kahless's labors at the Kri'stak Volcano."

Picard nodded. "Yes, of course . . . the one in which he dips a strand of his hair into the lava." His brow wrinkled as he tried to remember. "After that, he plunged the flaming lock into Lake Lusor—and twisted it into a

15

revolutionary new form of blade, which no Klingon had ever seen before."

Worf had to return the human's smile. Without a doubt, Picard knew his Klingon lore—perhaps as well as the average Klingon. And in this case even better, because this particular legend had been nurtured by a select few until just a few years ago.

"That is correct," he confirmed.

Pointing to the northern slope of the volcano, he showed the captain Kahless's position. The emperor-to-be had hurled himself across the deep channel again—this time with a bit less effort, perhaps, thanks to the improvement in the terrain he was leaping from—and was descending the mountainside, his trophy still in hand.

It was only after much hardship that he would come to the lake called Lusor. There, he would fashion from his trophy the efficient and graceful weapon known as the *bat'telh.*

Picard made an appreciative sound. "Hard to believe he could ever have made such a climb in fact."

Worf felt a pang at the captain's remark. He must not have concealed it very well this time, because Picard's brow furrowed.

"I didn't mean to question your beliefs," the human told him. "Only to make an observation. If I've offended you—"

The Klingon waved away the suggestion. "No, sir. I am not offended." He paused. "It was only that I was thinking the same thing."

Picard regarded him more closely. Obviously, he was concerned. "Are you . . . having a crisis of faith, Lieuten-

ant? Along the lines of what you experienced before
Kahless's return?"

Worf sighed. "A crisis of faith?" He shook his head.
"No, it is more than that. Considerably more." He
watched the distant figure of Kahless descend from the
mountain, making improbable choices to defy impossible
odds. "A few years ago," he explained, "it was a personal
problem. Now . . ."

He allowed his voice to trail off, reluctant to give the
matter substance by acknowledging it. However, he
couldn't avoid it forever. As captain of the *Enterprise,*
Picard would find out about it sooner or later.

"You see," he told the human, "these myths—" He
gestured to the terrain below them, which included not
only the volcano but the lake as well. "—they are sacred
to us. They are the essence of our faith. When we speak of
Kahless's creation of the *bat'telh* from a lock of his hair,
we are not speaking figuratively. We truly believe he did
such a thing."

Worf turned his gaze westward, toward the plains that
formed the bulk of this continent. He couldn't see them
for the smoke and fumes emerging from the volcano, but
he knew they were there nonetheless.

"It was out there," he continued, "that Kahless is said
to have wrestled with his brother Morath for twelve days
and twelve nights, after his brother lied and shamed their
clan. It was out there that Kahless used the *bat'telh* he
created to slay the tyrant Molor—and it was out there
that the emperor united all Klingons under a banner of
duty and honor."

"Not just stories," Picard replied, demonstrating his
understanding. "Each one a truth, no matter how impossible it might seem in the cold light of logic."

"Yes," said Worf. "Each one a truth." He turned back to his captain. "Or at least, they *were.*" He frowned, despite himself.

"Were?" Picard prodded. He hung there in the shifting winds, clouds writhing behind him like a monstrous serpent in terrible torment. "What's happened to change things?"

The Klingon took his time gathering his thoughts. Still, it was not an easy matter to talk about.

"I have heard from the emperor," he began.

The captain looked at him with unconcealed interest. "Kahless, you mean? I trust he's in good health."

Worf nodded. "You need not worry on that count. Physically, he is in fine health."

In other words, no one had tried to assassinate him. In the corridors of Klingon government, that was a very real concern—though to Worf's knowledge, Kahless hadn't prompted anyone to want to kill him. Quite the contrary. He was as widely loved as any Klingon could be.

"The problem," the lieutenant went on, "is of a different nature. You see, a scroll was unearthed alongside the road to *Sto-Vo-Kor.*"

Picard's eyes narrowed. "The road the historical Kahless followed when he took his leave of the Klingon people. That was . . . what? Fifteen hundred years ago?"

"Even more," Worf told him. "In any case, this scroll—supposedly written by Kahless himself—appears to discredit all the stories that concern him. It is as if Kahless himself has given the lie to his own history."

The captain mulled the statement over. When he responded, his tone was sober and sympathetic.

"I see," he said. "So, in effect, this scroll reduces Klingon faith to a series of tall tales. And the emperor—"

"To a charlatan," the lieutenant remarked. "It was one thing for the modern Kahless to be revealed as a clone of the original. My people were so eager for a light to guide them, they were happy to embrace him despite all that."

"However," Picard went on, picking up the thread, "it is quite another thing for the historical Kahless to be nothing *like* the legend."

"And if the scroll is authentic," Worf added, "that is exactly the message it will convey."

Below them, the volcano rumbled. The wind howled and moaned.

"Not a pretty picture," the captain conceded. "Neither for Kahless himself nor for his people."

"That is an understatement," the Klingon replied. "A scandal like this one could shake the empire to its foundations. Klingons everywhere would be forced to reconsider the meaning of what it is to be Klingon."

Picard's brow furrowed. "We're speaking of social upheavals?"

"Without a doubt," Worf answered. "Kahless revived my people's dedication to the ancient virtues. If he were to fall from grace . . ."

"I understand," said the captain. His nostrils flared as he considered the implications. "For a while there, Kahless seemed to be all that kept Gowron in his council seat. If that were to change, the entire diplomatic landscape might change with it. It could spell the end of the Federation-Klingon alliance."

"It could indeed," the lieutenant admitted.

He saw Picard gaze at the volcano again. Down below, Kahless had reached its lowermost slopes, though it looked to have cost him the last of his strength. Still, according to the legends, he would make it to the lake somehow.

"So that is why you constructed this program," the captain remarked out loud. "To play out the myths before your eyes. To test your faith in the face of this scroll's revelations."

Worf confirmed it. "Yes. Unfortunately, it has only served to deepen my doubts—to make me wonder if I have been fooling myself all along."

Still gazing at Kahless, Picard took a breath and expelled it. "I suppose that brings me to the reason I barged in on you like this." He turned to the Klingon again. "A subspace packet has arrived from the Klingon homeworld. It seems to be a transcript of some sort. I would have notified you via ship's intercom. . . ."

"But you were concerned," the Klingon acknowledged, "about the possible political implications."

"Yes," the captain confirmed. "Anything from Qo'noS makes me wary—perhaps unnecessarily so." He paused. "Any idea what it might be?"

Worf nodded. "I believe it contains the contents of the scroll," he rumbled. "As I requested."

"I see," said Picard.

At that point, he didn't ask anything of his officer. Nonetheless, the Klingon sensed what the captain wanted.

"After I have read it," he said, "I will make it available to you."

Picard inclined his head. "Thank you," he replied. "And please, continue what you were doing. I won't disturb you any further."

Worf grunted by way of acknowledgment and turned to watch Kahless begin his trek toward the lake. Out of the corner of his eye, he saw the captain make his way through the clouds and exit from the holodeck.

The Klingon sighed. He would read what was written in the cursed scroll soon enough. For now, he would track the emperor's progress from his place in the sky, and try again to stir in himself some feeling of piety.

KAHLESS

CHAPTER 2

The Heroic Age

The chase was over, Kahless thought, bringing his lean, powerful *s'tarahk* to a halt. And a long, arduous chase it had been. But in the end, they had cornered their quarry.

The outlaws milled about in the foothills of the towering Uhq'ra Mountains, wary as a cornered *targ* and twice as restless. Sitting at the head of the emperor's forces, Kahless listened to his mount gnashing its short yellow tusks while he considered the enemy. As they were upwind, he sampled their scent. His nostrils flared with surprise.

There was not the least sign of fear in the brigands. In fact, when Kahless tried to make out their faces, he thought he could see their teeth glinting in the sun.

They were not to be taken lightly, he told himself. But then, cornered beasts were always the most dangerous kind.

"Kahless!"

Turning, he saw Molor riding toward him on his proud, black s'tarahk. Out of heartfelt deference to his master, Kahless pulled hard on the reins of his own beast. It barked loudly as it reared and clawed at the air, red eyes blazing, muscles rippling beneath its thick, hairless hide.

After all, Molor was no petty land baron. He was a monarch among monarchs, who in the course of his lifetime had seized half the world's greatest continent. And before long, if all went well, he would no doubt lay claim to the rest of it.

"My liege lord," said Kahless.

He had served Molor for seven years, almost to the day. And in that time, he had gradually won himself a post as one of the ruler's most trusted warchiefs. So when Molor rode up to him, his pale green eyes slitted beneath his long, gray brows, it was with a measure of respect.

"What are they doing?" asked Molor, lifting his chin-beard in the direction of the outlaws.

"Waiting," Kahless grunted.

"For us to make the first move," his lord suggested.

The warchief nodded his shaggy head. "It looks that way, yes."

Molor's s'tarahk pawed the ground and rumbled deep in its throat. "Because our numbers are about even," the ruler observed. "And because, with their backs guarded by the hills, they have the strategic advantage. Or to be more accurate, they *think* they do."

Kahless eyed him. "You believe otherwise?"

As Molor's steed rose up on its hind legs, the monarch's lip curled back. "What I believe," he said, "is that strategies only go so far. More important is what is in *here*." He pounded his black leather breastplate, for emphasis. "Our hearts. And their hearts. That is what a battle is about."

The warchief couldn't help but acknowledge the truth of that. He said as much.

Gazing at the outlaws, Molor laughed. "I will confide something to you, Kahless, son of Kanjis—for you have earned it."

The warchief made a sound of gratitude. "And what is that, my lord?"

"Battles are won and lost," said Molor, "before they ever begin. It is not the strength of one's sword arm that carries the day, but the manner and the timing of one's attack. And the look in one's eyes that says he will suffer nothing less than victory."

Kahless had never looked at it that way. But if it came from his lord, could it be anything but wisdom?

"The enemy may seem fearless now," Molor observed. "Eager, even. But then, they expect us to spend the afternoon talking, planning what we will do next. If we were to strike swiftly and unexpectedly, like a bird of prey, and show not an ounce of mercy . . ."

Molor grunted. "It would be a different story entirely, I assure you of that. Before they recovered from our first charge, you would see it in their faces—the knowledge that they will not live to see another dawn." He chuckled in his beard. "Fear. There is no more powerful emotion," he grated. "And to us, no more powerful friend."

As if they had heard and understood, the first line of *s'tarahkmey* rumbled and poked at the ground with their forelegs. A smile on his face, Molor nodded approvingly.

"Prepare yourself," he told Kahless, "and see if I am not right."

Suddenly, he raised his right hand. All eyes were drawn

to it, instantly, as lightning is drawn to an iron rod in the midst of a thunderstorm. Then, with an ululating cry to spur them on, Molor dropped his hand.

Like bristling, black death itself, the emperor's first rank sprang forward as one. Molor himself served as its spearhead, with Kahless right beside him, their war-axes held high.

His heart beating like a drum, even harder and louder than the thunder of his *s'tarahk*'s charge, the warchief tightened his grasp on the haft of his weapon. Up ahead, the outlaws loomed in the lap of the hills, scrambling about to brace themselves for the unexpected onslaught.

Then, almost before he knew it, Kahless was among them, slashing and cursing, whirling and rending. He could hear the bellows of warriors seeking their courage and the clangor of clashing weapons. He could smell the sweat of their beasts and the metallic scent of blood, feel the numbing impact of the enemy's weapons on his own.

This was battle. This was what it felt like to be a warrior, to pit strength against strength and fury against fury.

And as Molor advised, the warchief's actions were swift and ruthless. The blade of his axe grew slick with the outlaws' gore—and still he smashed and cut and clawed, meeting savagery with even greater savagery. He refused to let up, refused to stop until the last of the brigands cried for mercy.

Nor was the enemy the only one who bled and fell, to be crushed under the hooves of the snarling *s'tarahkmey*. Many of Molor's men perished that day as well. Kahless bore witness to it.

Then again, it was a good day to die. It was *always* a good day to die.

Only Molor had to live. It would be the greatest shame to Kahless and the rest of their army if their monarch fell in battle. It would be a failure that would haunt them the rest of their days.

So, even while he was trying to preserve his own life, the warchief was keeping an eye out for Molor. It was a good thing, too, or Kahless wouldn't have seen the outlaw giant cutting and slicing his way in the master's direction.

Of course, Kahless had noticed the giant before, catching sight of him as they pursued the brigands across the plains of Molor's kingdom. It would have been difficult *not* to notice; the man stood a full head taller than most of the other outlaws and had shoulders like crags.

Warriors that tall were often clumsy and plodding, but this one was an exception. As immense as he was, as difficult to knock down, he was also as quick with a blade as anyone Kahless had ever seen.

No one could seem to slow the giant down, much less stop him. And before long, he had hacked away the last of Molor's defenders, leaving the emperor alone to face his fury.

No—not quite alone. For as the giant's sword whistled for Molor's head, Kahless leaped from his *s'tarahk* and dragged his lord to earth, saving his life in the process.

When they hit the ground, Molor was stunned. But Kahless was not. Rising in his emperor's stead, he challenged the outlaw.

"My name is Kahless," he roared, "son of Kanjis. If you wish to kill my lord, you must kill me first!"

The giant leered at him, revealing a mouthful of long, stakelike teeth. "It will be my pleasure!" he spat.

He had barely gotten the words out before he lifted his blade and brought it slicing down at Kahless. But the warchief was quick, too. Rolling to one side, he got to his feet again and launched an attack of his own.

The giant parried it in time, but had to take a step back. It was then, in a moment of strange clarity, that Kahless remembered Molor's words: *"Strike swiftly and unexpectedly, like a bird of prey, and show not an ounce of mercy."*

Surely, the giant wouldn't expect him to press his attack—not when they were so clearly mismatched. But, heeding his master's advice, that is exactly what the warchief did.

He rushed forward and swung his axe with all his might. To his surprise as well as the giant's, he buried it deep in the place where the outlaw's neck met his shoulder.

The giant screamed, dropped his own weapon, and tried to pull the axehead free. But with his life's blood soaking his leather armor, he no longer had the strength. He sank to his knees, still striving with the axe.

Kahless didn't have the luxury of watching his enemy's blood pool about him on the ground. There was still work to do. Plucking up the giant's sword, which was not that much bigger or heavier than those he was used to, he whirled it once around his head.

Then, in a spray of blood, he used it to decapitate the mighty outlaw. As the giant's head rolled off his shoulders, it was trampled under the hooves of a riderless *s'tarahk*.

After that, the outlaws seemed to lose their lust for battle. And before the sun met the horizon, Molor's men had carried the day.

In the aftermath of the fighting, the monarch embraced Kahless and awarded him first choice of the spoils for his work that day. Molor slapped the warchief on the shoulder and said out loud that Kahless, son of Kanjis, was his fiercest and most loyal warrior.

In Kahless's ears, there could have been no more pleasing sound than the praise of his master, or the resultant cheers of his men. He had wrapped himself in glory. What else was there?

CHAPTER 3

The Modern Age

When the Muar'tek Festival comes to Tolar'tu, even the heavens lift their voices in celebration.

Kahless reflected on the uncanny accuracy of the saying as he made his way through the milling crowd toward the town square. The afternoon sky, packed tightly with low, brooding clouds, rumbled softly, as if in willing accompaniment to the brave sounds sent up by the festival musicians.

The Klingon felt himself drawn to the tumult—to the hoarse whistling of the long, tapering *abin'do* pipes, to the insistent strumming of the harps, and to the metallic booming of the *krad'dak* drums that echoed from wall to age-stained wall.

If all went well, the coming performance in the square and the mounting storm would pace one another like a matched pair of hunting animals, reveling in their power and their beauty as they ran down their quarry—only to reach it at the same time.

As Kahless edged closer to the ancient plaza and the space that had been cleared out in the center of it, he caught the briny scent of the fresh serpent worms offered by the street vendors. And as if that were not enough to set one's belly grumbling, one-eyed Kerpach—whose shop was set into the western wall of the square—was bringing out a particularly pungent batch of *rokeg* blood pie.

Glancing around, he saw that few of those who'd come here for the festival wore their everyday dark clothes without embellishment. That was a change. Just a few years ago, one might see only a few of the elderly sporting a blood-red glove or band in keeping with the festival's traditions. These days, even the smallest children wore red headbands as a matter of course.

But then, to this square which had seen so much, these were *all* children—young and old, traditionalist or otherwise. And it welcomed them with open arms, as long as there was joy and honor in their hearts.

After all, this was the oldest part of Tolar'tu, the only part that escaped the ravages of Molor more than fifteen hundred years ago. The town's ancient center, where—it might be said—Klingon civilization first took hold. And had it not been for Kahless, he mused, even this place would have been consumed by the tyrant's greed.

He took considerable pride in that accomplishment. Perhaps he was not the historical Kahless, as he'd once believed. Perhaps he was only a clone of that warrior-prince, created by the clerics of Boreth from the blood on an ancient dagger to restore a sense of honor to the Empire.

Still, he felt responsible for everything the first Kahless had accomplished. And why not? Could he not remember the salvation of Tolar'tu as if he had *been* there? Could he not recall in detail his every stroke against Molor's armies?

Thanks to the clerics, he had all his predecessor's memories—all his wisdom and ethical fiber. And, of course, all his good looks.

That was why he had to conceal his face under a hood sometimes—today being a case in point. Most days, he was glad to be the Empire's icon, a symbol held high for all to emulate. But even an icon had to be by himself once in a while, and now was such a time.

No sooner had Kahless edged up near the front rank of onlookers than the musicians changed their tune. The music became louder—more strident, more urgent. It sounded more and more as if the instruments were *yearning* for something.

And then that very *something* had the grace to appear. With a great, shrill burst of delight from the *abin'do* pipes, the afternoon's performers darted out into the center of the square. One was dressed all in red, the other all in blue. They glared at each other, feigning hatred, as if already in the midst of a savage combat.

To the audience's delight, the performer in red bellowed his purpose in a deep baritone: to teach his opponent a lesson about honor. A moment later, his opponent answered in just as deep a voice, echoing the words that had been handed down through the centuries. . . .

"I need none of your wisdom, brother."

The crowd cheered with mock intensity—and awaited the gyrations sure to follow the brothers' challenges. For this was no choreographed ritual, predictable in its every gesture. Though no injury was intended, there was no telling who would do what to whom.

And yet, when the performance was over, the actor in red would somehow emerge victorious. That was the only certainty in all of this, the only predictability—that in the end, Kahless would exact from his brother Morath the price of telling a lie.

Needless to say, this was only symbolic of the combat in which the *real* Kahless had engaged—a combat that lasted twelve days and twelve nights. Kahless recalled it as if it were yesterday—at least, the beginnings of it. The rest was all but lost in a stuporous haze, born of sleep deprivation and lack of nourishment.

But Morath had learned his lesson. And from that point on, he had never compromised the honor of his brother or his clan.

There in the square, the actors wove in and out of each other's grasp. They barely touched one another, but their grunting and their flexing gave the impression of unbridled exertion. Sweat poured from their temples and ran down their necks, turning their tunics dark with perspiration.

Up above, the stormclouds shouldered one another, as if to get a better view of the performance. Lightning flashed and thunder cracked unmercifully. And the musicians answered, not to be outdone, as the first fat drops of rain began to fall.

A second time, the actor in red called out to his adversary, demanding that he regret his act of betrayal. A second time, the actor in blue refused to comply, and the audience roared with disapproval.

As well they should, Kahless remarked inwardly. The

only thing worse than incurring dishonor was refusing to recognize it as such.

He wished that puny excuse for a cleric—the one who claimed to have discovered that damned *scroll* on the road to *Sto-Vo-Kor*—could have been here to witness this. He wished the little *p'tahk* could see what *real* honor was.

Then, perhaps, he might understand the gravity of what he had done—the purity of the faith he had assailed, and the disgrace that attended such a bald-faced lie.

The scroll was a fake. No one knew that better than Kahless, who had lived the events it attempted to question.

For whatever reason, Olahg was lying through his teeth. But there were those who seemed to take stock in his blasphemy. After all, he was one of the clerics of Boreth, wasn't he? And as a result, beyond reproach?

In the end, of course, Olahg would be brought low for his deception. Kahless promised himself that. And like Morath, the damned initiate would pay the price for his crimes.

As Kahless emerged from his reverie, he realized the rain had begun to fall harder. Some of the onlookers, mostly old women and little children, went rushing for cover, of which there was blessed little in the square. But most stayed for the balance of the performance, which they sensed was not all that far off.

Sure enough, as the ground turned dark with heavy, pelting raindrops, the actor in red struck his adversary across the face—or so it seemed. Then again. And again. The actor in blue sank to his knees, defeated.

"I yield," he cried, again citing the ancient words.

Finally, the Klingon in red lifted the exhausted figure of Morath to the heavens and bellowed his triumph. It was echoed by the *abin'do* pipes and the *krad'dak* drums. And as the music rose to a harsh, discordant crescendo, lightning blanched the sky in a great, white burst of glory, blinding them all for a single, dizzying moment.

They were still blinking when the thunder descended on them like a horde of wild *s'tarahkmey*, crashing about their ears and drowning out all else. Only when it finally showed signs of relenting did the actor in red let his "brother" down, and both of them bowed deeply to the crowd.

The people thrust their fists into the air and beat on one another's shoulders, delirious with approval. Even Kahless found himself butting heads with a young warrior who'd been standing beside him, enjoying the performance.

The clone laughed. He was right to have come here, he told himself. This was what he had needed to lift his spirits. A reaffirmation of his legacy, an assurance that this was still Kahless's world and not that of some mewling degenerate seeking an undeserved place in the sun.

As the rain let up a bit, the actors gave way to a big, bald-headed Klingon in a large black robe. Kahless recognized him as Unarrh, son of Unagroth, a powerful member of the high council and one of Gowron's staunchest supporters.

Unarrh lived near Tolar'tu, in a place called Navrath. It must have been he who had sponsored the street drama. If so, it was only proper that he should address the crowd afterward.

"I trust you enjoyed the performance," said Unarrh, his teeth exposed in a broad, benevolent smile, his voice deep and inexorable as the tides of the Chu'paq Sea.

"However, let us not forget the meaning of what we have seen—indeed, the meaning of the entire festival."

Good, thought Kahless. That is what the people needed to hear, now more than ever. It was to Unarrh's credit that he should be the one to remind them of this.

"Let us rejoice in the tradition handed down to us by our fathers," the council member intoned. "Let us place honor above all else, despite the temptations laid in our path by treacherous men—"

"How do you know?" called one of the warriors on the fringe of the crowd.

Heads turned with a rustling of cloaks and hoods. The rain beat a grim tattoo on the hard ground.

"How do you know," the man repeated, "that the cleric Olahg is treacherous? How do you know he's not speaking the truth?"

"That's right," called another warrior, from elsewhere in the assemblage. "He says he has proof."

"What if Kahless was a fraud?" asked a woman. "What if all the myths about him are lies—as dishonorable as those for which Morath was punished?"

"They are *not* lies," Unarrh maintained, anger flashing in his dark, expressive eyes. "The stories are as true now as they have ever been. In time, this upstart initiate will be exposed for the fraud he is. But until then, I will continue to believe in the virtues Kahless taught us—and more than that, in Kahless himself."

Well said, the clone cheered inwardly. Surely, that would silence the doubters in the crowd.

But it didn't. If anything, it made their voices stronger as they rose to meet Unarrh's challenge, their protests louder than the grumble of thunder from the persistent storm.

"What if Kahless did not invent those virtues?" asked the first man. "What if that was a lie too?"

"All our lives," shouted the woman, "we've believed in him, worshipped him . . . never suspecting our beliefs were based on falsehoods which bring dishonor to us all. What will we believe in now?"

"Rest assured," shouted Unarrh, "your beliefs were based on *truth*. Nothing can change that—certainly not a corrupt cleric, whose imagination exceeds his sense of propriety."

He darted a glance at a subordinate who was standing off to the side. Kahless knew the meaning of the gesture. Before long, the protesters would be picked out of the crowd and taken bodily from the gathering.

As they should be. Yet, the prospect was of no comfort to him. The spirit of the occasion had been ruined, at least from his point of view.

Kahless snarled. His joy turned to bile, he left the square and headed for his favorite dining hall.

Kahless grunted as he walked in, still hooded, and felt the warmth of the firepit on the exposed portion of his face. It was a good feeling.

Not that he was cold—at least, not on the outside. It wasn't even close to being winter yet. The fire felt good because it was a diversion—because it took his mind off what had happened in the main square.

Also, the clone was comfortable here. He had eaten his midday meal in this hall for the last week or so, having become a creature of habit since his "return" a few years ago.

There were three empty tables. One was near the firepit, used every day by an elderly man whose name he

KAHLESS

didn't know. The other two were located in the corners by the back wall.

One of them was *his*. Without removing his hood or his cloak, Kahless crossed the room and sat down.

In most places, a hooded man would have attracted attention. Stares of curiosity, perhaps a taunt or two. But not in this place.

It was run by an old woman whose husband had been killed long ago in the Romulans' attack on Khitomer. Widowed, left with little or no property, she had opened a dining hall in her native Tolar'tu, on one of the narrow, twisting streets leading to the main square.

Because of the location, the woman's first customers had been of the less-than-respectable variety—the kind with secrets to keep. She hadn't done anything to discourage them, so more showed up. And more.

It was the fastest way to build a business that she could think of. More importantly, it worked. Before long, the widow was dishing out more bloodwine and gagh— serpent worms—than anyone else in Tolar'tu.

And if the fare wasn't the best, and the walls were bare of decoration, so what? It was a refuge for those in need of one, and there was always someone with that kind of need.

Besides, Kahless had never felt comfortable lording it over others. Here, he didn't have to worry about that. And though the customers were rough-hewn, they weren't the kind to give up on tradition because of some worm-eaten, fungus-ridden scroll.

Before long, the serving maid approached him. She was a comely sort, though a bit too short and stocky for his taste. Then again, she *did* have a nice sharp mouthful of teeth. . . .

37

"What do you want?" asked the serving maid.

Kahless shrugged. "You?" he asked playfully. Even a man in a hood could enjoy flirting. Particularly now, when his spirits were low.

"Not if you were the emperor himself," she replied. "Now, if you're not hungry, I can—"

"No," he said, holding up a hand in surrender. "I know what it's like to incur your wrath. One can sit here until he dies of old age and never get a chance to order." He sat back in his chair. "How's the *targ?*"

"It was still alive a couple of hours ago." The serving maid looked around at the patrons. "Which is more than I can say for some of the clientele. But there's no heart left."

"Of course not." Kahless thought for a moment—but *just* a moment. "The liver, then. And bring it to me bloody."

She chuckled. "Is there another way?"

He watched the swing of her hips as she left him, then nodded appreciatively. He liked this place. He liked it a lot.

Out of the corner of his eye, he noticed two men walk in, their cloaks as dark with rainwater as his own. Like him, they left their hoods up to conceal their faces.

One of the men was tall, with an aristocratic bearing. The other was broad and powerful—almost as broad as Kahless himself. They looked around, then headed straight for the elderly man's table.

Apparently, the serving maid had noticed too. Halfway to the kitchen, she veered off and wound up at the table in question. The two men, who were about to sit down, turned to her.

"We're not ready to order yet," said the tall one.

The maid shook her head. "You misunderstand. I wasn't asking for your order." She pointed to the table. "This is taken."

The tall man glanced at the table, then at her, then laughed. "Taken, is it? You're joking, right?"

"Not at all," she replied. "There's a man named T'lanak who sits here every day. I don't know much else about him, but he's a steady customer, and we stand by our steady customers."

The broad man took a step toward the serving maid. He was smiling, but it was a forced smile, and Kahless had the impression it could easily become something else.

"This T'lanak isn't here now—and we are. Nor are we any less hungry than he's likely to be. Now go see to your other customers while we decide what we want to eat."

The clone frowned. He didn't like the way this Klingon was talking. As much as he would have liked to keep to himself a while longer, he wasn't going to stand here while two cowards bullied a serving wench.

He got up and approached the men. He wasn't more than halfway there before they noticed and turned to face him.

His voice was low and unmistakably threatening. "The serving maid gave you some advice. I suggest you take it."

The broad man tilted his head to get a better look at Kahless, though he couldn't see his face very well because of the cloak. Likewise, the clone couldn't see much of his adversary.

Then again, he didn't have to. Kahless didn't back off from anyone. In fact, he was actually hoping the situation would come to blows. As emperor, he seldom got the opportunity to engage another Klingon in combat. But as a hooded man in a place where everyone had a secret, it wouldn't be at all inappropriate for him to crack a few skulls.

"This is none of your business," the broad man told him.

Kahless grunted. "I've made it my business."

"Even if it involves the spilling of blood?"

The clone smiled. *"Especially* if it involves the spilling of blood."

The broad man's hand drifted toward his waist. Under his robes, no doubt, he had a weapon tucked into his belt.

Kahless prepared himself for his adversary's move. But before the broad man could start anything, his companion clamped a hand on his arm.

The clone looked at the tall man. For a moment, as their eyes met, he caught a glimpse of a long, lean face, with a clean-shaven chin and a wispy moustache that began at the corners of the man's mouth.

Then, perhaps realizing that he was exposed, the tall man lowered his face. Again, his cowl concealed him.

"This isn't worth killing over," the man said, his voice deep and throaty. "It's just a table, after all. And there's another for us."

The broad one hesitated, lingering over the prospect of battle. But in the end, he relented. Without another word, he followed his companion to the empty table and sat down.

Out of the corner of his eye, Kahless noticed that the serving maid was looking at him. Gratefully, he imagined. The clone turned and nodded, as if to say, *you're welcome.* With a chuckle, the wench stirred herself and went about her duties.

Kahless returned to his seat, quite pleased with himself. It was satisfying to engage an opponent eye to eye and stare him down. Not as satisfying as drawing his blood, perhaps, but pleasing nonetheless.

And yet, as he reflected on it, there was something about the encounter that didn't seem right. Something that didn't ring quite true. He glanced at the newcomers, who were conversing across their new table with their heads nearly touching. Only their mouths were visible.

They didn't look the least bit shaken by him. Nor should they have been, considering there were two of them, and neither looked feeble in any way. So why had they backed down so easily?

Unless, perhaps, they had even more reason to hide behind their cowls than he did? The clone nodded to himself. That must have been it.

In his mind's eye, he reconsidered his glimpse of the tall one's features. Long chin. Wispy moustache. The more he thought about it, the more it seemed to him there was something familiar about what he'd seen— something he couldn't put his finger on.

He scoured his memory. The man wasn't one of the clerics, was he? No, not that. A bureaucrat on one of the moons? He didn't think so. A retainer to some great House, then? Or a crewman on the vessel that had carried him to the homeworld from the *Enterprise*?

Then it came to him. The man was Lomakh, a high-ranking officer in the Klingon Defense Force. They'd met less than a year ago, at a ceremony honoring Gowron's suppression of the Gon'rai Rebellion.

At the time, Lomakh had been very much in favor— held in high esteem by both the Council and the Defense Force hierarchy. So why was he skulking about now? And who was he skulking *with*?

Pretending not to be interested in the pair any longer,

the clone looked away from them. But every few seconds, he darted a glance in their direction, hoping to catch a smattering of their conversation.

After all, he had been created by the clerics with a talent for reading lips—one of the skills of the original Kahless. As long as he could see the men's mouths, he could make out some part of what they were saying.

Of course, in ancient times, a great many people could read lips, as it was essential to communication in battle and, thus, critical to their survival. It was only in modern times that the practice had fallen into disuse.

Fortunately, the two men were so intent on their own exchange, they didn't seem to notice the clone's scrutiny. With increasing interest, Kahless watched their lips move, shaping an intrigue that caught him altogether off-guard—an intrigue so huge and arrogant in its scope, he could scarcely believe it.

Yet there it was, no mistake. Sitting back in his chair, he took hold of his reeling senses. This was something he had to act to prevent—something he couldn't allow at any cost.

Abruptly, he saw a plate thrust before him. Looking up, he saw the serving maid. She was smiling at him with those remarkable teeth of hers.

"I hope you like it," she said, then turned and left.

Kahless glanced at the conspirators, whose heads were still inclined together. He shook his own from side to side. "No," he breathed. "I *don't* like it. I don't like it at *all.*"

The question was . . . what would he do about it?

CHAPTER 4

The Heroic Age

As Kahless entered the village of M'riiah at the head of his men, he saw a flock of *kraw'zamey* scuttling like big black insects over a mound of something he couldn't identify. It was only when he came closer, and the *kraw'zamey* took wing to avoid him, that he realized the mound was a carcass.

The carcass of a *minn'hor*, to be exact. A burden beast, prized in good times for its strength and its ability to plow a field. By its sunken sides and the way its flesh stretched over its bones, Kahless could tell that the beast had died of hunger. Recently, too.

It was not a good sign, he thought. Not a good sign at all. And yet, he had found it to be pitifully common.

With a flick of his wrist, Kahless tugged at his *s'tarahk's* head with his reins and urged it with his heels around the *minn'hor*. Otherwise, the *s'tarahk* might have been tempted to feed on the carcass, and there was still a possibility of contagion in these lands.

Riding between the huts that made up the village, he saw the central square up ahead. It was nothing more than an empty space with a ceremonial cooking pot set up in the center of it. At the moment, though it was nearing midday, there was nothing cooking. There wasn't even a fire under the pot.

Again, he had seen this before, in other villages. But that didn't make it any more pleasant.

Behind him, Kahless heard a ripple of haughty laughter. Turning, he saw that it had come from Starad. Truth to tell, he didn't like Starad. The man was arrogant, cruel and selfish, and he used his raw-boned strength to push others around. But he was also Molor's son, so Kahless put up with him.

Unfortunately, Starad wasn't his only problem. Far from it. There were others who grumbled at every turn, or whispered amongst themselves like conspirators, or stared hard at one another as if they'd break out into a duel at any moment.

That was what happened when one's warriors came from all parts of Molor's empire, when they had never fought side by side. There was a lack of familiarity, of trust, of cameraderie. And the wretched tedium of their mission only made matters worse.

As Kahless stopped in front of the pot, he saw that the villagers had finally noticed him. They were starting to emerge from their huts, some with children in their arms. A few looked almost as bony as the *minn'hor*.

An old man in a narrow, rusted honor band came out of the biggest hut. His cheekbones looked sharp enough to cut leather, and his ribs stuck out so far Kahless could have counted them at a hundred paces.

This, apparently, was the headman of the village. Its leader. It was to him Kahless would present his demands.

Nudging his *s'tarahk* in the man's direction, Kahless cast a shadow over him. "I've come on behalf of Molor," he spat. "Molor, who claims everything from the mountains to the sea as his domain and demands tribute from all who live here." He indicated the circle of huts with a tilt of his head. "You've neglected to pay Molor what's due him, either the grain or the livestock. Where is it?"

The headman swallowed, visibly shaken. Even before he opened his mouth to speak, Kahless had a fair idea of what the old one would tell him—and he wasn't looking forward to hearing it.

"We cannot give you the grain due our lord, the matchless Molor." The headman's voice quavered, despite his painfully obvious efforts to control it. "Nor," he went on, just as painfully, "can we submit to you the livestock required of us."

Kahless's stomach tightened. Give me an enemy, he thought. No—give me ten enemies, all armed and lusting for my blood—and I will not complain. But this business of squeezing tribute from a scrawny scarecrow of a headman was not to his liking.

Off in the distance, the *kraw'za* birds picked at the *minn'hor*'s corpse. Right now, Kahless felt he had a lot in common with those *kraw'zamey*.

He leaned forward in his saddle, glaring at the headman as if his eyes were sharpened bores. "And how is it that you cannot pay Molor his rightful tribute?" he asked, restraining his annoyance as best he could.

The man swallowed again, even harder than before.

"Because we do not have it." He licked his dry, cracked lips. "You must know what it has been like here the past two years. First, the drought and the famine that followed it. Then the plague that ravaged our beasts." He sighed. "If there was nothing for us to eat, how could we put aside anything for tribute?"

Before Kahless knew it, Starad had urged his mount forward and turned its flank to the headman. Lashing out with his foot, Starad dealt the villager a solid blow to the head with the heel of his boot.

Unprepared for it, the headman fell like a sack of stones and slammed into the hard-packed ground of the square. A moan escaped him.

"You put aside your tribute *before* you eat," Starad snarled, "out of respect for your lord Molor."

Eyeing Starad carefully, a couple of the females moved to help the headman, who waved them back. Dusting himself off, he rose stiffly and faced Kahless once more.

"Starad," said Kahless, though he still stared at the villager.

He could see out of the corner of his eye that Molor's son was grinning at those he called his companions in the group. He had entertained them with his attack on the headman.

"Yes?" replied Starad, the grin still in place.

"Another stunt like that one," Kahless said evenly, but loud enough for all to hear, "and I'll put your damned head on a post—no matter *who* your father is."

The wind blew ominously through the village, raising spiraling dust demons as it went. For several long moments, Starad's eyes narrowed gradually to slits, and it looked as if he might carry the matter further. Then he whirled and maneuvered his *s'tarahk* back into the ranks.

A wise decision, thought Kahless. He'd had no choice but to reprimand the youth. Just as he'd have had no choice but to physically discipline Starad, even in front of these lowly tribute-dodgers, if Molor's son had piled a second affront on top of the first one.

A leader had to lead, after all. And like it or not, Kahless was the leader of this less-than-inspiring expedition.

Turning back to the headman, he saw that there was a dark bruise already evident on the side of the man's face. But it was not out of pity that Kahless pronounced his judgment—just a simple acceptance of the facts.

"There is no excuse for failing to pay your taxes," Kahless rumbled. He could see the headman wince. "But I will exact no punishment," he said, glancing sideways at Starad, "that has not been exacted already."

The villagers looked at one another, incredulous. Kahless grunted. "Do not rely on the *next* collector's being so lenient," he added and brought his mount about in a tight, prancing circle.

With a gesture for the other warriors to follow, he started to put some distance between himself and the village square—until he heard someone call out his name. A moment later, Starad rode past him and planted himself in Kahless's path, giving the older man no other option but to pull up short.

"What are you doing?" Kahless grated.

His tone of voice alone should have been enough to make Starad back down. It was a tone that promised bloodshed.

But Molor's son gave no ground. "There's no room for mercy here," he bellowed, making fast his challenge in the sight of the other warriors. "Molor's instructions were specific—collect the full amount of the village's taxes or burn it to the ground."

"There's no glory in such work," Kahless spat, sidling his steed closer to Starad. "I didn't come here to terrorize women and striplings, or to drive them from their hovels. If that's what Molor requires, let him find someone *else* to do it."

"What has glory got to do with it?" asked Starad. "When one pays homage to Molor, one demonstrates obedience to him."

Kahless leaned toward the younger man, until their faces were but inches apart, and he could smell Starad's breakfast on his breath. "You're a fool," he told Molor's son, "if you think I'll take obedience lessons from the likes of *you*. Now get out of my way."

Kahless's father was long dead, the victim of a cornered *targ*. But while he lived, Kanjis had imparted to his only child one significant bit of wisdom.

In every life, his father had said, there were moments like a sword's edge. All subsequent events balanced on that edge, eventually falling on one side or the other. And it was folly, the old man had learned, to believe one could determine on which side they fell.

Kahless had no doubt that this was such a moment. Molor's whelp might back down or he might not. And if he did *not*, Kahless knew with a certainty, his life would be changed forever.

As luck would have it, Starad's mouth twisted in an expression of defiance. "Very well," he rasped, his eyes as hard and cold as his father the tyrant's. "If you won't do your job, I'll see it done for you."

Spurring his mount, he headed back toward the center of the village. As he rode, he pulled a pitch-and-cloth-swaddled torch out of his saddlebag. And he wasn't the only one. Several others rode after him, with the same damned thing in mind.

Kahless felt his anger rise until it threatened to choke him. He watched as Starad rode by one of the cooking fires, dipped low in the saddle to thrust his torch into the flames, and came up with a fiery brand.

"Burn this place!" he thundered, as his *s'tarahk* rose up on its hind legs and pawed the air. "Burn it to the ground!"

Before Starad's mount came down on its front paws, Kahless had spurred his own beast into action. His fingers closed around the hilt of his sword and dragged it out of his belt.

Molor's son made for the nearest hut. Kahless measured the distance between himself and Starad's objective with his eye and feared that he wouldn't be in time. Digging his heels into his animal's flanks, he leaned forward as far as he could. . . .

And as Starad's torch reached for the hut, Kahless brought his blade down, cutting the torch's flaming head off. Wrenching his steed about sharply, Kahless fixed Starad on his gaze.

"Stop," he hissed, "and live. Or continue this mutiny and die."

With a slithering of his blade from its sheath, Molor's son chose the latter. "If I'm to die," he said slowly and dangerously, "someone will have to kill me. And I don't believe you have the heart to do it."

In truth, Starad was immensely strong, and skilled in swordplay beyond his years. After all, he'd had nothing but the best instructors since he was old enough to stand.

But Kahless had had a crafty old trainer of his own: the

long, drawn-out border wars, which taught him more than if he'd had a courtyard full of instructors. He was willing to pit *that* experience against *any* man's.

"Have it your way," he told Starad and swung down from his beast, sword in hand. On the other side of the square, Molor's son did the same. In the next few seconds, their riding companions dismounted as well, forming a circle around them—a circle from which the villagers backed away, one of them having already grabbed the cooking pot.

It was understood by every warrior present that only one combatant—either Kahless or Starad—would leave that battleground on his feet. This would clearly be a fight to the death.

There was no need for formal challenges or ceremonies—not out here, in the hinterlands. Without preamble, Starad uttered a guttural cry and came at Kahless with a stroke meant to shatter his collarbone.

The older warrior saw it coming, of course—but it was so quickly and powerfully delivered that he still had trouble turning it away. As it was, it missed his shoulder by a mere couple of inches.

Starad's momentum carried him past his adversary. But before the echoes of their first clash had a chance to die down, Molor's son turned and launched a second attack.

This time, Kahless was better prepared for Starad's power. Bracing his feet wide apart, he flung his blade up as hard as he could. The younger man's blow struck sparks from the hard-cast metal, but could not pierce Kahless's defense. And before Starad could regain his balance, Kahless had sliced his tunic from his right shoulder to his hip.

No, thought Kahless, with a measure of satisfaction. More than just the tunic, for there was a hint of lavender along the edge of the ruined leather. He'd carved the upstart's flesh as well, though he didn't think the wound was very deep.

For his part, Starad didn't even seem to notice. He came at Kahless a third time, and a fourth, matching bone and muscle with his adversary, until the square rang with the meetings of their blades and dust rose around them like a dirty, brown cloud.

It was the fifth attack on which the battle turned. It started out like all the others, with Molor's son trying to turn his superior reach to his advantage. He began by aiming at his enemy's head—but when Kahless moved to block the stroke, Starad dropped his shoulder and tried instead to cut him at the ankles.

Kahless leaped to avoid the blow, which he hadn't expected in the least. Fortunately for him, it missed. But when he landed, he stumbled.

He was just starting to right himself when his heel caught on something and he sprawled backward. At the same time, Starad came forward like a charging beast, his sword lifted high for the killing downstroke.

Kahless knew that someone had taken advantage of his vulnerability to trip him. He even knew who it was, though the man might have concealed it from the others. But there was no time for accusations—not with Starad's blade whistling down at him.

He rolled to one side—but not quickly enough. Before he could escape, the finely honed edge bit deep into his shoulder, sending shoots of agony through his arm and leaving it senseless as a stone.

Striding forward, Starad brought his blade up again—

apparently his favorite line of attack. Kahless could see the purplish tinge of gore on it—the younger man's reward for his last gambit.

The sight of his own blood was maddening to Kahless. It gave him the manic strength to get his legs underneath him, to try to lift his weapon against this new assault. But again, he saw, he wouldn't be fast enough. Starad would crush his other shoulder, leaving him completely and utterly defenseless.

He clenched his teeth against the expected impact, knowing it was treachery that had cost him this battle. But treachery, he knew, was part of life.

Then something flashed between him and Starad— something small and slender and bright. It caught the younger man in the side, forcing him to loosen his grip on his weapon and hit the ground instead of his target.

Out of the corner of his eye, Kahless saw a warrior step back into the crowd, lighter by the weight of a throwing dagger. He vowed to remember the man, just as he would remember who had caused him to lose his footing a moment earlier.

In the meantime, there was still a battle to be fought. Kahless scrambled to his feet and raised his blade before him, albeit with one hand. By then, Starad had pulled out the dagger in his side and balanced it in his left hand. It was clear what he intended to do with it.

Seeing that he had no time to lose, Kahless lunged as quickly and forcefully as he could—closing the distance between them so the dagger couldn't be thrown. With a scowl, Starad brought his blade across to intercept his enemy's.

But just this once, he was too slow. In one continuous

motion, Kahless thrust his sword deep into the younger man's side and followed it with his shoulder, bringing Starad down like a tall tree at a land-clearing feast.

They landed together, Kahless on top of his enemy—and his first thought was of the dagger. Taking a chance, he let go of his hilt and used his right hand to snatch at Starad's wrist.

There was still a lot of strength left in Molor's son—so much, in fact, that Kahless nearly lost the struggle for the dagger. But in the end, he forced Starad to plunge the thing into the ground.

Weaponless, hampered by the sword in his side, Starad clawed at Kahless's face, scoring it with his nails. But the older man managed to squirm free, to lurch to his feet, and to grab hold of the sword that still protruded from between Starad's ribs.

He pulled on it, eliciting a groan from Molor's son. With a sucking sound, the blade came free.

Kahless felt the weight of the sun on his face. His wounded shoulder throbbed with pain that was only just awakening. Breathing hard, sweat running down the sides of his face into his beard, he bent to recover the dagger that had preserved his life and thrust it into his belt. Then he paused to survey his handiwork.

Starad was pushing himself backward, inch by painful inch—trying to regain his sword, which had fallen from his hands at some point and still lay a meter or so beyond his grasp. There was gore running from his mouth and his nose, and his tunic was dark and sticky where Kahless had plunged his sword in.

Molor's son was no longer a threat. Left to his own devices, he would perish from loss of blood in a matter of minutes. But despite everything, Kahless was inclined to give him one last chance—for by doing so, he'd be giving himself a chance as well.

A chance that Molor would forgive him. A chance that he might still have a place in the world.

Approaching Starad, so that his shadow fell across the man, Kahless looked down at him. Molor's son looked up, and all the hatred in him was evident in his bulging, bloodshot eyes.

"Yield," Kahless barked, "and I'll spare your life."

Starad kept on pushing himself along, though he never took his eyes off his enemy. Obviously, he had no intention of giving in.

Kahless tried again anyway. "Did you hear me, warrior? I'll let you live if you admit your mistake."

"I admit nothing," Starad croaked. "If I were you, Kahless, I would kill me—because otherwise, I *swear* I'll kill *you.*"

The older man scowled. There was no point in dragging this on. He was weak with blood loss himself and needed stitching. Raising his blade with his one good hand, he brought it down as hard as he could. Molor's son shuddered as the spirit passed out of him.

But Kahless wasn't through yet. Removing the dagger from his belt, he turned and threw it. Nor did the warrior who'd tripped him realize what was happening in time to avoid it.

There was a gurgling sound as the man tried to pull it from the base of his throat. He'd only half-succeeded when his legs buckled and he fell to his knees, then pitched forward face-first on the ground.

Kahless grunted. There was silence all around him, the kind of silence that one might fall into and never be heard from again. Withdrawing his blade from Starad's body, Kahless wiped it clean on the tattered sleeve of his wounded arm. He could feel the scrutiny of his warriors, but he took his time.

Finally, he looked up and commanded their attention. "Molor ordered me to burn this place if its taxes were not paid. I will not do that, nor will I allow anyone else to do it. If there is a man among you who would dispute that with me, as Starad has, let him step forward now. I do not, after all, have all day for this foolishness."

The bravado of his words far exceeded his ability to back them up. He was already beginning to feel light-headed, and he doubted he would survive another encounter. However, he knew better than to say so.

"Well?" he prodded. "Is there not one of you who thinks ill of me for breaking my promise to Molor?"

No one stepped forward. But one of them, the one who had thrown the dagger at Molor's son, drew his sword from his belt and held it high, so it caught the sun's fiery light.

A moment later, another of Kahless's charges did the same. Then another, and another, until every warrior in the circle was pledging his allegiance to the wounded man. Even those who'd ridden with Starad, and laughed at his jokes, and drawn their torches when he did. Their swords were raised as well.

Kahless nodded. It was good to know they were behind him.

But at the same time, he recognized their foolishness. He had made a pariah of himself. He had begun a blood feud with the tyrant Molor, the most powerful man in the world.

Kahless had nowhere to go, no place he could call

home. And no idea what he would do—in the next few minutes, or hours, or days.

No—that wasn't quite true. There was one thing he knew he would do. Eyeing the warrior who had taken the dagger in his throat, he walked over to him, ignoring the mounting pain in his shoulder.

Bending, Kahless withdrew the blade from below the man's chin. Then he walked over to the warrior who had thrown it in the first place.

"Here," he told the man. "I believe this is yours."

"So it is," the warrior replied. He accepted the dagger and replaced it in its sheath, which was strapped to his thigh.

"What's your name?" asked Kahless.

The warrior looked at him unflinchingly, with dark, deep-set eyes. "Morath," he answered. "Son of Ondagh."

Kahless shook his head. "To follow me is to invite Molor's vengeance. You must be a cretin, Morath, son of Ondagh."

Morath's dark eyes narrowed, but there was no spite in them. "No more than you, Kahless, son of Kanjis."

The warchief couldn't help smiling at that. Then, out of the corner of his eye, he saw someone approaching. He turned.

It was the village headman. Behind him, a couple of women had come out with wood for the cooking pot. Another man was setting it up again in the center of the square.

"Your wound," said the old man. "It must be cauterized and bathed, or it will become infected and you will lose the arm."

Kahless couldn't help but see the wisdom in that. Bad

enough to be hunted by Molor, but to do so with only one hand . . .

"All right," he said, loud enough for all his warriors to hear. "We'll wait long enough to lay hot metal against my wound. Then we will ride."

But he still had no idea where they would go or what they would do. Unfortunately, he had never been an outlaw before.

CHAPTER 5

The Modern Age

As Kahless marched the length of the long corridor that led to the Klingon High Council Chamber, he could hear the resounding clack of each footfall. He had grown to like that sound, to look forward to it—just as he had grown to appreciate the venerating looks he got from the warriors standing guard along the way.

It was right that his footsteps should resound. It was right that warriors should look at him with respect and admiration in their eyes. After all, he was *Kahless*.

But even here, the emperor saw, the scroll had taken its toll on him. The guards didn't look at him quite the same way as he passed. Instead, they peered at one another, as if asking: Is it true? Can he be the utter fraud they've made him out to be?

The muscles in Kahless's jaw tightened. He wished he had Olahg's scrawny neck in his hands, for just a minute.

He would repay the initiate tenfold for the damage he had done.

Regaining control, he saw the doors to the central chamber were just ahead. Kahless resolved not to glance at anyone else along the way, but to keep his gazed fixed on the entrance. Remember who you are, he told himself. Remember and be proud.

He didn't pause at the doors, as other Klingons did. It was his right as emperor—even one who wielded no political power—to come and go as he pleased. Laying a hand on either door, he pushed them open.

Gowron was sitting in the leader's seat at the far end of the chamber, conferring with one of his councilors. When he saw Kahless make his entrance, he paused for a moment, then dismissed the councilor with a gesture.

Kahless stopped, allowing the echoes of the man's footfalls to become lost under the dark, vaulted roof. Gowron sat back in his seat and assessed his visitor, his eyes giving no clue to his emotional state.

The emperor grunted softly. Gowron was very good at that, wasn't he?

"What do you want?" asked the council leader, his voice—like his eyes—as neutral as possible.

Kahless straightened to his full height. "I would speak with you privately, son of M'rel."

Gowron considered the request for a moment. Then he looked to the guards who stood at the door and made a sweeping motion with his arm. Kahless didn't look back to see how it was done—but a moment later, he heard the heavy, clanging sound of the doors as they were shut.

It was quiet in the chamber now. The only sound was that of their breathing—until Kahless spoke up again.

"I believe there is a conspiracy," he said, seeing no reason to be circumspect. "A plot against you and your regime—and therefore, against me as well."

Gowron's brows met over the bridge of his nose. He started to smile as if it were a joke, then stopped himself. "And who do you believe is conspiring against us?"

Kahless told him about the incident in the dining hall. About Lomakh, and the things he had seen Lomakh say. And, finally, he told Gowron what he thought it all meant.

The council leader stared at him. "Why *them?*" He tilted his head. "They have always been among my greatest supporters. Why would they see fit to turn against me now?"

"One might look at a *thranx* bush for seven years," said Kahless, "and conclude it was incapable of flowering. But if one came back in the eighth year, one would see a vast profusion of flowers."

Gowron scowled. "In other words, they've been nurturing a plot against me for some time? And I was simply not aware of it?"

"It is certainly possible," Kahless agreed. "The question is—what are you going to do about it?"

Gowron's scowl deepened, his eyes like flat, black stones. "I will do nothing," he replied at last.

If this was humor, the emperor didn't appreciate it. "Nothing?" he barked, his words echoing around him. "Against a threat of this magnitude?"

The council leader leaned forward in his chair. "If there *is* a threat," he rejoined. "I have seen no evidence. All I have to go on is the account of a single individual—an individual with a great deal on his mind right now, who may have perceived a conspiracy where none existed."

Kahless could feel the old anger rising inside him. It was all he could do to keep from challenging Gowron to combat.

"You doubt my *word?*" he seethed. "You think I've made this up?"

"I think you believe what you believe," the other man responded, leaning back ever so slightly. "However, under the circumstances, your beliefs may not be grounded in reality. And I cannot accuse my right hand of clawing at my throat until I have seen its fingers reaching for it."

Kahless felt the anger bubble up inside him, refusing to be denied. "I saw what I saw!" he thundered, until the rafters shook with it. "And if you will not defend your Empire, I will!"

Gowron's eyes flashed with equal fire. But before he could answer, the emperor had turned on his heel and was headed for the exit.

Had it been anyone else, Kahless knew, the council leader would have rewarded his impertinence with a swift and violent death. But scroll or no scroll, he was still Kahless. Gowron didn't dare try to kill him, no matter how great the insult.

What was more, Kahless had suffered the greater affront. The accuracy of his observations had been questioned, as if he were some drooling half-wit, or a doddering old warrior who had outlived his usefulness. Gowron's words stung him like *pherza* wasps as he threw open the doors and stalked back down the long corridor beyond.

Seeing his anger, the guards on either side of him

looked away. A wise move on their part, he thought. He was in no mood for further impudence on the part of his inferiors.

Until recently, Kahless told himself, Gowron's regime had benefited mightily from the emperor's popularity. Only now, as the controversy concerning the scroll reached new heights, did Gowron seem eager to disassociate himself from Kahless—to keep the clone at arm's length.

Kahless's mouth twisted into a silent snarl. Regardless of how Gowron had treated him, he could not let the Empire fall. And yet, he couldn't very well face the threat of Lomakh and his conspirators alone.

He needed help. But from whom? Who could he enlist in his cause?

Not the clerics who created him. They were thinkers and philosophers, useless in a situation like this one. And there was no one else he could trust implicitly, within the council chamber or without.

No . . . wait. There *was* someone he could place his faith in.

Someone *outside* the empire . . .

CHAPTER 6

The Heroic Age

There was a village in the distance, the largest one they'd seen since Kahless and his men had fallen afoul of Molor's power. The dark tower of its central keep danced in the heat waves that rose off the land, surrounded by equally dark walls.

A deep, slow-moving river irrigated the fields and the groves of fruit trees that radiated from the village like the spokes of a wheel. The wind brought the smell of the *minn'hor* droppings commonly used as fertilizer. Swarms of blue-gray treehens scuttled across the land, screeching as they hunted for parasites.

Kahless used the back of his hand to rid his brow of perspiration. Removing his water bladder from his saddle, he untied the thong that held its neck closed, lifted, and drank. At least they'd had no shortage of water as they traveled north, away from Molor's capital—and the river up ahead would provide them with even more.

He wished the same were true of their food supplies. Their military provisions had run out long ago, and thanks to the famine the year before, it was almost impossible to find fresh game for the fire. As a result, they'd had to subsist on a diet of groundnuts and stringy *yolok* worms.

"I wouldn't mind stopping here," said Porus, the eldest of them. He'd been in Molor's service longer than even Kahless himself, but he hadn't liked their orders back in M'Riiah any better than the warchief had. "I'm weary of slinking around like a *p'tahk,* and this place looks prosperous. I'll wager they have plenty to eat, and then some."

Morath, who sat on Kahless's right flank, nodded wistfully. "I'll wager you're right. Their location on this broad old river must have helped them during the drought." He bit his lip. "But we don't dare stop here."

"Why not?" asked a third warrior, a wiry, one-eyed man called Shurin. "What harm could it do to cajole some bread from the local baker? Or better yet, to swipe it while he's not looking?"

Kahless shook his head slowly from side to side. "No," he said, "Morath is right. Once the villagers get an idea we're outlaws, they'll report our whereabouts to the tyrant. And then a good meal will be the *least* of our problems."

With that, he pulled on the reins and pointed his beast's head toward a bend in the river. There were plenty of trees and bushes there to conceal them while they filled their waterskins. As his men fell into line behind him, he could hear them moaning about what they'd missed.

"I wonder how these people prepare *rokeg* blood pie," Porus sighed. "Baked in spices? Or in its own juices?"

"Spices," decided Shurin. "Definitely."

"How do you know?" asked Porus.

"Because that's the way I like it," returned Shurin. "If I can't have it in any case, why not imagine I'm missing the best?"

Kahless cursed the circumstances that had put him and Molor at odds. After all, he'd been as loyal a soldier as anyone could ever want. He'd been brave and effective. He deserved better.

Why couldn't he have been sent to collect taxes from a village like this one, where they had enough to pay and be done with it? Then he might have been gnawing on *bregit* lung and heart of *targ* instead of dreaming about them.

But fate had given him no choice in the matter. How could he have burned M'riiah, with all the misfortunes it already had to endure? Molor might as well have asked him to flay the flesh from his shoulders.

Given a second chance, he knew, he would do the same thing all over again. He would like it no better than the first time, he would drag his feet—but he most certainly would do it. And if *that* was not some particularly virulent form of insanity, he didn't know what *was*.

Kahless grunted pensively—then looked around at his companions. And yet, he thought, if I am insane, I am not the only one. If I am diseased, my men are doubly so. And Morath most of all.

The man had risked his life for a warchief he barely knew, just to ensure a fair fight. Given Starad's size and prowess, Morath had to have believed he was wagering on a losing cause. But, fool that he was, he had wagered nonetheless.

And when the fight was over, and Morath had had

MICHAEL JAN FRIEDMAN

every chance to fade into obscurity, he had chosen to raise his sword and lead the cheer for Kahless instead. The warchief shook his head.

Unlike the others, Morath was closemouthed, his motivations difficult to plumb. He didn't speak much of where he came from or how he had been raised, or how he had come to join Molor's forces.

Nor would Kahless make an attempt to pry the story from him. If the younger man wished to keep his own counsel, he would have every opportunity to do so. The warchief owed him that, at least.

Up ahead, the gray and yellow *micayah* trees swayed in the wind, their slim, brittle leaves buzzing like strange insects. Kahless urged his mount toward an opening between two of the largest specimens, through which the glistening surface of the river was blindingly visible.

The animal trotted along cheerfully, for a change. The prospect of a good watering would do that to anyone, thought Kahless. Cool shadows caressed him as he ducked his head to avoid a low-slung branch.

He had almost reached the river bank when he heard a cry downstream, to his left. His first thought was that he'd led his men into an ambush. His second was that Molor would have fewer outlaws to worry about tonight when he took his evening bath.

However, as Kahless slipped his sword free, he saw it wasn't an ambush at all. Not unless Molor's warriors were all females these days, and naked ones at that.

What's more, they hadn't noticed his approach. They were too busy shrieking with glee, too busy pounding at the surface of the water in an effort to drench one another—though they were already as drenched as one could be. Clearly not the behavior of steely-eyed assassins.

Kahless couldn't help smiling. The females were so lovely, so tempting as they raised rainbow-colored sprays with their splashing, their dark hair making slapping sounds as it whipped about their heads. He'd had precious little time for lovemaking these past few years, in Molor's employ. Now he was forcibly reminded of what he'd missed.

"What have we here?" murmured Shurin, as he caught up with his chief.

Porus chuckled. "Something tastier than blood pie, my friend. Our reward, perhaps, for sparing M'riiah?"

"Not likely," grunted Kahless, putting his cohorts on notice. He wasn't about to let anyone take advantage of these females. They had enough enemies without making more.

On the other hand, there was no harm in watching, was there? Certainly, Morath didn't think so. He was so intent on the females as he nudged his beast up near the bank, Kahless thought the man's eyes would boil.

"Look at you," Porus jibed, elbowing Morath in the ribs. "One would think you'd never seen a wench before."

Morath shot him a look that was altogether too serious. "That would be none of one's business," he hissed.

But before he could say anymore, his mount gave in to temptation—and surged forward over the riverbank, landing with a noisy *plash* in the shallow water beyond.

Suddenly, the females' heads turned. For a moment, no one moved and no one spoke, each group seemingly paralyzed as it took stock of its situation. Then the naked ones struck out for the nearest bank.

For no reason he could identify at the time, Kahless brought his animal about and guided it through the trees. Up ahead, he could see the females scrambling for their garments in a little clearing, where they had hung them on the lower branches.

Without even bothering to put their clothes on, they scampered away through the woods. Not that there was any reason to flee, thanks to Kahless's prohibition—but they had no way of knowing that. Amused, he watched them run, fleet as any animal and twice as graceful.

All except one of them. The tallest and most beautiful stood her ground all alone, having grabbed not her clothes but a long, deadly dagger. As Kahless spurred his *s'tarahk* to move closer to her, he saw her eyes flash with grim determination.

He knew that look. This female had the heart of a warrior. He liked that. He liked it a lot.

Kahless heard his men emerge from the woods to assemble behind him. The female's eyes darted from one to another of them, but she didn't run or drop her weapon or plead for mercy. Yes, a warrior's heart indeed.

"My father warned me that Molor's warriors might be about," she said, with just a hint of tremulousness in her voice. "Collecting Molor's stinking taxes," she went on. "But foolish me, I didn't listen—and this is the result." She raised her chin in a gesture of defiance. "Still, I'll make some of you sorry you thought to lay a hand on me."

Kahless heard his men laugh deep in their throats. With a gesture, he silenced them, though he himself was grinning like a *kraw'za*.

"We were once Molor's warriors," he told the woman. "But we're not that anymore. In fact, he would be happier if we were hanged with our own intestines. And rest assured, we have no intention of laying a hand on you."

The female's eyes narrowed. "Not Molor's men? Then you must be . . . ."

"Outlaws," said Kahless, confirming her suspicions. "And since I have spared your life, I ask a favor in return."

"A favor?" the female echoed.

He nodded his head. "We could use some food and a comfortable place to sleep for the night—somewhere we'll be safe from the lord of this place. We don't want to find ourselves his prisoners in the morning." He paused. "That is, if it's not asking too much."

For the first time, a smile tugged at the corners of the female's mouth. "I think I can give you what you want," she said. "But I'll make no guarantees about keeping your presence here from Lord Vathraq. After all, it's his hall you'll be sleeping in."

"His hall . . . ?" Porus muttered.

The female nodded. "He is my father."

CHAPTER 7

The Modern Age

As Worf entered the captain's ready room, he had expected only Picard to be waiting for him. He was surprised to see that there was another figure as well—a figure whose drab, loose-fitting garb marked him as one of the clerics of Boreth.

And not just *any* cleric. Closer scrutiny showed Worf that the shadowed face beneath the cowl was that of Koroth—chief among those who had dedicated their lives to the preservation of Kahless's traditions.

Koroth inclined his head out of respect for the lieutenant. After all, it was Worf who had forced a meeting of the minds between Gowron and the clone, affording the emperor an honorary place in the council hall.

The security chief returned the gesture of respect. Then he looked to his superior for an explanation.

"I am as much in the dark about this as you are," Picard informed him. Casting a glance in the cleric's direction, he added: "Our guest asked that you be present before he told us what his visit was about."

There was just the slightest hint of resentment in the captain's voice, but Worf noticed it. After one had served with a commanding officer for more than seven years, one came to know his reactions rather thoroughly. However, the Klingon doubted that their visitor had picked up on it.

Koroth fixed Worf with his gaze. "I've come on behalf of Kahless," he declared. "The *modern*-day Kahless."

"The clone," Picard confirmed.

The cleric nodded, though it was clearly not the description he would have preferred. "Yes. You see, he is in need of help—and he hopes you two will be the source of it."

The captain shifted in his seat. "Why *us?*" he asked.

"Because he knows he can trust you," Koroth told him. He was still looking at Worf. "After all, you were the ones who helped him come to an understanding with Gowron. If not for you, the Empire might have split into bloody factions over their conflict."

True, thought Worf. Though it was Gowron, as leader of the High Council, who still wielded the real power.

"What *exactly* does Kahless wish us to do?" Picard inquired.

The cleric shrugged. "Unfortunately, he did not provide me with this information. Nor did I press him for it, as he seemed reluctant to speak of the matter. My mission was simply to alert you to Kahless's need . . . and to give you the coordinates of a Klingon colony in the Nin'taga system, where Kahless wishes to meet you at a designated time."

The captain eyed his security chief. Worf knew that

look as well. It meant Picard had come up with some answers of his own, which he would no doubt wish to test.

"I don't suppose this has anything to do with the *scroll?*" the captain ventured.

Koroth scowled. "I would be surprised if it did not. The scroll has been a source of great discomfort to him. In fact, to all of us. I wish Olahg had never found the cursed thing."

"Has it been authenticated?" Picard asked.

The cleric shook his head. "Nor do I believe it will be. I have publicly demanded that it be subjected to dating technologies, to prove its fraudulence. However, it may be too late to bury the controversy the scroll has created." Koroth sighed audibly. "One thing is certain—Kahless needs your assistance now, before things get any worse."

Worf didn't doubt it. Kahless would not have called on them for any small problem. Whatever trouble the scroll had birthed, it was something big. He hated to think *how* big.

But in the end, it didn't matter *why* Kahless had requested their help—only that he *had*. Surely, Picard would see that.

"Will you honor the emperor's request?" asked the cleric.

The captain drummed his fingers on the desk in front of him as he looked from Koroth to the lieutenant and back again, mulling the situation over. After a while, he stopped.

"All right," he told the cleric. "If there's a problem in the Empire, I suppose I must investigate it, at least. Give me the time and coordinates of the rendezvous and I'll be there."

Koroth turned to Worf. "And you, Lieutenant?"

Worf indulged himself in a typically Klingon remark: "Can I let my captain risk his life alone?"

The cleric smiled a thin-lipped smile. "No," he said softly. "Not if you are the sort of a warrior the emperor believes you to be."

The lieutenant grunted. As Picard's duty was clear, so was his—to respond to Kahless's summons as quickly as possible, and to gauge the danger to both the Empire and the Federation.

But despite his brave remark, he didn't feel inspired by the undertaking. Not when all he believed about Kahless seemed to have been built on a foundation of lies.

Commander William Riker was sitting in the center seat on the bridge, staring at the Byndarite merchant ship hanging off their port bow. He didn't like the idea that something was going on and he didn't know what or why.

First, the Byndarites had hailed the *Enterprise*—an unusual event in itself, given the aliens' customary lack of interest in dealing with the Federation. Then the commander of the Byndarite vessel had asked to speak with Captain Picard—and Picard alone, though it was Riker who had command of the bridge at the time.

Naturally, the first officer had alerted the captain as to the request. Understandably intrigued, Picard had asked Riker to put the communication through to his ready room.

But the captain wasn't the only one curious about the Byndarites' intentions. And the first officer only became more curious when Picard gave the order to lower shields.

To Riker, that meant only one thing. Someone was beaming aboard.

Someone who insisted on a certain amount of secrecy, the first officer discovered a moment later. Otherwise, the visitor would have arrived in one of the ship's several transporter facilities, instead of beaming directly into the captain's ready room.

Trying to contain himself, Riker had remained patient—even when he saw the turbolift open and deposit Worf on the bridge. A little taken aback, he had watched the Klingon join Picard.

What did Worf have to do with the Byndarites? he had wondered. He was still wondering some ten minutes later when the aliens retrieved their mysterious envoy—or so his monitor indicated.

A moment later, as the first officer watched, Worf had emerged from the captain's ready room. But he hadn't provided an explanation. He hadn't even glanced at anyone on the bridge. The lieutenant had simply reentered the turbolift and disappeared.

Which left Riker where he was now, staring at the Byndarite as it ran through some engine checks. Apparently, it was about to depart, taking its mystery along with it—and leaving the first officer in the dark.

Of course, the captain wouldn't let him languish there for long. There were few matters he didn't share with his senior staff, no matter how sensitive or restricted they were.

That was one of the advantages of serving under someone with as much clout as Jean-Luc Picard. He could bend the rules a little, and no one at Starfleet Command was likely to complain.

Not that he would let just anybody in on a high-priority matter. Only those officers he trusted.

Abruptly, the captain's voice flooded the confines of the bridge. "Number One?" he intoned.

Ah, thought Riker. Right on time. "Yes, sir?"

"I'd like to see you in my ready room as soon as possible."

"Right away, sir," said the first officer.

Relinquishing the bridge to Commander Data, he got up, circumnavigated the curve of the tactical console and made his way to the ready room door. A moment later, he heard the single word, "Come." Right now, it was a welcome word indeed.

As the door slid open, it revealed Picard. He was sitting at his desk, chair tilted back, looking contemplative. Lifting his eyes, he gestured to the chair opposite him.

"Have a seat, Will."

Riker complied. "This is about our mysterious visitor?" he asked. It wasn't really a question.

The captain nodded. "Koroth. One of the Klingon clerics we had aboard a year and a half ago."

"Ah," said the first officer. So *that's* who it was. "One of the people who created the Kahless clone."

"Precisely. And since the clerics have no ship of their own, and Koroth wished to remain anonymous, he took advantage of his familiarity with the Byndarites to secure passage."

Riker understood. Boreth was on the outskirts of the Empire—and therefore nearly in the path of one of the Byndarite trade routes.

"But that doesn't explain what Koroth was doing here," the first officer pointed out. "Or why he felt compelled to be so secretive."

"No," Picard conceded. "Apparently, he was acting as

a go-between. It seems Emperor Kahless desires a meeting with myself and Mister Worf."

Riker looked at the captain. "Why couldn't Kahless tell you that himself?"

Picard frowned. "I don't know—though Koroth implied we would find that out in due time. We have only one clue. Not long ago, a scroll was discovered on the Klingon homeworld—a scroll that seems to debunk a great many Klingon legends. Particularly those dealing with the historical Kahless."

"I see," said the first officer.

"Mister Worf received the content of the scroll via subspace communiqué recently. He's agreed to make it available to you and the other senior officers, in case it becomes necessary to familiarize yourselves with it. I recommend you take a glance at it—just in case."

Riker smiled uncertainly. "In case *what?*"

The captain sighed. "I don't know that either, I'm afraid. If I were you, I would be ready for anything."

The first officer grunted thoughtfully. "If you say so, sir."

"I do. Dismissed, Number One."

But Riker didn't leave. He just sat there, trying to decide how best to phrase what he wanted to say.

Picard's brow wrinkled. "Was there something else, Will?"

"Yes, sir. I don't suppose you've forgotten why you chose me to be the first officer of the *Enterprise?*"

The captain considered the question for a moment. "Because of that incident on Altair Three, you mean. The one where you forbade your captain to go on an away mission on the grounds it was too dangerous. When I read about it in your file, it showed me what you were made of—that you had the guts to stand up for what you believed in."

"That's right," Riker confirmed. "You might say a bell went off in my brain back on Altair Three. A warning bell."

Picard smiled. "Any reason that incident should come to mind right now?"

The first officer nodded. "That bell is going off again. You're responding to the request of someone who tried to deceive you once before."

It was hard to argue with that. Koroth and his clerics had tried to convince not only the captain, but the entire quadrant, that Kahless the clone was in fact Kahless the Unforgettable. And they had nearly gotten away with it.

"Even if you think you can trust him," Riker went on, "you're headed for the Klingon Empire—hardly the safest venue in the quadrant. And on top of it, you don't know what you'll find when you get there."

Picard met his gaze. "All true, Number One. And if the situation were different, I would feel compelled to consider your argument. However, Kahless specifically asked for *me* to meet with him. Also, I have visited the homeworld before. I will hardly be a babe in the woods there."

"And if it turns out to be a trap?" Riker suggested.

The captain's mouth became a thin, hard line. "Then I shall no doubt wish I had listened to you. But my instincts tell me it's not a trap, Will. And there is a Klingon expression . . ."

The first officer saw where Picard was going with his remark. *"DujIIj yIvog,"* he declared.

"Trust your instincts," Picard translated. "Exactly."

Riker thought for a moment. "All right," he agreed at last. "We'll *both* trust your instincts, sir."

Alexander was doing his quantum mechanics homework—or trying to—when he heard the whisper of an opening door and saw his father walk in. Right away, the boy knew that something was up. After all, Lieutenant Worf didn't normally visit in the middle of his shift.

Then, just in case Alexander had any doubts, he saw the expression on his father's face. It was an expression he'd seen before, a funny mixture of reluctance and determination.

The reluctance part had to do with his having a son on board—someone he had to raise and protect—and that meant not exposing himself to danger any more than he had to. He hadn't shared any of that with the boy, but Alexander had figured it out all the same.

As for the determination . . . the boy wasn't quite sure about that. But he could guess.

Sighing, Alexander leaned back from his computer terminal. "You're going on a mission, aren't you?"

His father looked at him. "Yes," he admitted. "And there is a chance I will be gone for some time."

The boy nodded. "Can I ask where you're going? Or has the captain asked you not to say anything?"

Worf scowled. "In fact, he has. But I can tell you this much—it involves the Empire."

"You're going to the homeworld?"

His father shrugged. "Possibly."

"In secret?" Alexander pressed.

"In secret," his father confirmed.

"How will you get there?"

"More than likely, we will be transported by the Pescalians."

Now it was the boy's turn to frown. "The Pescalians? But I thought you said their ships were held together with spit."

Worf harrumphed. "Perhaps I was exaggerating. In any case, we will rendezvous with one of their vessels in an hour."

Alexander felt a lump in his throat—the one he got whenever his father left on some dangerous assignment. And by the sound of it, this one was pretty dangerous.

"Who's *we?*" he asked.

"The captain and I," Worf replied.

Well, that was a bright spot. Alexander trusted the captain. He was a smart man. And Starfleet wasn't eager to lose him if they could help it.

"Okay," the boy said, not wanting his father to see his fear. "Have a good trip."

Not that Worf would have scolded him for being afraid. They had come to an understanding about Alexander's human side, the quarter of his heritage he had received from his mother's mother. But it was considered bad luck for a Klingon to leave in the midst of sorrow.

"I will try," his father agreed. "In the meantime, keep up your schoolwork. And your *bat'telh* practice."

Alexander nodded. "I will."

"And if you need anything, you can turn to Counselor Troi. She will be glad to help in any way she can."

The boy knew that without Worf's having to say it. He liked Counselor Troi. And so did his father, though he sometimes didn't seem eager to admit it—even to himself.

"Don't worry," said Alexander. He smiled. "I'll be fine."

Worf looked at him. His eyes gleamed with a touch of pride. "Good. I'll see you when I get back."

"Sure," the boy told him, faking an assurance he didn't quite feel. "When you get back."

A moment later, his father was gone.

CHAPTER 8

The Heroic Age

Hungry as he was, Kahless had a hard time keeping his mind on the food that writhed and steamed and bled on Lord Vathraq's table. Of course, his men had no such problem.

They heaped their plates high with heart of *targ* and serpent worms, with warm, soft *tor'rif* bread and dark, sweet *minn'hor* cheese. They slacked their thirst with fragrant bloodwine, poured by Vathraq's servants. And they gorged themselves as if they didn't know where their next meal was coming from, which was no more or less than the truth.

Kahless, on the other hand, was too busy watching Vathraq's daughter to pay much attention to food.

Her name was Kellein, and in all his years he had never seen anything like her. At first glimpse, back at the river, he had appreciated her courage above all—despite her nakedness. Now, as he watched her move from table to table, seeing to it that everyone was amply served, he took time to appreciate her more obvious attributes.

The way her hips swayed beneath her long, belted tunic, for instance. Or the sharpness of her teeth. Or the shape of her eyes, as brown and oval as *en'tach* leaves in the spring.

Kahless would have guessed that she was twenty years old, perhaps twenty-two. Yet she was wearing a *jinaq* amulet on a silver chain, signifying that her parents had only in the last year deemed her old enough to take a mate.

By that sign, the warrior knew her to be only eighteen. It made her defiance in the river seem even more impressive to him.

Instinctively, he tried to catch her eye. To communicate without words his body's yearning for her. But Kellein didn't look his way.

Cursing himself, Kahless drained a goblet full of bloodwine. Why should she? he asked himself bitterly. All I am is a stinking outlaw, a man with no standing and no future. She'd be better off with a half-wit for a mate than a man marked for death by Molor.

Abruptly, the warchief heard a clamor at the far end of his table. Turning, he saw Vathraq standing with a goblet in his hand, pounding on the wooden boards for silence.

It took a while, but he got it. Smiling like someone who'd had too much bloodwine—which was true, if the stains in his ample gray beard were any indication—Vathraq raised his goblet in Kahless's direction.

"For my guest," he bellowed. "Kahless the Unconquered, Bane of the Emperor Molor. May he feed the tyrant his own entrails!"

There was a roar from Vathraq's people, most of whom were as drunk as he was. As they echoed the toast, they drummed their fists against their tables, making the rafters ring with their noise.

But Kahless didn't like the sound of his host's words. Getting up, he felt himself sway a little—a sign that he'd had more wine than he thought. But he spoke nonetheless.

"I have no intention of going anywhere near Molor, much less feeding him his entrails. In fact, I want to stay as far away from him as I can."

Vathraq roared with laughter. "Whatever you say," he replied. "Don't worry about us, brave Kahless. We'll keep your secret." He turned to his some of his people. "Won't we?"

They howled their approval. Kahless shook his head, intent on dispelling any illusion they had created for themselves.

"No," he shouted. "I mean it. We're outlaws, not idiots. No one can get within a mile of Molor, anyway."

But Vathraq and his people only laughed even louder. Dismissing them with a wave of his hand, Kahless sat down again. Obviously, they would believe what they wanted to, no matter what he said.

But as he poured another goblet full of bloodwine, the warchief saw Morath looking at him from across the room. Of all his men, only Morath seemed clear of eye, free of the wine's influence. And he had a distinct look of disapproval on his face.

Kahless could guess why, too. If he had learned one thing about Morath, it was that the man had principles—

the kind that didn't allow him to let a falsehood go uncorrected.

The warchief grunted. Some falsehoods weren't worth worrying about, he mused. Turning away from Morath, he drained his goblet, allowing his troubles to drown themselves one at a time.

CHAPTER 9

The Modern Age

Picard materialized on a smooth, black plateau open to a glorious, red-orange sky. The air was cool, with a strange, spicy scent to it. Beyond the precipice before him, a good hundred and fifty meters below, a Klingon colony sprawled across a ruddy brown landscape.

Turning to his left, he saw that Worf had taken shape beside him. That was something of a relief. He hadn't particularly trusted the transporter unit in the Pescalian cargo ship that had brought them here.

Then again, they hadn't had much choice in the matter. The captain couldn't have taken the *Enterprise* into Klingon territory without notice—not unless he wished to start a war with Gowron.

"Worf!" boomed a deep voice from behind them. "Captain Picard!"

The captain turned—and saw Kahless emerge from behind a rock formation. The clone grinned. As he closed with them, a curious-looking amulet swung from a thong around his neck.

"It is good to see you again," he said. "Both of you. In fact, you don't know *how* good."

"It is good to see you as well, Emperor," Worf responded.

Kahless clasped his fellow Klingon by the forearm, then repeated the gesture with Picard. The captain winced. The clone was as strong as ever.

"You look well, Emperor," Picard said.

Kahless shrugged. "I am well," he replied, "despite what you may have heard." He looked past the human at the installation below them. "Strange. I have never been to this world before, but it feels familiar here."

He paused to consider the place for a moment. Then, slowly, a smile broke out on his face.

"T'chariv," the clone whispered.

"In the north?" asked Worf.

Kahless nodded. "Of course, the sky was this color only at sunset. But the shape of the settlement, the way it nestles in the hills . . ." He grunted. "It's T'chariv, all right. The place where the original Kahless called the outlying provinces to his banner."

Picard didn't say anything. Neither did Worf.

The clone looked at them. "Yes," he added, responding to their unspoken question. "I am *sure* the original Kahless visited T'chariv. Any person or thing that says otherwise is a liar."

Again, the captain withheld comment. Until the scroll was determined to be authentic or otherwise, he couldn't offer any encouragement. What's more, the clone knew it.

"In any case," Kahless went on, "I didn't bring you here to reminisce with me. There is treachery afoot.

Treachery which will tear apart the Klingon Empire if left to run its course."

Picard couldn't help but be interested. "Treachery from what quarter?" he inquired evenly.

The emperor grunted. "I take no pleasure in saying this—but it is my duty as emperor." He paused for effect. "Apparently, the Klingon Defense Force is undertaking a military coup designed to unseat Gowron and the rest of the council."

"How do you know this?" asked Worf.

"I know," said Kahless, "because I saw two of the conspirators whispering in a dining hall in Tolar'tu, during the Festival of Muar'tek—and nearly every day since. Fortunately, I can still read lips as well as ever."

Picard looked at him skeptically. "But the leaders of the Defense Force were handpicked by Council Leader Gowron. They have sworn to defend him with their very lives."

Kahless's eyes blazed. "That," he told the human, his voice thick with revulsion, "is why they call it *treachery.*" He turned his head and spat. "Believe me when I say there's a scheme against Gowron. And certainly, that would be bad enough. But the conspirators also mentioned Olahg's scroll—said it had enabled them to get their rebellion under way."

"How so?" asked Worf.

The clone made a gesture of dismissal. "The rebels are embracing it as evidence that I am not worth their respect. That Kahless the Unforgettable is not what he seems—and never was."

Worf scowled. "And in many instances, you were all that kept the people from rising up against Gowron."

"Exactly," said the clone. "Without me to bolster him,

Gowron is all too vulnerable. Mind you, he's not my idea of a great leader, but he's a damned sight better than the alternative."

Picard agreed. Gowron, at least, was still an ally of the Federation. The next council leader might not be so inclined.

His eyes losing their focus, Kahless pounded his fist into his other hand. "I wanted to confront the conspirators right then and there. I wanted to stand on their conniving necks and watch their blood run out on the floor." He sighed. "Then I realized I wouldn't be tearing down the rebellion—only lopping off one of its limbs."

"And that's when you came to us?" the captain asked.

The clone shook his head. "First I went to Gowron, for all the good it did. He didn't believe I'd uncovered a threat. He thought I was seeing these things because I wanted to—because I needed to feel important."

Picard didn't want to say so, but he had some doubts himself. And so would Worf, the captain thought, if he knew the Klingon's mind.

This business with the scroll was clearly making Kahless wary. More than likely, he was imagining things. Lots of people whisper in dining halls, but that doesn't mean they plan to overthrow the government.

"You don't believe me," the clone said suddenly, noticing some nuance in Picard's expression. He looked at Worf, then back to the captain again. "Neither of you. You're as incredulous as Gowron was."

"Forgive me," Picard replied, "but there's no proof—"

"I know what I'm talking about!" Kahless thundered. "You want proof? Come with me to the homeworld and I'll *give* you proof!"

The captain didn't think that would be a good idea. He said so. "It was a risk just coming to this colony world. Returning with you to Qo'noS would place Federation-Klingon relations in considerable jeopardy."

The clone's nostrils flared. "They are in considerable jeopardy already, Picard, though you refuse to see it. Knowing me as you do, how can you place so little trust in me? How can you ignore the possibility that I'm right—and that the Empire stands on the brink of revolution?"

Picard had to admit the Klingon had a point. With little or nothing in the way of facts at this juncture, he would be taking a risk either way. And if there was a conspiracy after all—and he ignored it—he would have to live with that oversight the rest of his days.

He turned to Worf. "What do *you* think, Lieutenant?"

The security officer didn't like to be put on the spot like this. The captain knew that from experience. On the other hand, Worf had the firmest grasp of the situation. If anyone could divine the truth about this "conspiracy," it would be the son of Mogh.

For a long moment, Worf looked Kahless square in the eyes. Then he turned to Picard. "I think we ought to go to the homeworld," he said at last.

The captain was still leery of the prospect. However, he had placed his trust in his security officer.

"All right," he concluded. "We'll go."

Kahless smiled. "You won't regret it," he said.

Tapping his wristband, he activated his link to whatever vehicle awaited him. It was the same kind of wristband Picard himself had used to maintain control of *Enterprise* shuttles.

At the same time, the captain tapped his communicator and notified the Pescalians they wouldn't be going back with them. At least, not yet.

"Three to beam up," the clone bellowed.

A moment later, Picard and the others found themselves on the bridge of a modest cruiser. As with all Klingon vessels, the place was small, stark, and lacking in amenities. Quarters were cramped and lights were dim. The bridge had three seats; Kahless took the one in the rear, leaving his companions the forward positions if they wanted them.

"Break orbit," the clone commanded, speaking directly to the ship's computer. "Set course for Qo'noS, heading three four six point one. Ahead warp factor six. Engage."

The captain felt the drag of inertia as the ship banked and leaped forward into warp. Even for a small and relatively unsophisticated vessel, its damper system left something to be desired.

Then again, Kahless probably preferred it that way. The rougher, the better, Picard mused.

"The journey will take a couple of days," the clone informed them. "When you tire, you'll find bunks in the aft cabin." He jerked a thumb over his shoulder for emphasis. "Back there."

Picard nodded. "Thank you."

He recalled the last time he was on a Klingon vessel. He had been on a mission to investigate Ambassador Spock's activities on Romulus. From what he remembered, his cabin had been sparsely furnished and eminently uncomfortable. He resigned himself to the likelihood that on a cruiser this size, the accomodations would be even worse.

Worf looked around. "Nice ship," he observed.

Kahless grunted. "Gowron gave it to me, though I

don't think he expected I'd use it much. And truthfully, I haven't."

Again, Picard found his eyes drawn to the amulet on the clone's chest. He was starting to think he'd seen such a thing before in his studies of Klingon culture, though he wasn't sure where.

"You like my amulet?" asked Kahless.

The captain was embarassed. "I didn't mean to stare."

"You need not apologize," said the clone. "It is called a *jinaq.*"

Picard nodded. He remembered now. Klingon men used to wear them when they were betrothed to someone. Did that mean Kahless intended to marry?

"I have no lover," the clone informed him, as if he'd read the captain's mind. "Not anymore, at least—not for fifteen hundred years or more. But I wear it still, out of respect for her."

"I see," said Picard.

He made a mental note to ask Worf about the applicable myth later on. It sounded interesting—and if it would shed more light on Kahless for him, it was well worth the time.

CHAPTER 10

The Heroic Age

Kahless sat back heavily in his sturdy wooden chair, his head spinning like a child's top. The food and the bloodwine had been more than plentiful. And in all fairness, Vathraq wasn't the *worst* storyteller he'd ever heard, although he came close.

But the warchief was restless under his host's vaulted roof. So, as the revelers' eyes grew bloodshot on both sides of the overladen table, and their speech thickened, and the hall filled with smoky phantoms born of the cooking fires, the guest of honor left the feast.

No one seemed to notice as he made his way out of the great hall, or as he crossed the anteroom and exited the keep. And if anyone did notice, they didn't care enough to say anything.

The evening air was cold and bracing after the warmth of Vathraq's feast—like a splash of melt from a mountain spring, clearing his head and tightening the skin across his face. Breathing it in deeply, he felt as if he'd regained some semblance of his wine-dimmed senses.

A dirt track began at his feet and twisted tortuously between a couple of dark, blockish storage buildings, then reached through the stronghold's open gates to the river road beyond. Kahless caught a glimpse of the cultivated *tran'nuc* trees that grew between the road and the riverbank, and the sweet, purplish fruit that drooped heavily from their thorny black branches.

Vathraq hadn't served the *tran'nuc* fruit because it wasn't ripe yet, nor would it be for a couple of weeks. Kahless knew that because his family had had a tree of their own when he was growing up.

Still, he hadn't bitten into a *tran'nuc* fruit since he left the capital months earlier. And he might not have a chance to taste one again, the way Molor was hunting him.

He could feel the warm rush of his own saliva making his decision for him. Wiping his mouth with the back of his fat-smeared hand, he set out for the gate and the trees beyond. The sentries on the wall turned at his approach. He called up to them, so there would be no surprises.

They swiveled their crossbows in his direction, just in case he was one of the tyrant's tax collectors trying to deceive them. Then one of them recognized him, and they let their weapons fall to their sides. It was unlikely that they'd have shot at him anyway, considering he was *leaving* the compound, and doing it alone at that.

Once past the gates, he felt the wind pick up. It lifted his hair, which he'd left unbraided. The broad, dark sky was full of stars, points of light so bright they seemed to stab at him.

Kahless grunted. What *wasn't* stabbing at him these days?

Leaving Vathraq's walls well behind him, Kahless crossed the road and approached the nearest *tran'nuc* tree. As he moved, the river unfolded like a serpent beyond its overhanging banks, all silver and glistening in the starlight. It seemed to hiss at him, though without malice, as if it too had had its fill this night.

Arriving at the foot of the tree, he reached up and tore a fruit from the lowest branch. In the process, he scratched himself on one of the long, jagged thorns. A rivulet of blood formed on the back of his hand, then another.

Ignoring them, he bit into the fruit. It was riper than he'd imagined, sweet and sour at the same time. But as he'd already gorged himself on Vathraq's food, he had no room for the whole thing.

Tossing the sweet, dark remainder on the ground, he waited for the *yolok* worms to realize it was there. In a matter of seconds, they rose up beneath it, their slender, sinuous bodies white as moonlight. The fruit began to writhe under their ministrations, and then to disappear in chunks as they consumed it with their pincerlike jaws.

Before long, there was only a dark spot on the ground to show that the *tran'nuc* fruit had ever existed. Kahless snorted; it was good to know there were still *some* certainties in life.

He turned to the river again, observing the ripple of the winds on its back. He had forgotten how good it could feel to have a full belly and the prospect of a warm place to sleep. He had forced himself to forget.

Of course, he could have had this every night, if only he'd gone along with Molor's orders back at M'riiah. If he had returned from his mission, the blood on his sword testament to his hard work, and remained the tyrant's most loyal and steadfast servant.

Molor treated his servants well. He would have given Kahless all the females he wanted, and all the bloodwine he could drink. And in time, no doubt, a hall of his own, with a wall for his trophies and a view of his vassals working in the fields.

But if he had torched the village as he was supposed to, all the bloodwine in the world wouldn't have soothed him at night. And the stoutest walls couldn't have kept out the ghosts of M'riiah's innocents.

The outlaw snorted. Why had the tyrant set such a task before him anyway? Why couldn't he have sent one of his other warchiefs—one with a quicker torch and a less tender conscience?

Kahless shook his head angrily. I've got to stop playing "what if" games, he told himself, or they'll drive me mad. What's done is done, for better or worse. And is that any different from what I—

Before he could complete the thought, Kahless realized he was not alone. His eyes slid to one side, searching for shadows; there weren't anyway. Nor could he find a scent, given the direction of the wind. But he sensed someone behind him nonetheless, someone who had apparently made an effort to conceal his approach.

Kahless's thumbs were already tucked into his belt, and his back was to his enemy. As subtly as possible, he moved his right hand toward the knife that hung by his thigh and grasped it firmly. Then he lifted it partway from its leather sheath.

Listening intently, he could hear the shallow breathing

of his assailant, even over the sigh of the wind. In a minute, maybe less, the *yolok* worms would have another meal—and a meatier one.

He waited for a few impossibly long seconds, the hunter's spirit rising in him, the blood pounding in his neck like a beast tearing loose of its chain. His lips curled back from his teeth, every fiber of his being caught in the fiery fever of anticipation.

Finally, the moment came. Clenching his jaw, Kahless whirled, blade singing as it cut the air, heading for the spot between his enemy's head and his shoulders. His eyes opened wide, drinking in the sight of surprise on the intruder's face, exulting in the prospect of the blood that would flow from his—

No!

Muscles cording painfully in his forearm, he stopped his blade less than an inch from its target. The oiled surface of the knife glinted, reflecting starlight on the smooth, gently curving jaw of Vathraq's daughter. Her neck artery pulsed visibly beneath the metal's finely honed edge.

And yet, she didn't flinch. Only her eyes moved, meeting Kahless's and locking onto them. They were pools of darkness, full of resentment and anger.

But nothing to match his own. Lightning-swift, Kahless flicked the blade back into its sheath and snarled like a wounded animal.

"Are you mad?" he rasped. "To sneak up on me like a—"

He never finished. Kellein's open hand smashed him in the face, stinging him as he wouldn't have imagined she could. He took a half-step back, stunned for the moment.

But she wasn't done with him. Slashing him with her

nails, oblivious to the knife he still held in his hand, she sent him staggering back another step. With his left hand, he caught one of her wrists and squeezed it hard enough to crush the bones within.

His intention was to make her stop until he could put his knife away, then use both hands to subdue her. But before he could carry it out, his back foot slipped on the uncertain ground of the riverbank. He felt himself falling backward and braced himself for the chill of the current.

But instead, he felt something hard rush up to meet him, half-pounding the breath out of him. Then there was another impact—that of a weight on top of him. *Her* weight.

It was only then he realized that they had fallen onto a gentle slope just beneath the bank. In the season of Growing, this ground would be submerged by the flood; now, it was dry.

Kahless found that he was still grasping Kellein's wrist with his free hand. Tightening his grip on it, he glared at her, his face mere inches below hers. He could feel the warmth of her breath on his face, smell the wildflowers with which she'd adorned herself for the feast.

Pleasant sensations, under other circumstances. But here and now, they only made him angrier. Remembering his knife, he plunged it into the soft earth beside him.

Kellein planted the heel of her hand on his chest and tried to get up—but he wouldn't let her. Though Kahless's strength was greater than hers, she tried a second time. And a third.

His lip curled. "You followed me out here," he growled accusingly.

"And what if I did?" she returned, her teeth bared in an anger that seemed every bit as inflamed as his.

"What were you thinking?" he thundered. "Why did you come up behind me without warning?"

Kellein's eyes narrowed, making her seem even more incensed than before. "Why," she asked—her voice suddenly husky with something quite different from anger—"do you *think?*"

Suddenly, Kahless understood. All too aware of the hard-muscled angles of Kellein's body, he caught her hair in his fist and drew her face down until her mouth met his.

He tasted blood—though it took him a moment to realize it was his own, wrung from a lip Kellein had just punctured with her teeth. He didn't care, not in the least.

In fact, it made him want her that much more.

In the aftermath of passion, Kahless lay with his back against the ground and Kellein's head on his shoulder. Lightly, she ran her fingernails across his cheek, tracing what seemed to him to be arcane emblems.

Praxis had risen in the east. In its light, Kellein's skin took on a blue-white, almost ethereal cast. She was too beautiful to be of this world, yet too full of life to be of the next.

"What?" she asked suddenly.

He looked at her. "How did you know I was thinking of something?"

Kellein grunted. "You are always thinking of something. If you weren't, Molor would have caught you a long time ago."

Kahless smiled at that. "But how did you know *this* thought had to do with *you,* daughter of Vathraq?"

She shrugged and looked up at the stars. "I just knew," she told him.

"Did you also know *what* I was thinking?"

Kellein cast him a sideways glance. "Don't play games with me, Kahless. I don't like games."

"I don't either," he admitted. "It is only that . . ."

"Yes?" she prodded.

"Where I come from, this means we are betrothed."

Kellein laughed. It was the first time he'd heard her do that. Normally, he would have liked the sound of it—except in this case, he felt he was being mocked. He said so.

"I am not mocking you," she assured him.

"It does not *have* to mean we're betrothed," the warchief told her, snarling as he gave vent to his anger. "It does not have to mean *anything.* We are not in my village, after all."

"I am not mocking you," Kellein repeated, this time more softly. "I was laughing with delight." She propped herself up on one elbow and looked deeply into his eyes. "What we did just now . . . it means the same thing to *my* people that it does to *yours.*"

His anger faded in the wake of another emotion—a much milder one. "You would betroth yourself to me? An outlaw with no future?"

"Not just any outlaw," Kellein said. "Only Kahless, son of Kanjis, scourge of hill and plain."

Kahless was filled with a warmth that had nothing to do with the bloodwine. Taking her head in his hands, he drew her to him again.

"You should do that more often," he told her.

She raised her head. "Do what?" she asked.

"Laugh," he answered.

"Oh," she said. *"That."* There was a note of disdain in her voice. "I have never been the laughing kind." And then, as if she had been carrying on a separate conversation in her own head, "I will make you a *jinaq* amulet just like mine. That way, everyone will know we belong to each other."

"Yes. Everyone will know. And all through the Cold, whenever I touch it, I will think of you."

For a moment, Kellein seemed surprised. "Through the Cold . . . ?"

Kahless nodded. "I mean for my men and I to lose ourselves in the mountains. To give Molor time to forget we exist. Then, when the hunt for me has abated somewhat, I will send them away to seek their separate fortunes, unburdened by their association with me. And you and I will go somewhere the tyrant can't follow."

"I could go with you *now*," she suggested. "To the mountains, I mean. I could remain at your side the long Cold through."

"No," he told her. "It wouldn't work for me to have a mate when none of the others do. It would cause jealousy, dissension. Besides, if Molor were to catch us, the worst he could do is kill us. A female, especially a strong one, would be handled much worse."

Kellein ran her long-nailed fingers through his hair. "But you'll come back in the Growing." It wasn't a question. "And then you'll ask the Lord Vathraq for his daughter's hand in marriage."

He grunted. "I will indeed. That is, if I'm still alive."

She eyed him with a forcefulness he had never seen in a woman before. It robbed him of his breath.

"You'll still be alive," Kellein told him, "if you know what's good for you."

CHAPTER **11**

The Modern Age

Alexander couldn't sleep. He stared at the ceiling, imagining fleecy sheep leaping over fences in a land of rolling, green hills. They leaped one at a time, making long, lazy jumps.

It didn't work. It had *never* worked. And it didn't make it any easier that he had never seen an actual sheep in his whole, entire life.

The only reason Alexander even tried counting sheep was that his mother had suggested it to him. He clung to things he remembered about her a little more than was absolutely necessary.

Like the way she used to sneak up on him and hug him when he wasn't expecting it. Or the way she would recite nursery rhymes to him, which she claimed were from Earth but sounded more Klingon than human.

Little Red Riding Hood, for instance. Didn't that one end with a woodchopper slicing a wolf into bloody bits?

Then there was Snow White, where an evil stepmother poisoned the heroine of the tale with a piece of fruit. K'mpec, who led the High Council before Gowron, died after being poisoned.

And what about the Three Billygoats Gruff? Unless Alexander was mistaken, that was about an animal who butted his enemy off a bridge and saw him drown in the waters below. If that wasn't Klingon, what was?

The boy sighed. He missed his mother.

And now, at least for a while, he missed his father as well. He wished Worf had been able to tell him something more about his mission. It would've made the darkness a little less dark if he knew something. *Anything.*

Suddenly, he remembered. His father had received a subspace message recently. Alexander hadn't thought to ask about it at the time, assuming it was something official or Worf would have discussed it with him.

But now he wondered. Could it have had something to do with the mission his father was on now? If that was the case, there would be some evidence of it in the ship's computer system.

Swiveling in bed, Alexander lowered his feet to the floor, got up, and padded over to the computer terminal in the next room. At the same time, he called for some illumination.

As the lights went on, the boy deposited himself on the chair in front of the computer screen. Then he accessed the log for this particular terminal. It showed him a long list of communications, the vast majority of them from other sites on the *Enterprise.*

There was only one from off-ship. And its origin was the Klingon Empire!

Alexander's hands clenched into fists. His instincts had

been right on target so far. Now it was a matter of bringing the message up on the screen.

If it was classified information, he would be out of luck. No one could get into those files without Starfleet priority clearance. And even if he could somehow hack his way around that fact, he wouldn't. He liked the officers on this ship too much to get in trouble with them.

With a few touches of his padd, the boy established that the message wasn't classified after all. But it *was* restricted to this terminal and one other—the captain's.

And Captain Picard had gone with Alexander's father on the mysterious mission. The pieces were starting to fall into place, thought Alexander. Whatever was in the message, it had something to do with Worf's being called away.

Of course, he could tear the cover off this mystery right now. Tapping again at his padd, he called up the file.

What he saw came as a surprise to him. There was no call for help. In fact, it wasn't really a message at all. It was a history of some kind.

Curious, he read a few lines. And then a few more. It talked about Kahless and the kinds of things he did when he was young, but it didn't seem to jibe too well with what Alexander knew of him. In fact, it seemed to be talking about someone else altogether.

Intrigued, the boy propped his elbows on his desk. Resting his face in his hands, he read on.

Picard couldn't help frowning a little as he followed Kahless and Worf into the dining hall in Tolar'tu. After all, his hood was hardly a foolproof disguise. Anyone who had an opportunity to peer closely inside it would realize in a moment he was no Klingon.

All the more reason not to attract undue attention. Keeping his eyes straight in front of him, the captain felt the warmth of the firepit as he crossed the room.

There was a table in the corner with room for three. Kahless gestured, and they all sat down. Taking a moment to survey the place, Picard decided it was just as the clone had described it.

Nearly everyone was wearing a hood. Most were sitting alone, minding their own business, but there were pairs and trios as well. And everyone spoke in such low voices it was difficult to hear what they were saying.

The captain turned to Kahless. "Are they here?" he whispered.

The clone shook his head. "Not yet. But soon." He eyed Worf. "And you will recognize Lomakh when you see him, I promise. That is, if you look closely enough."

Picard and his security officer exchanged glances. Worf sat back in his chair and frowned.

No doubt, the lieutenant was wondering if he'd done the right thing encouraging his captain to come here. The closer they'd gotten to the dining hall, the more skeptical Worf's expression had become.

Still, Picard mused, they had ventured this far. As the expression went, in for a penny, in for a pound.

He had barely finished the thought when the door opened and two men walked in. One was tall, the other shorter and broad. Like everyone else here, they wore cowls to conceal their features.

Kahless turned to his companions. Picard could tell from the gleam in the Klingon's eye that these two were the ones he'd warned them about. Nonetheless, Kahless felt compelled to underline the point.

"It's them," he breathed.

Worf looked past him at the newcomers. They sat down at a table on the other side of the room and bent their heads until they were almost touching.

"You see?" Kahless commented. "Do they not look like conspirators?"

The captain sighed. The newcomers looked no more conspiratorial than anyone else in the place. "You said Mister Worf would recognize one of them."

The clone nodded. "Yes. The tall one."

Worf's eyes narrowed in the shadow of his hood. "I cannot tell from here," he decided. "I will need a better look."

"Then by all means, take one," Kahless urged.

His frown deepening, the security officer got up and crossed the room to the firepit. Once there, he made a show of warming his hands by its flames. Then he returned to the table.

"Well?" Kahless prodded.

Worf paused for a moment, then nodded. "I believe the tall one is Lomakh. I do not recognize the other."

"Then you see what I am saying," the clone hissed, triumphant. "What would Lomakh be doing in a place like this, concealing his face with a hood . . . unless it was to plan Gowron's overthrow?"

"Unfortunately," said Picard, "he could be doing a great many things." He was still unconvinced.

"I told you," Kahless insisted. "I read their lips. I saw them speak of plucking Gowron from the council like a fattened *targ.*"

As on the colony world, the captain turned to Worf, relying on his judgment and his expertise. "What do you think?" he asked.

The lieutenant sighed. "As an officer in the Defense Force, Lomakh is taking a risk coming here. It does not make sense that he would do so—unless he deemed it a greater risk to conduct his conversation elsewhere."

"In other words," said Picard, "you agree with the emperor's assessment of the situation."

Again, Worf paused a moment, ever cautious. "Yes," he replied at last. "For now, at least, I agree."

The captain absorbed the response. As far as he was concerned, they had seen enough. They could go.

But if they left without eating, Lomakh might notice and wonder about it. And if he really was part of a conspiracy, it might then dig itself an even deeper hole, from which it would be impossible to extricate it. So they hunkered down within their cowls and stayed.

A couple of minutes later, a serving maid came over. The clone ordered for all three of them. Fortunately, Picard was a connoisseur of Klingon fare, so he would arouse no suspicion in that regard.

His only disappointment was the lack of fresh gagh. Apparently, he would have to settle for the cooked variety.

The food wasn't long in coming. But at Kahless's request, they lingered over it, giving him more time to read lips and gather information. In the end, he failed to discover anything useful.

After a rather extended stay, Lomakh and his crony paid for their meals and left the place. The captain felt a bit of tension go out of him. Lomakh hadn't seemed to pay any undue attention to them. Apparently, they had been careful enough to avoid suspicion.

Finishing their food, which was as tasty as the clone had predicted, they gave Lomakh enough time to make himself scarce. Then Kahless took care of their bill and they departed.

Outside, the air was chill and the sun was beginning to set, turning the sky a few shades darker in the west. Obviously, they had been in the dining hall longer than Picard had imagined.

As they retraced their steps toward the main square, which was a good half-kilometer distant, the captain asked "Now what?"

Kahless looked at him. "I was hoping you would have a suggestion, Picard. After all, the captain of the *Enterprise* must wield considerable power."

Picard understood the implication—or thought he did. "Not the kind you need, I'm afraid. We can't exactly assume orbit around Qo'noS, beam down a security team, and place Lomakh under arrest. That is, if we even believed that was a good idea."

"Which it is not," the clone agreed. "As I myself pointed out, Lomakh is only a part of this. If we were to arrest him, we would never expose the rest of the conspiracy." His eyes narrowed beneath his bony brow. "I was speaking more in terms of your influence, Picard. Surely, the Federation maintains spies within the Empire, who would—"

The captain looked at him. "Spies?" he repeated. He laughed. "Whatever gave you that idea?"

Kahless returned the look. "It is only logical. With the surgical techniques available, I imagine—"

"The Empire and the Federation are *allies*," Picard asserted. "We have no spies among the Klingons."

The clone smiled a thin smile. "Either you are naive or you seek to conceal the truth, human. I will give you the benefit of the doubt and embrace the first possibility."

The captain shook his head. "I am neither concealing anything nor am I naive. We conduct no espionage within the Empire, period."

Kahless harrumphed. "Then your Starfleet Headquarters informs you of every move it makes—without exception?"

Picard could see this was getting them nowhere. "Believe what you like," he said. "The bottom line is I have no influence here, no resources. If we are to expose Lomakh's conspiracy, we will have to resort to other means."

The clone frowned. "Very well. If you won't help, or can't, we can always call on our—"

Picard looked at him, wondering why he'd stopped in midsentence. Then he saw the masked figures emerging from the alleyway to Kahless's right, each of them clutching a three-bladed *d'k tahg* in either hand.

Even as the captain prepared himself for their onslaught, he spared a glance in the opposite direction—and saw more trouble coming from the alley opposite. Altogether, it looked to be six or seven against their three. Fortunately, Picard and his allies weren't entirely unprepared.

They hadn't been able to carry phasers off the *Enterprise,* for fear of being identified by them—and disruptors might also draw undue attention. But everyone carried a blade of some sort, and Kahless had seen to it they were no exception.

Slipping his *d'k tahg* free of the sheath on his thigh, the captain braced himself. Before he knew it, one of their assailants was on top of him. Twisting quickly to one side, Picard narrowly avoided disembowelment. And as the

Klingon's momentum carried him past, the human slammed his hilt into the back of the warrior's head.

The masked one hit the ground and lay still. Picard barely had time to kneel and pick up a fallen *d'k tahg* before the next assault came. This time, perhaps seeing what the captain had done already, his adversary approached more slowly and deliberately.

Then, with a viciously quick and accurate lunge, he stabbed at Picard's throat. The human fended off the attack with one of his own blades and countered with a backhand slash of his own. The Klingon leaped back, and the slash fell short.

Almost too late, Picard turned and realized what was really happening. The frontal assault was only a decoy, so a second Klingon could stab him from behind. Reacting instantly, he ducked—and the second assailant sailed over his head, confounding the first.

That gave the captain a chance to see how his companions were doing. He noted with relief that they were both still alive. There was blood running down the side of Worf's face and Kahless had a wet, dark rent in the shoulder of his tunic, but their wounds weren't slowing them down.

Picard watched as Worf lashed out with his foot, cracking an opponent's rib, then faced off with another. And Kahless wove a web of steel with his dagger, keeping two more at bay.

As the captain turned back to his own assailants, he found them separating in an attempt to flank him. A sound strategy, he thought. Cautiously, he backed off, hoping to buy some time.

It would have been the right move, if not for the

recovery of the Klingon he thought he'd knocked unconscious. Hearing the scrape of the warrior's boots, Picard whirled in time to catch a downstroke with crossed blades—but the maneuver left him open to the other two.

The captain could almost feel the shock of cold steel sinking into his back. But it never came. Instead, he saw his adversary withdraw into the alley that had spawned him. Turning, Picard saw the other masked ones retreating as well.

Then he saw why. A group of warriors were approaching from the direction of the dining hall, eager to even the odds. Fortunately, there was nothing a Klingon disliked more than an unfair fight.

Kahless started after the masked ones, caught up in a bloodlust, but Worf planted himself in the clone's way and restrained him. Seeing that his officer would need some help, Picard added his own strength to the effort.

"Let me go!" bellowed Kahless, his eyes filled with a berserker rage.

"No!" cried Worf. "We have got to get out of here, before people start asking questions!" Then he caught sight of the captain and his lips pulled back from his teeth. "Sir!" he hissed. "Your hood!"

Picard groped for it—and realized it had fallen back, exposing his all-too-human face to those around him. He pulled it up again as quickly as he could and looked around.

As far as he could tell, no one had seen him. The newcomers were far too eager to plunge after the attackers to notice much else.

Worf turned back to the clone. "Now we have even more reason to leave," he rasped.

Kahless scowled and made a sound of disgust deep in his throat. Thrusting Worf away from him, he probed the wetness around his shoulder with his fingers. They came away bloody.

"The *p'tahkmey*," he spat. "This was a perfectly good tunic. Mark my words, they'll pay for ruining it."

"You'll need medical attention," remarked Picard.

The Klingon looked at him and laughed. "For what?" he asked. "A flesh wound? I've done worse to myself at the dinner table."

Then he gestured for Picard and Worf to follow, and started for the square again. Behind them, their rescuers were still hooting and shouting, but there was no din of metal on metal. Apparently, the attackers had gotten away.

The captain saw Worf turn to him, his brow creased with concern.

"Are you all right, sir?"

Picard nodded. "Better than I have a right to be. And you?"

The Klingon shrugged. "Well enough."

The captain cast a wary glance down an alley as they passed it. "It seems we were not as circumspect as we believed. Someone realized we were on Lomakh's trail and sent us a message."

Worf grunted in agreement. "Stay clear of the conspiracy or die."

Kahless looked back at them. "Is that what you'll do, Picard? Stay away, now that I've shown you the truth of what I said?" His eyes were like daggers.

The captain shook his head. "No. Staying away is no longer an option. Like it or not, we're in the thick of it."

The clone smiled, obviously delighted by the prospect. "You know," he told Picard, "we'll make a Klingon of you yet."

Then he turned his massive back on them and walked on with renewed purpose. After all, his point had been made, albeit at the risk of their lives.

CHAPTER 12

The Heroic Age

Kahless cursed deep in his throat. His breath froze on the air, misting his eyes, though it couldn't conceal the urgency of his plight.

Up ahead of him, there were nothing but mountains, their snow-streaked flanks soaring high into wreaths of monstrous, gray cloud. As his *s'tarahk* reared, flinging lather from its flanks, the outlaw chief turned and saw the army less than a mile behind them.

Molor's men. With Molor himself leading the hunt.

Again, Kahless cursed. The tyrant had come out of nowhere, surprising them, rousting them from their early Cold camp. He had forced them to fly before his vastly more numerous forces, and the only direction open to them had been this one.

So they'd run, and run, and run some more, until their mounts were slick with sweat and grunting with exhaustion. And all the while, Kahless had had the feeling they were being herded somewhere.

His feeling had been right. Now they were pinned against a barrier of steep, rocky slopes, which their *s'tarahkmey* had no hope of climbing. They had no choice but to turn and fight, and acquit themselves as well as possible before Molor's warriors overran them.

Nor would their deaths be quick—Kahless's, least of all. Molor had to be half-insane with his thirst for vengeance. Starad had been the most promising of his children, after all. The tyrant would make his son's killer pay with every exquisite torture known to him.

As Molor's forces grew larger on the horizon, the outlaw glanced at his men. They were watching their pursuers as well, wondering how they could possibly escape. Kahless wondered too.

No doubt, the tyrant had been tracking them for some time, feeding on rumors and *s'tarahk* prints, edging ever closer. That was the way he stalked those who defied him—with infinite patience, infinite care. And then he struck with the swiftness of heat lightning.

And this trap—this too was in keeping with Molor's method. Many was the time Kahless had engineered just such a snare, in his days as the tyrant's warchief. And to his knowledge, no one had ever escaped.

"Tell everyone to be ready," he barked, eyeing Morath and Porus and Shurin in one sweeping glance. "Molor won't hold any councils when he arrives. He'll pounce, without warning or hesitation."

For emphasis, Kahless drew his sword, which had become nicked from hewing tough, gnarled *m'ressa* branches. But he had had little choice. It was either that or go without cover from the snow and rain.

"Kahless!" called a voice.

He turned and saw Morath sidling toward him on his *s'tarahk*. His deepset eyes were darker than ever—but not with hopelessness, the outlaw thought. It seemed to him the younger man had an idea.

Kahless couldn't imagine what it might be, or how it could possibly help. But he wasn't about to reject it out of hand.

"What is it?" he snapped, never quite taking his eyes off the approaching line of Molor's men.

Morath came so close their mounts were nearly touching. "I've been in these hills before," he said. "At least, I think I have. It was a long time ago."

Kahless had no time for fond reminiscence. "And?"

"And I think there's a way out," Morath declared.

The outlaw looked at him. "What way?" he asked. "Are you going to sunder the mountains and let us through? Because there's no way I can see to get *over* them."

Morath ignored the derision in the older man's voice and pointed to the gray slopes towering behind them. "We don't have to make it *over* them," he insisted. "We only have to make it *into* them."

Kahless was sure Morath had gone insane, but there was no time to argue with him. Scowling, the outlaw signaled to the others to follow. Then Morath took off, with Kahless right behind him.

Despite his leader's skepticism, the younger man seemed to know exactly where he was going. Turning first this way and that, as if negotiating an invisible trail, he urged his *s'tarahk* ever upward. And if the slopes grew steeper as he went, that didn't seem to faze him in the least.

From behind, Kahless could hear the cries of Molor's

men. They were gaining on them now, perhaps half a mile away at most. If Morath was going to work some magic, it would have to come soon.

Suddenly, though the outlaw chief had had his eye on Morath from the beginning of their ascent, the younger man seemed to drop out of sight. Thinking Morath might have fallen into an unseen crevice, Kahless dug his heels into his *s'tarahk*'s flanks and urged the beast forward.

But it wasn't a crevice that had devoured Morath. It was a narrow slot in the mountainside, just big enough for a warrior and his mount to fit through. Morath stopped long enough to beckon his comrades—to assure them with a gesture that he knew what he was doing.

Then he vanished into the slot.

Still wondering where Morath was leading them, Kahless guided his *s'tarahk* into darkness. The walls of the slot scraped his legs where they straddled his beast, but he got through.

Further in, there was a strange sound, almost like the sighing of the north-country wind. It took the outlaw a few seconds to realize it was the murmur of gently running water.

It was shattered by a splash. As Kahless's eyes adjusted to the scarcity of light, he saw Morath moving forward like a shadow, a web of perfect ripples spreading out around him. Gritting his teeth, Kahless followed him into the icy water. Behind him, others were doing the same.

It was some kind of underground stream, flowing from a high point in the mountains. A mysterious black river which had carved a path for itself over the centuries, known only to the tiny creatures who must have inhabited it. And, of course, to Morath.

After a while, there wasn't any light to see by, no matter

how well Kahless's eyes had adjusted. He was forced to travel blind, listening for the snuffling of Morath's mount up ahead and heeding the man's occasional word of guidance.

Fortunately, they didn't have to remain in the river for long. When several minutes had gone by, it seemed to Kahless that the level of the water was dropping. A couple of minutes more and they were on solid rock again.

"Morath," the outlaw rasped, careful to keep his voice low.

Molor couldn't have reached the opening in the mountainside yet, but even so, he didn't want to take a chance on making any noise. Why give the tyrant any help in discovering their exit?

"What is it?" asked the younger man.

"Where does this lead?"

"To another stream," Morath told him, "more treacherous than the first. And from there, to a beach by the sea."

Kahless could scarcely believe what he'd heard. "But the sea . . ."

"Is ten miles distant," the younger man finished. "I know."

The outlaw would normally have been annoyed by the prospect. However, the trek might well prove to be their salvation.

Molor would have a hard time finding the slot. And when he finally discovered it and realized what had happened to them, it was unlikely he'd follow them into what could easily turn out to be an ambush.

Despite himself, the outlaw laughed softly. "That's twice you've saved my hide now," he whispered to Morath.

There was silence for a while. Then Morath spoke again.

"I would have preferred to stay and fight," he said, "if our forces had been more equal."

The chief shook his head. Morath was still young. With him, it was easy to forget that.

"As far as I'm concerned," Kahless replied, "each morning I wake to is a victory. There's no shame in running if it allows you to survive."

Morath didn't speak again as he led them through the darkness. But Kahless could tell that his friend disagreed.

CHAPTER 13

The Modern Age

Despite his acquisition of a seat on the High Council, which had brought with it the governorship of the colony world Ogat, Kurn didn't seem to have changed much since Picard saw him last. The Klingon was still lankier than his older brother, favoring what the captain understood to be their mother's side of the family.

As they entered the garden of standing rocks, Kurn was conversing in bright sunlight with a shorter, stockier Klingon, whose jutting brow was easily his most distinguishing characteristic. Both men wore stately robes, which gave them an air of haughty authority.

At least in Kurn's case, that illusion was quickly dispelled. When Worf and his companions caught his eye with their approach, Kurn grinned like a youth reveling over his first hunting trophy.

"Worf! Brother!" he bellowed, so that the greeting echoed throughout the garden. "Let me look at you!"

Picard's security chief was just as glad to see Kurn. However, as always, he was somewhat less demonstrative in his enthusiasm.

Growing up in an alien culture—that of Earth, for the most part—Worf had learned all too well to hide his innermost feelings. His stint on the *Enterprise* had encouraged him to open up somewhat, but old habits were hard to break.

Kurn pounded Worf on the back and laughed: "It is good to see you, brother. I miss your companionship."

"And I, yours," the lieutenant responded. "Though I see you have managed to keep busy, with or without me."

Kurn grunted and made a gesture of dismissal. "Serving on the Council is more drudgery than I had expected. It leaves little time for my more pleasant duties—like the inspection I've agreed to carry out today."

Picard saw Kurn's companion approach them then, as if that had been his cue. He inclined his head respectfully—though his dark, deepset eyes were clearly drawn to Kahless more than to Worf or the captain.

"This," said Kurn, "is Rajuc, son of Inagh, esteemed headmaster of this academy. You will find him to be a gracious host."

Rajuc smiled, showing his short, sharp teeth. "My lord governor is too generous with his praise. Still, I will do what I can to make you comfortable here." He turned to Kahless. "I have long been an admirer of your exploits, Emperor. This institution is honored beyond measure by your presence."

Kahless shrugged. "Tell me that after I've bloodied your furnishings and ravaged your women," he instructed.

For a moment, the headmaster seemed to take him

seriously. Then his smile returned. "You may do your worst, great one—and I will be honored to be the first to match blades with you."

Beaming, the clone slammed his fist into Rajuc's shoulder. "That's the spirit," he hissed. "Give ground to no one."

"I never have," the headmaster informed him, warming to the subject. "Especially not to the rumor-mongers who would have us believe Kahless was a fraud. I assure you, Emperor, I place no credence at all in the scroll they claim to have found. As far as I am concerned, the stories we learned as children contain the truth of the matter."

Kahless looked as if someone had rammed him in the stomach with the business end of a painstik. "Indeed," he said tightly. "I am grateful for your loyalty, son of Inagh."

No doubt true, thought Picard. However, the clone didn't seem to like being reminded of the scroll—not in any context. It was quite simply a sore subject with him.

"You will be interested to know," Rajuc continued, "that our eldest students plan to reenact Kahless's departure for *Sto-Vo-Kor* in two days' time." For the sake of protocol, he included Worf and Picard in his glance. "Perhaps you can stay long enough to see it."

"I am afraid not," Kahless replied. "As much as I enjoy such dramas, we have business elsewhere which cannot wait." He turned his attention to Kurn. "Which is what we came to speak with you about, Lord Governor."

Worf's brother inclined his shaggy head. "Of course, Emperor." He gestured to a remote cul-de-sac in the garden, obscured by tall, oblong boulders on three sides. "I believe you will find that spot over there to your liking." Placing his hand on Rajuc's shoulder, he added:

"I will see you shortly, Headmaster. There is still much we need to discuss."

Rajuc inclined his head again—first to Kurn, then to Kahless, and finally to Worf and Picard. Then he departed.

"He does good work here?" asked the clone.

Kurn nodded. "Fine work. He turns out warriors of the highest caliber."

"Good," Kahless remarked.

Then, taking Kurn's arm, he led him toward the cul-de-sac. Nor did he wait until they reached it and took their seats to tell the governor why they had come. He began as soon as they were out of the headmaster's earshot.

As Picard watched, Worf's brother listened to Kahless's suspicions. It took a while, but Kurn didn't comment until he was certain the emperor had told him all he wished to tell.

"These are grave accusations," he said at last. "Had they come from someone else, I would have dismissed them out of hand. But from emperor Kahless, the Arbiter of Succession, and my own brother . . ." Kurn scowled. "I will conduct an investigation through my contacts in the Defense Force. Then we will speak of a next step, if one is required of us."

Kahless nodded. "Thank you, son of Mogh. Worf told me you would not fail us."

Kurn flashed a smile at his brother. "Yes, he *would* say that." With that, he rose. "Unfortunately, I must complete my review of the Academy. But if you can linger a while, we'll eat together. I know of a feasting hall in town where the heart of *targ* is worth dying for."

"Done," replied Kahless, obviously cheered by the prospect. "We'll meet back here just before dusk."

"Before dusk," Kurn agreed. He acknowledged Picard, then Worf. "I will see you later, Brother."

"Yes, later," the lieutenant repeated.

He watched his brother leave them with a vaguely uncomfortable expression on his face—one which didn't escape the captain's notice. What's more, Picard thought he knew the reason for it.

"He was holding something back," he said to Worf. "Wasn't he?"

The lieutenant was still watching his brother withdraw. "Or covering something up," he confirmed, with obvious reluctance. "But what?"

Kahless looked at them. "What are you saying?" he asked.

Worf drew a deep breath, then let it out. "I am saying," he explained, "that my brother lied to us when he said he would help. There is something preventing him from doing so—though I cannot imagine what it would be."

The clone eyed him. "You're sure of this?"

The lieutenant nodded. "Regretfully, I am sure of it. And I intend to confront him with it when the opportunity presents itself."

"Dinner would be such an opportunity," the captain suggested.

Kahless made a sound of disgust. "Why wait for dinner? Let us pin him down now, while his lie is still fresh on his lips. Who knows? Maybe he's part of the damned conspiracy."

Worf grabbed him by his arm. Instinctively, Kahless spun around, ready for anything.

"My brother is not a traitor," the lieutenant snarled.

The emperor's eyes narrowed. "Then let him prove it."

And without waiting to see if his companions would

follow, the clone took off after Kurn with that swaggering, ground-eating pace by which he'd become known.

Worf made a noise deep in his throat and followed. Picard did his best to keep up, though it wasn't easy. Klingons were damned quick when they wanted to be.

But just as Kahless caught up with his prey, Kurn was swarmed by a group of young admirers—warriors-in-training, wearing the black-and-crimson colors of their academy. The governor had barely expressed his surprise before he was assailed with questions—mostly about his encounters with the Romulans following Gowron's succession.

Kurn would likely have answered them, too, had Kahless not shooed the youngsters away like a gaggle of young geese. When the emperor wanted something, he tolerated no delays.

Worf's brother looked at Kahless, no doubt trying to conceal his displeasure at the students' dismissal—but falling short. "Is something wrong?" he asked.

Worf answered for the emperor. "You *know* there is, Brother. You lied to us when you said you would investigate Kahless's concerns. And I want to know why."

"Yes," the clone added. "Unless you're a conspirator yourself. Then you may want to go on lying."

Kurn bared his teeth. For a moment, he glared at Kahless and then Worf, apparently liking his brother's challenge even less than the emperor's audacity. Then his temper seemed to cool.

"All right," he said. "I *was* deceiving you. But I had the best of intentions. And I am *not* a conspirator."

"There is a Terran expression," Picard remarked, "about the road to Hell being paved with good intentions. I'd like to hear more before I decide to exonerate you."

Kurn's nostrils flared. Obviously, this was information he wasn't eager to part with. He looked around and made certain they were alone before continuing.

"Very well," the governor growled. "But this must not become common knowledge, or I'll *truly* have become a traitor."

Worf thrust his chin out. "You *know* none of us will repeat anything you tell us."

Kurn thought for a moment, then nodded. "I believe you're right." He heaved a sigh before he began. "The reason I wished to dissuade you from investigating the Defense Force is simple. Close scrutiny of its activities would have revealed a significant number of concurrent absences on the parts of two particular officers—a male and a female, each one with a mate outside the Defense Force."

Picard grunted. The Klingon family was held together by almost feudal bonds. Such philandering was a violation of those bonds—at least, on the part of the male Klingon involved.

The female's situation was different. She could have initiated a divorce anytime she wanted—though she apparently had her reasons for not doing so.

Kurn turned to Picard. "This is not a thing to be taken lightly," he explained, just in case the captain didn't understand. "The response of the cuckolded husband, in this case, must be to seek revenge—as if a challenge had been made. Worse, the cuckolded wife in this situation may have her husband slowly drawn and quartered by four powerful burden beasts—while his lover is forced to watch."

"And yet," said Picard, "they risked this. And despite

the fact that your society frowns on it, you yourself condone it."

Kurn scowled at the remark. "You must understand, Captain. These philanderers are members of prominent Houses, which have long been allies of Gowron. If their affair became public, it would drive a wedge between their families and severely erode Gowron's power base."

Kahless snorted. "So these liaisons must be kept secret?"

"Exactly," said Kurn. He turned to his brother. "Of course, if you and your companions had proof of your claims, that would be a different story. But until you do, I cannot help you."

Picard looked to his lieutenant, but Worf said nothing. Apparently, he accepted Kurn's answer as sufficient. Morality aside, the captain wasn't sure he disagreed, given the importance of Gowron's survival as Council Leader.

This time, Kurn didn't bother with niceties. He merely turned his back on them and resumed his progress toward the academy's main hall.

In other words, Picard thought, they had gained nothing at all. Frowning, he watched Worf's brother disappear into the building—and with him, their best hope.

Kahless looked to Worf, then Picard. "What now?" he asked. "Who else can we turn to, if not Kurn?"

The words were barely out of his mouth when an explosion ripped through the academy building like a fiery predator, shattering the peacefulness of the grounds and sending debris flying in every direction.

Worf's eyes flashed with anger and fear. "Kurn!" he wailed—and went running toward the site of the explosion, where flames were already starting to lick at the ruined masonry.

A moment later, the captain and Kahless took off after him. Picard could hear shouts of fury arising from the building. Also, cries of agony. Unfortunately, all of them were the voices of children.

Before they could reach the building, a door burst open and a gang of students came rushing out, carrying an adult—Rajuc. The captain winced at the sight of the headmaster. The man was half-covered with blood and his arm hung limply at his side, but at least he was still alive.

Brushing past the students and their burden, Picard followed Worf into the edifice itself—or what was left of it. A ruined corridor stretched out in either direction, choked with rubble.

At one end of it, the captain could see a gaping hole in the ceiling, where daylight tried to lance its way through a curtain of rising smoke and flames. As he approached it, following Worf's lead, he caught a glimpse of the carnage behind the curtain.

A lanky figure was hauling smaller ones away from the blaze. He raised his head at their approach, his face smeared with soot and taut with urgency.

It was *Kurn*.

"There are more of them back there!" he bellowed over the roar of the fire and the screams of the injured. "Some may still be alive!"

But it was clear that some were not. The bodies of dead students littered the hallway, having come to rest wherever the explosion cast them. Their postures were painfully grotesque.

Picard wanted to rearrange them, to give them some measure of dignity in death. But there was no time. His priority had to be the survivors.

For what seemed like an eternity, the captain pulled out child after child from the burning building. Some were conscious, some were not. Some were badly wounded, others only dazed.

There were still others to be saved—no one knew how many. But just as Picard was running back inside for another survivor, an even bigger explosion wracked the building.

He was deafened by it, thrown off his feet as the floor beneath him shivered with the impact. He found himself pressed against a slab of stone, the skin of his cheek scraped and bloody.

As the captain rose and regained his bearings, he saw a huge ball of fire blossom into the sky. In its wake, all was silent. There were no screams from within, no sound of life at all. And by that, he knew there was nothing more they could do in this place.

But if he stayed, the fire would consume him. So Picard dragged himself outside, where the surviving students had been arrayed on the short, red *en'chula* grass.

That's when he saw Worf heading toward him, the Klingon's countenance full of horror and rage. The captain waved his officer back.

"There's no one left in there," he shouted, striving to be heard over the groans of the wounded. "If they weren't dead before, they're dead now."

But Worf didn't stop. Wild-eyed, he kept on going, aiming for the burning pile of rubble that was all that remained of the academy.

"Lieutenant!" Picard cried. "Worf!"

His officer didn't heed him. Instead, as if bent on suicide, he plunged into the maze of flames.

The captain started after him, but he felt himself grabbed from behind. Whirling, he saw it was Kahless who had grabbed him, and Kurn wasn't far behind.

"Let me go!" Picard shouted. "It's Worf! He's gone back into that inferno!"

"Then he's dead!" the clone roared back at him. "You cannot throw your life after his!"

Kurn didn't say a thing. He just stared at the blazing ruin. But by the look in his eyes, the captain could see Worf's brother had given up hope as well.

Cursing beneath his breath, Picard tried to pull away from Kahless. But the clone was too strong, and the human was too drained from his rescue efforts. In time, the captain ceased his struggles and gazed narrow-eyed at the academy building.

He could feel the heat of the conflagration on his face. Even here, it made the skin tighten across his face.

By then, Picard told himself, Worf had to have perished. No one could have survived. He didn't want to believe it, but he couldn't see any way around it.

Suddenly, against all common sense, the captain caught sight of something moving in the debris. Something that made a path for itself between the flames. Something that staggered out through a gap in what had once been a wall.

It was Worf.

His face was blackened with soot, his clothing full of smoke and red-hot embers. And somehow, against all odds, he had not one but *two* young Klingons slung over his shoulders.

Rushing to him, the captain helped relieve Worf of his

burden. With Kurn's help, he lowered one of the students to the ground. Though badly burned and bleeding from half a dozen places, the child was still breathing. He had a chance to live.

Not so with the other one, the youth Kahless had wrested from Worf's shoulders. He was blackened beyond recognition, a lifeless husk. But in the chaos within the building, there couldn't have been any way to tell that. Worf had just grabbed him and run.

As for the lieutenant himself, he was on all fours, helplessly coughing out the acrid fumes that had invaded his lungs. As someone came and took the living child away, Picard went to Worf and laid a hand on his powerful shoulder.

The Klingon's head came about sharply, his eyes smoldering no less than the inferno from which he'd escaped. Shrugging the captain off with a growl, he got to his knee and turned away.

Picard wasn't offended. He understood. His security officer had been reduced to instincts in his attempt to save those children. And his instincts were not pretty by human standards.

No, he realized suddenly—there was more to it than that. A great deal more. Standing, he recalled the story he had read several years earlier in Worf's personnel file.

As a child of six, Worf had accompanied his parents to the Khitomer outpost, on the rim of the Klingon Empire. It was an installation devoted to research, to scientific pursuits. Nonetheless, the Romulans attacked the place without warning, brutally destroying the four thousand Klingons who lived there—Worf's parents included.

Buried in the rubble, in danger of suffocation, Mogh's son would have died too—except for the Starfleet vessel

Intrepid, which arrived in time to search for survivors. A team located a faint set of life signs in the ruins and began digging. It was Sergey Rozhenko, a human, who saved the Klingon's life and later adopted him.

The captain could only imagine what it had been like to be trapped in all that debris, small and alone, despairing of assistance yet hanging on anyway. Or how Worf had felt when he'd seen the stones above him coming away, to reveal the bearded face of his savior.

That's why he had refused to leave those two children behind. That was the force that had impelled Worf from the conflagration against all odds. The Klingon remembered the horrors of Khitomer. He could not do less for those students than Sergey Rozhenko had done for him.

Even as Picard thought this, he heard a call go up, a wail of pure and unadulterated pain. A moment later, a second call answered it, and then a third. Before he knew it, every survivor, child and adult, was crying out to the smoke-stained sky above them. Worf too.

This wasn't the death song the captain had heard before—the ritual howl of joy and approval meant to speed a warrior's soul to the afterlife. This was an admixture of fury and anguish, of ineffable sadness, that came from the darkest depths of the Klingon heart.

Those who died this day had been denied the chance to become warriors. They had been slaughtered like animals on the altar of greed and power. And no one here, Picard included, would ever forget that.

The murderers of these children had to be brought to justice. There was no other way the captain would be able to sleep at night.

"Whoever did this," said a hollow voice, "was without honor."

Picard turned and saw it was Kahless who had uttered the remark, his throat raw from crying out. And he was standing beside Kurn—hardly an accident.

Worf's brother didn't turn to look at the clone. But in his eyes, the captain could see the reflection of the burning academy. Kurn's jaw clenched, an indication of the emotions roiling within him.

"Obviously," said the governor, in a soft but dangerous voice, "the conspiracy is real. And this attack was directed at *me,* on the assumption I would move to help you uncover it." He grunted. "Me, a member of the High Council—as if that meant anything."

"The question," Kahless responded pointedly, "is what you are going to do about it."

This time, Kurn looked at him. "What I will do," he said, "is put my loyalty to the lovers aside—and help in whatever way I can."

The clone nodded, satisfied. Then, despite the weariness they all felt, he went back to see to the survivors, who were being tended to by those adults who had survived unscathed.

Suspecting that Worf and his brother might have several things to say to each other, the captain fell in behind Kahless. After all, Picard had a brother too. He knew how exasperating they could be.

CHAPTER 14

The Heroic Age

Snow was falling in great, hissing dollops, making it difficult to see the trees even thirty meters in front of them. But it wasn't falling so heavily Kahless couldn't see the hoofprints between the drifts, or catch the scent of the wild *minn'hor* herd that had made them.

"We're gaining on them," Porus observed with some enthusiasm, his ample beard rimed with frost.

"Slowly," Shurin added. He snorted. "Too slowly."

Kahless turned to the one-eyed man. Like the rest of them, his cheeks were sunken from not having eaten in a while.

"We're in no hurry, Shurin. It's only the middle of the day. Why push the *s'tarahkmey* if we don't have to?"

Morath said nothing. That wasn't unusual. He only spoke if he really had something to say.

As the outlaw chief negotiated a path through the forest, he became aware of the *jinaq* amulet pressed

133

against his chest by the weight of his tunic. And that made him think about Kellein.

Around her father's village, it would be Growing season in another month or so—time to pursue the promise he had made to her by the riverbank. And pursue it he would.

It was madness, of course. Though he wanted Kellein as he'd never wanted anything or anyone in his life, all he could give her was the life of an outlaw. And he had learned how hard that life could be.

All Cold long, he and his band had been on the move, always looking back over their shoulders, always wondering when Molor would swoop down on them like a hunting bird. Hell, Kahless hadn't gotten a good night's sleep since he killed the tyrant's son—except for the night he'd spent by Vathraq's keep.

If he stayed in this realm, Molor would track him down. If not in Cold, then in Growing; if not during the day, then at night. Kahless had no illusions about that.

That was why he had to reach the southern continent. True, it was a harsh and backward place, largely untouched by civilization. Life there would be punishing, and rewards few.

But at least he and Kellein would be safe from the tyrant's hatred. With luck, they might find some measure of happiness together. And if they were truly lucky, if the ancient gods smiled on them, their children would never have to know the name Molor.

All Kahless had to do was make his way into one of the tyrant's port towns. And hire a vessel with a greedy captain, who knew his way across the sea. And when he had done that, he would—

Suddenly, the outlaw realized how absurd it all

sounded. How impossible. Chuckling to himself, he shook his snow-covered head.

How would he pay for their passage? And what seafarer would defy the all-powerful Molor to help a scraggly renegade?

It was an illusion, a pipedream. And yet, it was one he would wrestle into truth. Somehow. For Kellein's sake.

"Kahless!" a voice hissed at him.

It was Shurin. The one-eyed man pointed through the sheeting snowfall at a wide brown smudge in the distance. Kahless sniffed the air.

It was the herd, all right. Perhaps a dozen of the beasts, enough to keep them fed for a week or more. Nodding at Shurin to acknowledge the sighting, Kahless reached for the bow he'd made, which was secured to the back of his saddle.

He could hear the flapping of leather as the others did the same. Of course, they didn't have to worry about the *minn'hormey* hearing them. They were still a good distance from the herd and the thick, falling snow dampened all sounds.

As long as Kahless and his men remained downwind of the beasts, they wouldn't have any trouble picking them off. An easy kill, he thought—though small compensation for the scarcity of such herds, or the painstaking time it took to find them.

Raising his hand, the outlaw gave the signal for his men to urge their mounts forward. Then he himself dug his heels into the flanks of his *s'tarahk*. The animal picked up its pace, gradually narrowing the gap between hunter and prey.

The *minn'hormey* didn't seem to suspect a thing. They maintained their slow progress through the wood, their shaggy hindquarters swaying from side to side, their horned heads trained squarely on what was ahead of them.

Kahless sighted a particularly slow *minn'hor* and was about to take it down when he felt a hand on his arm. Turning, he saw Morath's ruddy, snow-covered face. In the swirling gray of the storm, the younger man's eyes looked like dark caverns.

"What?" asked Kahless.

Morath pointed—not at the herd, but at something off to the left of it. Something that moved with a purpose similar to their own.

There were four-legged predators in this place, but they didn't hunt in packs. And besides, these shapes were too tall to be animals. Klingons, then. Mounted, like Kahless's men. And after the same *minn'hormey.*

The other band must have spotted them at about the same time, because the riders hung back from the herd. With another hand signal, Kahless gestured for his own men to slow down.

The *minn'hormey* kept going, still unaware of their danger. The wind howled and writhed, sending spindrifts whirling through the forest. And all the while, the two hunting parties sat their mounts, eyeing one another.

Sizing one another up. After all, they were Klingons.

Finally, Kahless spoke, shouting to make himself heard over the storm. "This herd is ours. If need be, we'll fight for it."

On the other side, one figure separated itself from the others. His hair was the color of copper, gathered in ice-encrusted braids. "So will we," came the answer.

Kahless licked his lips. The last thing he wanted was to lose men over a meal. But he didn't know when the next one would come along, and he had no stomach for *s'tarahk* meat.

Morath and Porus had positioned themselves on either side of him. He glanced at them, making sure of their alertness. They held their bows at the ready, waiting for him to give the word.

But the leader of the other band acted first. With a bloodchilling cry, he raised his arrow to eye level and let it fly.

It sliced through the snow, missing Kahless by no more than an inch, and buried itself in a tree behind him. The outlaw chief's teeth clenched. Roaring a challenge of his own, he shot back.

A moment later, the forest was alive with swarms of wooden shafts. There were grunts of pain and angry curses, all muffled by the storm. The *s'tarahk* under Porus shrieked, spilling him in its agony.

Kahless didn't like this. They could fire back and forth for hours, with no clearcut victor—except the damned *minn'hormey,* who would go free in the meantime. It was time to remember Molor's advice and take the bloody battle to the enemy.

Replacing his bow on the back of his saddle, Kahless took out his blade and spurred his mount forward. The animal responded with a gratifying surge of speed, putting him face to face with the enemy leader before anyone could stop him.

Another of Molor's lessons sprang to mind—cut the serpent's head off and the rest of it will die. With this in mind, Kahless took a swipe at the enemy leader's chest.

But the man was quicker than he looked. Ducking low, he let the blade pass over him. Then he reached out and grabbed Kahless's wrist.

At the same time, he drew a weapon of his own—a sword which had clearly seen better days. But it was still sharp enough to sweep a warrior's head off his shoulders.

Kahless had no intention of being the head in question. Lunging forward, he grabbed his enemy by the forearm.

The two of them struggled for a moment, whirling about on their *s'tarahkmey*, neither daring to let go of the other. Then, as one or both of them lost his balance, they toppled into the snow.

By then, Morath and Porus and the others had come crashing after their chief, breaking branches and trampling saplings in their way. But the other band leaped forward to meet them.

Kahless and his adversary were like a rock in the middle of a strong current. The battle raged around them as they rolled on the ground, each struggling for leverage with savage intensity.

Suddenly, Kahless's foot slipped out from under him, and the other man gained the upper hand. Twisting his wrist free, he smashed Kahless across the face with the hilt of his sword. A second time. And again.

For Kahless, the world swam in a red haze. And when it cleared, his enemy was sitting astride him, sword raised high, ready to plunge it deep into his naked throat.

Kahless groped for the handle of his weapon, but it wasn't there, and he was too dazed to search for it. He tried to push his enemy off, but it was no use. His strength had left him along with his senses.

"Tell me your name," said the man, "so I may honor it when I speak of our battle around the campfire."

The outlaw chief laughed at his own helplessness, spitting out the blood that was filling his mouth. "You'd honor me?" he grated, his voice sounding a hundred miles distant. "Make it Kahless, son of Kanjis, then. Or Molor himself. Or whoever you want."

What did he care? He'd be dead by then.

But as Kahless's words sank in, a change came over his enemy's face. A look of uncertainty, the outlaw thought. At any rate, the sword remained high.

"You are . . . Kahless?" the man demanded sharply. "In truth?"

The outlaw nodded. "I am." He squinted through the prismatic snow that had gathered on his eyelashes. "Do I know you?"

His enemy shook his head from side to side, his copper-colored braids slapping at his cheeks. "No," he said. "But I know *you.*"

Suddenly, the man was on his feet, waving with his sword at the other combatants. "Stop," he cried. "All those who follow Edronh, put down your weapons. These warriors are our friends!"

Kahless thought he was dreaming, or addled by all the punishment he'd taken. Klingons didn't stop in the middle of a life-or-death struggle to declare their enemies their allies.

Or did they?

All around him, the enemy stopped fighting. Kahless's men looked at one another, unsure what to make of this. And as the outlaw chief himself got to his feet, he didn't know what to tell them.

Then the leader of the other band knelt before Kahless and laid his sword at Kahless's feet. When he spoke again, it was in a voice filled with deep shame and embarassment.

"We yield to bold Kahless, who leads the fight against the tyrant. Had we known from the beginning whom we faced, we would never have raised our bows against him."

The son of Kanjis began to understand. Edronh and his men were outlaws too—the kind Kahless had hunted when he was still in the tyrant's employ. And like Vathraq to the south, they believed Kahless was leading a revolt against Molor's rule.

He was about to correct the notion when he realized how foolish it would be. The truth would only start their bloody battle all over again. And by keeping his mouth shut, by going along with the lie, he would get them the *cob'lat*'s share of the hunt.

Grabbing a tree for support, because his head still swam with the other man's blows, Kahless dismissed the conflict with a sweep of his arm. "It was an honest mistake. I will not hold it against you, nor will my men."

To cement his promise, he eyed as many familiar faces as he could find with a single glance. They seemed to understand, because to a man they nodded back. All except one, that is.

Only Morath looked away from him, reluctant to be part of the falsehood. The younger man was scowling as he stuck his sword in his belt. It was all right, Kahless thought. Some day, Morath would learn.

A young warrior, even younger than Morath, approached Kahless. Like his chief, he laid his sword in the snow.

"It is an honor to meet you," he said.

The enemy leader—no longer an enemy at all now, it seemed—grinned at the young one. Then he turned to Kahless.

"My youngest son," he explained. "His name is Rannuf."

Kahless nodded. "In that case, I'm glad we didn't kill him. Now, my friend, about the herd . . ."

"We'll take it down together," suggested Edronh. "But you may take the bulk of the provisions. We know these hills as we know our own swords. We can always find another herd."

Kahless smiled. This was better than leaving corpses in the snow. Much better. And all it had cost them was a single lie.

CHAPTER 15

The Modern Age

Deanna Troi spotted the boy in the corridor outside the ship's classrooms, on his way to the turbolift. She hurried after him, calling his name.

"Alexander?"

The boy turned and stopped to wait for her. The Betazoid smiled.

"I almost missed you," she told him. "I meant to be here ten minutes ago, but my work ran a little long today."

Alexander looked at her, his dark brows coming together at the bridge of his nose. "Is everything all right?"

She knew exactly what he was asking. Damn, she thought. Here I am, trying to ease Worf's absence, and I find a way to alarm the poor kid. *Some counselor you are, Deanna.*

"Everything's fine," she assured him, "as far as we know."

Troi had to add the caveat, just in case. After all, away missions included their share of tragedies, and the Klingon Empire was more perilous than most other destinations.

Alexander seemed to relax a little, but not completely. "So why were you in such a hurry to see me?"

The counselor shrugged. "No reason in particular. It's just that I haven't had a chance to spend any time with you since your father took off, and I thought you might like to keep me company while I have a sundae in Ten-Forward. Of course, you *could* have one yourself, so I don't look like too much of a glutton."

The boy normally smiled at her silliness, but not this time. "Okay," he said without enthusiasm. "I guess."

"That's the spirit," she told him, wishing she meant it.

Worf looked around the bridge of Kurn's ship. It wasn't much bigger or more comfortable than the one in which Kahless had brought them to Ogat. But it had four seats, one in the center and three on the periphery, and that made it possible for them all to be on the bridge at once.

At the moment, Kurn was in the center seat, checking to make certain they were still on course. After all, Klingon vessels of this size had a tendency to veer slightly at high speeds.

Kahless was pacing the corridor that led to the vessel's sleeping quarters, occasionally striking a bulkhead with a mere fraction of his strength. It was as if the ship were a *s'tarahk* and he was urging it into a gallop, eager to get on with his self-appointed mission.

Captain Picard was sitting at the station closest to the main viewscreen, his blunt, human features illuminated by the lurid light of his control panel. He seemed absorbed in the readings of the alien monitors.

Sitting next to the captain, one panel over, Worf watched him. There was something he needed to say, but he was having difficulty finding the words to say it.

After a moment or two, he gave up. He would just have to say what he felt, and hope that would be enough.

"Sir?"

The captain turned to him, so that the control lights lit up only half of his face. "Yes, Lieutenant?"

Worf frowned. "Sir, I must apologize for the way I acted on Ogat. At the academy, I mean."

Picard nodded. "After you emerged from the burning building, and I attempted to console you."

"Yes," said the Klingon. "I pulled away from you in a most unseemly manner. But I assure you, it was not my intention to offend you. Or to seem ungrateful for your—"

The captain winced and held up his hand. "Please, Mister Worf. There is no need for you to go on. First off, it's much too painful for me to watch. And second, I was not offended."

The lieutenant looked at him. "But the way I acted was hardly in keeping with Starfleet protocol."

Picard leaned closer. "That is true. However, you were under a great deal of strain at the time. We all were. And as you have no doubt noticed, we are not now wearing Starfleet uniforms. It occurs to me we can make some allowances if we wish."

The Klingon breathed a little easier. "Thank you, sir."

For a second or two, the captain smiled. Then he said,

"You are quite welcome, Lieutenant," and went back to scrutinizing his control panel.

His duty discharged, Worf sat back in his chair. He was fortunate to have a commanding officer who understood—at least in some small measure—what the Klingon was going through.

Normally, he would have been able to control his more feral instincts, no matter the provocation. Serving on the *Enterprise* had made him skilled at that. But this was different.

The killing of children was a provocation that went to the heart of his being—and not just because it was dishonorable, or because it stirred the memories of his experiences on Khitomer.

Worf was a father. And not so long ago, he had considered sending his son to the academy on Ogat, to make him more of a Klingon.

That was why the faces of those children had cut him so deeply, with their bloodless lips and their staring eyes. That was why he had lost control of himself and reverted to savagery.

Because to him, every one of those faces had been Alexander's.

Troi found Will Riker in the captain's ready room, taking care of ship's business at the captain's computer terminal. As she entered, he leaned back in his chair, his expression speaking volumes.

"And people ask me why I turned down my own command," he sighed.

"Red tape?" she asked.

"By the cargo hold full," he said. "What can I do for you, Deanna?"

"It's about Alexander," she told him. "He's not himself lately. And I think I know why."

Riker guessed at the answer. "The boy's having a hard time coping with his father's absence?"

"Certainly," said Troi, "he's worried about his father coming back in one piece—but not as much as you might think. He has a lot of confidence in Worf, after all."

"Then what's on his mind?" the first officer asked.

The counselor frowned. "Alexander wouldn't tell me, of course. It's as if he's trying to be like his father—strong and silent. So on a hunch I checked the computer log, to see if he'd been exposed to anything disturbing."

"And?" said Riker.

Her frown deepened. "I found out he had read those scrolls the captain told us about. The ones concerning Kahless."

The first officer regarded her, then leaned forward and tapped out a few commands on his padd. A moment later, he read the information contained on the screen.

"I see what you mean. Alexander accessed the contents of the scrolls night before last. And it seems he spent quite a bit of time with them." He shrugged. "Now what? Are you going to confront him with this?"

Troi shook her head. "No. As much as he likes me, as much as he trusts me, I don't think I'm the one he wants to talk to."

It took the first officer a moment or two to figure out what she meant. "You mean you want *me* to talk to him?"

"It would be a big help," the Betazoid noted. "Besides, it'll give you a chance to see how much fun my job is."

Riker eyed her. "If I'd wanted to be a counselor, Counselor, I would've applied to the University of Betazed." His features softened. "On the other hand, I can't let poor Alexander swing in the wind. Just what is it you'd like me to do?"

Troi told him.

CHAPTER **16**

The Heroic Age

It was the season of Growing.

The river that led to Kellein's village was swollen with flood, rushing between its banks as if it had somewhere important to go. The overhanging *micayah* trees were sleek and heavy with dark green nuts, which somehow managed to hover just above the glistening water.

As Kahless led his men along the same path he'd traveled the year before, Vathraq's village loomed ever closer. He recognized the dark walls, the dark keep, the dark tower. The rows of fruit trees that extended in every direction. And of course, the smell of manure.

It was just as he remembered it. More than ever, he was aware of the *jinaq* amulet his betrothed had given him. It lay against his chest, a promise yet to be fulfilled.

Kahless smiled at the thought of his betrothed. He imagined the look on her face when she spotted the outlaw band making its way down from the hills. The joy in her sharp-toothed grin, the quickening of her pulse.

He almost wished he could catch her bathing again and surprise her as he had before. But that would be too much to ask, he knew. It was ample cause for thanks that he had made it through the Cold.

As he led his men closer, the track dipped and then rose again, lined now on the river side with *tran'nuc* trees. Their purplish fruit were still puny things, waiting for late in the season to grow fat and flavorful.

He remembered how he had staggered out of Vathraq's house and tasted one—just before he'd tasted Kellein, and she him. Perhaps, he thought, I should bring one with me as a luck charm. Then he again felt the amulet under his tunic and knew that was all the luck he needed.

"Kahless," said Morath, who had come up beside him.

The outlaw was smiling as he turned to his friend. "Yes? What is it?"

Morath seemed intent on something in the distance. He squinted in the sunlight. "Something is wrong."

"Wrong?" Kahless echoed. He could feel his heart start to beat faster. "In what way?"

Following Morath's gaze, he saw what the man was talking about. One of the gates in the wall ringing the keep had been left ajar.

"It's only a gate," said the outlaw.

But he knew better. And so did Morath, by his expression.

"Where are the sentries?" asked the younger man.

Kahless repeated the question to himself. Granted, it was the middle of the day, but danger could appear at any time. Vathraq wouldn't tolerate such an oversight . . . if that was all it was.

Placing his hand on the hilt of his sword, he eyed the place in a new light. The quiet, which had seemed so natural only a few moments ago, seemed ominous now. And Vathraq's house, which had been so inviting, began smelling a lot like a trap.

If Molor discovered Kahless was taken in by these people, he might have left some men there to watch for the outlaw's return. Certainly, stranger things had been known to happen.

"A wise man would withdraw," Morath remarked.

Kahless looked at him. "Turn from a fight? That's not like you, my friend."

The younger man grunted. "I said a *wise* man would withdraw—not that *we* would. And if I know you, we will not."

True, thought the outlaw. After all, this wasn't simply a matter of their own preservation. If the keep had been taken by Molor's men, Kellein was a captive—perhaps worse. Kahless couldn't tolerate the thought of that.

"Follow me," he advised Morath. "But be wary."

"I am always wary," his friend replied.

Little by little, Kahless urged his *s'tarahk* up the river road, toward the open gate. His senses prickled with awareness, ready for the least sign of an ambush. But he couldn't find any.

At least, not at first. However, as they came closer to the gate, he distinctly heard something rustling within the walls. The swords of Molor's men, perhaps, as they drew them from their belts? Their arrows, as they fit them to their bowstrings?

The outlaw had to make a decision, and quickly.

Should I charge the gate, he asked himself, in an effort to surprise the *p'tahkmey?* Or continue this slow progress, waiting to see how far I can get before they stop me?

Before Kahless could come to a conclusion, the whisper of movement within the walls became a storm of activity, punctuated by high-pitched cries of annoyance. Before his eyes, a huge, black cloud erupted around the keep.

A flock of *kraw'zamey,* protesting loudly as they headed for the slopes beyond the river. The outlaw swallowed, his mouth as dry as dust.

This was no trap. Carrion birds didn't abide the presence of Klingons. Nor did they gather except where there was sustenance for them.

If Molor's men had been here, they were gone now. But that was no comfort to Kahless. Clenching his jaw so hard it hurt, he dismounted and walked the rest of the way to the gate. Then he went inside.

What greeted his eyes was a slaughterhouse. Vathraq's warriors choked the space between the walls and the keep with their gutted, lifeless bodies. Fleshless skulls grinned up at him with bared teeth and hollowed-out eyes, picked to the bone by the beaks of the *kraw'zamey.*

Molor's men could still have been inside the keep, awaiting them, but Kahless no longer cared. He was too overcome with fear for his beloved, too caught up in a current of dread and fascination to worry about himself.

Crossing the courtyard, he tore open the doors to the keep. Inside, it was silent as a tomb. Putting one leaden foot in front of the other, he made his way past the antechamber into the great hall.

Vathraq was sitting on his high wooden throne, just as Kahless remembered him. Except now he was slumped to one side, a blackened hole in his chest where an arrow had pinned him to the chair, and his eyes were sunken and staring.

His people lay scattered about, draped over serving tables or crumpled on the stone floor, cut down at the brink of the firepit or tossed inside to char and burn. No one had escaped, young or old, male or female.

No one except Kellein. Try as he might, Kahless couldn't find her body. It gave rise to a single, reckless hope.

Perhaps she had eluded Molor's hand. Perhaps she had been away at the time. Or she had seen the tyrant's forces in time to hide herself.

Perhaps, against all odds, she still lived.

Kahless felt a hand on his shoulder. Whirling, he saw that it was only Morath. But his friend had a grim expression on his face, even grimmer than was called for.

Suddenly, the outlaw knew why, and his heart plummeted. "Kellein . . . ?" he rasped, his throat dry with grief.

Morath nodded. "Upstairs," he said.

Rushing past him, staggering under his load of anguish, Kahless left the feast hall and found the steps that led to the higher floors. His men, who had been searching the place while he lingered downstairs, stood aside for him as he barreled his way up.

At the head of the stair, he found her. She was sprawled in a pool of dried blood, a sword still clasped tight in her hand.

Kellein's eyes were closed, as if she were only sleeping. But her skin was pale and translucent as *pherza* wax, and there was a track of blackened gore from the corner of her mouth to the line of her jaw.

The outlaw didn't have the heart to inspect her

wounds. Slowly, carefully, he touched his fingertips to her lips. They were cold and stiff as stone. Sorrow rose up in him like a flood.

Only then did he notice the thong around her neck and reach inside her tunic to take out her *jinaq* amulet. Cradled in his hand, it sparkled gaily in the light from a nearby window, affirming her vow.

Clumsily, with fingers that barely seemed alive, Kahless took out his own amulet and held it beside hers. As intended, they were identical. He and Kellein had planned to wear them at their mating ceremony.

Without meaning to, he began whispering the words he would have spoken. "I pledge my heart and my hand to you, Kellein, daughter of Vathraq, and no other. I am your mate for the rest of my days."

They were more than words to him, though his beloved had passed through the gates of Death. Kahless knew then and there he would never take another mate as long as he lived.

Indeed, why live at all? Why bother? With Kellein gone, what was there to live for?

Nothing, the outlaw screamed in the darkness of his despair. "Nothing!" he bellowed, making the hallway ring with his anger and his pain.

Blind with bitterness, Kahless drew his sword from his belt and raised it high above his head. Then, with all his strength, he hacked at the floor beside Kellein. One, twice, and again, raising white-hot sparks, until the gray metal of the blade finally relented and shattered on the stones.

The pieces skipped this way and that, then were still. As still as Kellein, Kahless raged. As still as the heart inside him.

Delirious, writhing inside with agony, he fled. Down the stairs, out of the antechamber and across the blindingly bright courtyard. He staggered past the corpses of Vathraq's defenders, through the gates to the walled town, and out to the river road.

His *s'tarahk* stood there with all the others, taut and nervous though it didn't know why. It raised its head when it saw him coming.

With a growl, he threw himself into the saddle and dug his heels into the animal's sides. Startled, it bolted forward, taking him down the road as fast as it could carry him.

He didn't know where he was going or why. He just knew he wanted to die before he got there.

CHAPTER **17**

The Modern Age

Kurn's estate on Ogat wasn't far from the academy. As dusk fell, Picard stood in its rambling main hall, a mug of tea warming his hands. He stared out a window at the darkening sky.

Several silvery shapes, each too big and irregularly shaped to be a star, reflected the light of the homeworld's sun. Testimonies, the captain mused, to the Klingon tendency to fragment themselves at every opportunity.

Once, more than seventy-five years ago, there had been a moon in these heavens. Called Praxis, it supplied the Klingons with more than three-fourths of their energy resources. Then, due to years of overmining and insufficient safety precautions, a reactor exploded—contaminating the homeworld's atmosphere, poking great holes in its delicate ozone layer, and creating a quirk in its orbit.

Klingon scientists had turned pale as they anticipated

the result. In half a century, Qo'noS would have become a lifeless husk, abandoned by its people. Of course, there were ways to save it, to preserve Klingon culture and tradition. But they were expensive ways—made implausible by the size of the Klingons' military budget.

There was but one option. The High Council opened a dialogue with the Federation, aiming for peace between the two spacefaring entities. Once that was accomplished, funds could be diverted from military uses to the rescue of the homeworld.

As it turned out, peace was not an easy row to hoe. Factions in both the Klingon hierarchy and the Federation tried to halt the process at every turn. There was considerable hardship, considerable violence. Nonetheless, by dint of courage and tolerance and hard work, a treaty was signed.

There would be peace between the Federation and the Klingon Empire. But that didn't mean the Klingons would stop warring with each *other*. Not by a long shot.

Over the next seventy-five years, the complexion of the High Council changed again and again. The story was always the same—some rising power challenging an established one at the point of a sharpened *bat'telth*. And no sooner was the upstart ensconced on the council than some newcomer appeared to challenge *him*.

As a young man, Picard had heard about the Klingons' overwhelming thirst for power, which made them tear at each other like ravening beasts. He had accepted it, but he had never truly understood it.

Now, he understood it all too well. It wasn't power that motivated the Klingons so much as instinct. It was in their nature to fight. If they couldn't battle an outside foe, they would battle each other.

Hence, this conspiracy to overthrow Gowron, which had begun to carve its bloody path to the council chamber. Perhaps the captain would not have been so angered by it, perhaps he could have accepted it better, if its victims had not been innocent children.

Turning, he saw Worf and Kahless standing by the hearth, staring into its flames. Picard could only imagine what they saw there.

Chaos? Destruction? The deaths of multitudes? Or the irresistible glory of battle? Even in his officer's case, he wasn't entirely sure.

Abruptly, the doors to the chamber opened and Kurn returned to them. Closing the doors behind him, he glanced at the captain.

"As you suggested," he said, "I've arranged with Rajuc to report my death in the explosion. Also, the deaths of several other adults. With luck, our enemies will believe you three perished as well."

Kahless nodded. "Well done, Kurn. If they think we're dead, they will lower their guards. And it will give us the opportunity to strike."

"Yes," the master of the house agreed. "But strike *how*, my friend? Where do we begin?"

The clone made a sound of disgust. "I had entertained the hope you could speak to Gowron for us. I thought you would have his ear."

Kurn shook his head. "Gowron has changed. He has forgotten who supported him when the House of Duras went for his head. I no longer understand what he is thinking half the time."

"Surely," said Picard, "the firebombing of the academy should be enough to arouse his suspicions."

"He will say it could have been an accident," Kurn

argued. "Or the work of someone other than a conspirator."

"Still," Worf maintained, "if we had proof, he would have to act on it. He would have no choice."

"Yes," Kahless agreed. "Something he can hold in his hands. Something tangible. But then, obtaining such proof has been our problem all along."

"Something tangible," the governor echoed.

There was silence for a moment. Picard was at a loss as to how to proceed. So were the others, apparently.

Finally, it was Worf who spoke. "If there was a bomb," he said slowly, still honing the idea in his own mind, "there will be fragments of it in the academy's wreckage. And while they are not the sort of proof we are looking for, they may provide us with a way to obtain that proof."

Kahless's eyes burned. He nodded. So did Kurn.

Unfortunately, the captain didn't quite know what Worf was talking about. But he imagined he was about to learn.

The broad, powerful leader of the conspiracy made his way through the hot, swirling mists of the cavern, his only garb a linen loincloth. The mists stank of sulfur and iron and the pungent lichen that grew here, and they were like fire on his skin.

But those who frequented the steambaths of Ona'ja'bur lived years longer than their peers. Or so it was said— mostly, the conspirator suspected, by the crafty merchants in the town down the hill, which profited greatly from the armies of visitors.

Of course, the conspirator had never put much credence in the tales about the baths. He would never have come here strictly out of concern for his health. Rather, it was the need for a meeting place far from the scrutiny of others that had drawn him here.

Not too long ago, he would have considered conferring with his comrades at the dining hall in Tolar'tu. But clearly, that was no longer an option. When his comrades were discovered there, it had rendered that venue useless to all of them.

Nor would this one be any more useful, were it not for the lack of visitors to the baths at this time of year. After all, they needed their privacy as well as their anonymity.

The conspirator sat and waited, as far from the battery-powered safety globes as possible. They were only vague, blue-white balls of incandescence in the distance. Fortunately, he didn't have to wait long before he saw a figure emerge from the mists.

It was Lomakh, looking thinner and considerably less distinguished in his loincloth than in his body armor. But then, the conspirator thought, that was probably true of everyone—himself included.

Lomakh inclined his head. "I am glad you could come," he said, his voice as harsh as ever, even subdued in a whisper.

"Likewise," said the conspirator. And then, because he was not by nature a very patient individual: "What news do you have?"

His companion sat down beside him. "Good news, most likely."

"Most likely?" the conspirator echoed.

Lomakh shook his head. "The groundskeeper at the academy, the one we hired to plant the bombs?"

"Yes? What about him?"

"He was killed in the explosion, the idiot. Therefore,

we have not been able to corroborate the deaths of our enemies."

The conspirator cursed. Some little thing was always going wrong. "What of our sources elsewhere on Ogat?"

"Those, at least, seem to confirm that our action was successful. So far as they can tell, Kahless and his friends are no more."

The conspirator relaxed somewhat—but not completely. "Continue your investigation," he said, "but keep it discreet. We don't want to give ourselves away as we did before."

Lomakh scowled at that. "It was the sheerest coincidence that Kahless spotted us in that dining hall."

"Of course it was," he replied, allowing a note of irony to creep into his voice. "I just want to make sure there are no *further* coincidences."

As it happened, Fate had been their friend as well as their enemy. After a couple of days of their dining-hall meetings, Lomakh had realized that he and Kardem were being watched, and had arranged for the watcher to be killed by street mercenaries.

But that was the day the watcher's allies had chosen to show up. In the melee that followed, one of them was revealed as a human—a human called "captain" by a comrade.

Few humans had ever set foot on Qo'noS. One of them, the famous Arbiter of Succession, fit the description provided by the street mercenaries. And of course, he was the *captain* of the *Enterprise*.

What's more, if Jean-Luc Picard was on the homeworld, could his Lieutenant Worf have been far behind? And would they not have enlisted the aid of Worf's brother Kurn in short order?

Still, it was not clear who had summoned them—who the mysterious, cowled watcher was in the dining hall—until they had gotten word from one of their sources at Gowron's court.

Apparently, the Kahless clone had come to the council leader with some interesting suspicions. But from what their spy could gather, Gowron had declined to help, asking for some proof of the so-called conspiracy.

Would Kahless have given up, then? Allowed a plot of some consequence to hatch without his doing something about it? Certainly not. But where else could he have gone for help?

To the captain of the *Enterprise,* perhaps? It made some sense. And it went a long way toward explaining Picard's presence in Tolar'tu.

Just in case, the conspirators had determined Kurn's schedule and planted their firebombs wherever they could—knowing the governor's estate was too well-guarded for them to reach him there. As a result, the academy hadn't been the only place targeted for destruction—just the place where Kurn had received his visitors.

With luck, their other bombs would go unused. But the leader of the conspiracy wasn't quite ready to concede that.

He sighed. "Even if we were successful on Ogat, Kahless may have managed to spread word of his suspicions. There may be others working against us even as we speak."

"Then we will find them," said Lomakh. He closed his fingers into a fist and squeezed. "And we will crush them."

"No," the conspirator declared. "That is not enough.

We must speed things up, if we are to accomplish our objective."

The other Klingon looked at him. "How much faster can we go, my lord? It is a tricky thing, this reshaping of public opinion—especially when it involves as beloved a figure as Kahless."

The conspirator had to acknowledge the wisdom of that. When the clone's death became common knowledge, he would become an even tougher adversary. Nothing was harder to fight than a memory.

He peered into the mists, as if seeking an answer there. "Nonetheless, there must be a way to accelerate our plan."

Lomakh grunted. "We cannot tamper with the testing of the scroll, if that is what you mean. If it proves authentic, as we believe it will, the finding must be beyond reproach."

The conspirator bit his lip. His companion had a point. Yet there had to be something they could do besides bide their time. Perhaps it would take some time to think of it.

As he thought this, he saw two vague figures striding through the sulfurous mists. Not toward them exactly, but close enough to overhear their conversation. The conspirator felt his jaw clench.

He did not wish to invite any more exposure. They had had more than their share already and been fortunate to get away with it. With a glance, he informed Lomakh that their meeting was over. Nor was Lomakh inclined to protest, silently or otherwise.

Instead, he got up and walked away, pretending they didn't know each other at all. A moment or two later, he vanished like a wraith into the roiling clouds of steam.

The leader of the conspiracy frowned. He would not

have to sneak around like a Ferengi much longer, he promised himself. Soon he would be sitting in the high seat in the central hall, where Gowron sat presently.

Then, he mused, things would be different. The Empire would shrug off its ties to the cursed Federation and find other allies. Not the Romulans—someone else. Allies of the Klingons' choosing, willing to observe Klingon rules and serve Klingon purposes.

That was the trouble with the rebellion the House of Duras had launched a couple of years ago. The Romulans had been pulling the strings, rendering Duras's sisters and his heir mere pawns in their scheme. And if Gowron had been toppled, the Romulans would have ruled the Empire.

Not so with *this* rebellion. The conspirator would be beholden to no one for his ascent to power. Not even Lomakh and Kardem and Olmai, and the others who did his bidding.

His ties with them were already growing strained. And the last thing he wanted was to surround himself with proven traitors. Better to find supporters among the well-fed and the content, and not have to look for the glint of a knife's edge in every mirror.

The conspirator smiled. Soon, he thought. Soon it would all be in his capable hands. And what did it matter if some blood was shed along the way, even the blood of innocent children?

What was a council leader, anyway, if he did not spill *someone's* blood from time to time? What was the use of being in the high seat if one did not hold the power of life . . . and death?

CHAPTER 18

The Heroic Age

As his *s'tarahk* left Vathraq's village behind, Kahless heard someone call out to him. Looking back over his shoulder, he saw that Morath was following on his own beast.

The younger man was only fifty meters behind and gaining. With a burst of speed, Morath closed the distance even more. But by then, Kahless had turned away again.

He wanted no part of what Morath wished to tell him. He wanted no part of anything except oblivion.

"Kahless!" the younger man cried out again.

Ignoring him, the outlaw kept on going. But soon, Morath pulled even with him. And though he didn't say anything, he stared at his friend with those dark, piercing eyes of his, until Kahless could take no more of it.

The outlaw glanced at Morath. "Leave me alone."

Morath shook his head. "I will not."

"And why not?" growled Kahless. "Why can't you let me suffocate in my misery, damn you?"

"Because it is your fault the villagers are dead," Morath replied. "Because it is you who murdered them. And you cannot leave until you have made retribution for your crime."

Kahless rounded on him, his anger rising high enough to choke him. "*Me*, you say? Did I take a blade to Kellein? Did I pin her father to his throne with my arrow?" His teeth ground together. "I had nothing but respect for those people. Respect and gratitude!"

Morath kept pace with him, relentless. "Then why did you allow them to become close to you, when all you could expect was the tyrant's hatred? Why did you let them believe in your rebellion, when none of it was true?"

Kahless didn't have an answer for that. He found that his hands had turned into tight white fists around his reins.

"I'll tell you why," said Morath. "To suit your purposes. To fill your belly. Or sate your lust."

The reference to Kellein filled Kahless with a blind, consuming fury. With a sound like a wounded animal, he threw himself at Morath and dragged the man off his mount.

Before Morath knew what was happening, Kahless struck him with all his strength. Again. And again, staggering him. The hills echoed with each resounding impact.

For the first time, Kahless saw anger in the younger man's eyes—a cold, deadly anger. The next thing he knew, Morath had taken his sword in his hand. Kahless stared at him, wondering if this was the way he was going to perish—and not much caring.

But a moment later, Morath's rage cooled. He tossed the sword away. And, with blinding speed, dealt Kahless a savage blow to the jaw.

The outlaw spun around and nearly fell, but he put out a hand to right himself. Then, like a charging *targ*, he went after his friend. Nor could Morath move in time to avoid him.

They hit the ground together, clawing and pounding at one another. Kahless grabbed his adversary by the hair and tried to dash his brains out on a piece of exposed rock. But Morath used both hands to push Kahless's chin back and finally broke the older man's hold.

They wrestled like that for what seemed a long time, neither of them gaining the advantage, neither coming close to victory over the other. Kahless felt as if he had fallen into a trance, as if his arms and legs were striving on their own without his mind to guide them.

But there was a struggle in his mind as well—not with Morath himself, but with Morath's accusations. He was grappling with shame and guilt, trying to free himself though he knew he would never be free again.

At last, exhausted in body and spirit, he and Morath fell apart from one another. As Kahless rolled on the ground, his muscles aching as if he'd wrestled a mountain instead of a man, he nonetheless found the strength to glare at Morath.

"Leave me," he demanded. "Go back to the others and let me drown in the depths of my pain."

His face scored and smeared with dust, Morath shook his head. "No," he rasped. "You've lied. You've shamed yourself and all your ancestors. The blood of an entire village is on your hands, as surely as if you had put them to death yourself."

Kahless closed his eyes against the accusation. "No," he insisted. "Molor killed them. *Molor!*"

"Not Molor," said Morath. "*You!*"

The outlaw couldn't listen to any more of the man's libels. Raising himself to his knees, he gathered one leg underneath him, then the other. Staggering over to his *s'tarahk*, who had been gnawing on groundnuts by the side of the trail, he pulled himself onto the animal's back.

Somehow, he sat up and took the reins in his hands. "Go," he told the *s'tarahk*. "Take me away from this place."

The beast began to move, its clawed feet padding softly on the ground. But after a while, Kahless heard a second set of clawed feet behind him.

With an effort, he turned and saw a haggard-looking figure in pursuit. It was Morath, sitting astride his own *s'tarahk*, only his eyes showing any life. But they accused Kahless as vigorously as ever.

The outlaw turned his back on his pursuer. Let Morath dog my steps all he likes, he thought. Let him follow me day and night. If he keeps at it long enough, he can follow me to *Gre'thor*.

CHAPTER **19**

The Modern Age

Alexander eyed the lanky Klingon standing not two paces away from him, armed with a wicked-looking *bat'telh*. A bar of light from a hole in the cavern roof fell across the Klingon's face, throwing his knife-sharp features into stark relief.

The boy moved sideways, placing a milk-white, tapering stalagmite between them. The scrape of his feet on the stone floor echoed throughout the dark, musty space. Chuckling to himself, the Klingon followed, shifting his weapon in his hands to allow him more reach.

"You shouldn't have come here," the Klingon rasped.

"I go where I please," the boy piped up, though his heart wasn't really in it.

Without warning, his adversary struck in a big, sweeping arc—one meant to separate Alexander's head from his shoulders. Somehow, the boy got his *bat'telh* up in time to block the blow.

The cavern walls rang with the clash of their blades, just as if this had been a real place and not a holodeck recreation. Alexander's opponent made a sound of disgust in his throat, just as if he were a real being and not an amalgam of electromagnetic fields and light projections.

Quickly, the boy moved to the other side, taking advantage of another stalagmite to buy himself some time. But, enraged by his failure to deal a mortal wound, the Klingon moved with him.

"You were lucky that time," he growled.

"We'll see about that," Alexander countered.

But he knew the Klingon had a point. The boy wasn't concentrating as hard as he should have been. He was too distracted, too concerned with events outside the program.

Even his retorts to the warrior's taunts seemed hollow. And usually, that was his favorite part of the exercise.

Alexander had received the program as a gift from his father on his last birthday. Of course, birthday gifts were a peculiarly human tradition, but Worf had grown up on Earth and was familiar with the practice.

"Tell me," his father had asked, "is there anything in particular you would like? Something from Earth, perhaps?"

The boy had shaken his head. "What I want," he'd said, "is another *bat'telh* program. I'm kind of getting tired of the one in the town square. I mean, it's so easy once you get the hang of it."

That seemed to have surprised his father. But it also seemed to have pleased him.

"I have just the thing," he told Alexander. "And you'll find it a lot more difficult than the one you have now, I assure you."

He was right. This one *was* a lot more difficult.

Actually, it was an adaptation of a program Worf himself had used when he first arrived on the *Enterprise*. Of course, a Klingon had been inserted in place of a Pandrilite and it was restricted to Level One, whereas Worf had bumped it up to Level Three at times. But otherwise, it was pretty much the same.

For instance, if his adversary's *bat'telh* connected, it would hurt like crazy. All the more reason, thought Alexander, not to let it do that.

The Klingon struck again, this time coming from above. Anticipating the move, the boy stepped to the side and launched an attack of his own—a swipe halfway between the vertical and the horizontal.

It wasn't the best countermove Alexander had ever made. Far from it, in fact. But fortunately for the boy, his opponent had overextended himself.

Before the Klingon could withdraw again, Alexander dealt him a nasty blow to the left shoulder. If an adult's strength had been behind the blow, it might have made a bloody ruin of the joint.

As it was, it didn't even pierce the Klingon's body armor. But it did make his arm twitch—an indication that the boy had done some damage after all. Gritting his teeth, the warrior switched his *bat'telh* to his other hand.

Alexander was about to try to capitalize on his enemy's weakness when he saw an irregular pattern open in the stone wall. Of course, that wasn't going to stop the Klingon.

He launched another assault, this time one-handed. Still, it was every bit as vicious as the first. The boy stepped back and nearly tripped on a stalagmite, but managed to keep his feet. And somehow, he deflected the attack.

Then, before he could be pressed any further, a voice said: "Freeze program."

The Klingon stopped moving. Alexander noted how much less threatening his adversary looked frozen in midmaneuver.

"Sorry to interrupt," said Riker, stepping through the opening. Behind him, one of the ship's corridors was visible. Bright, austere, and streamlined, it provided a jarring contrast to the subterranean depths of the cavern. "I just thought I'd look in on you. See how you were doing, you know?"

The boy looked at him. "I guess."

The first officer indicated Alexander's *bat'telh* with a tilt of his chin. "You've gotten pretty good with that thing."

Alexander knew it was less than the truth. His friend was just being kind. "Not as good as I'd like," he said.

Riker regarded him. "In that case, maybe I can help." He looked up at the ceilingful of stalactites. "Computer. I'd like a *bat'telh*, appropriate size and weight."

A moment later, a blade materialized in his hands. He hefted it, then nodded his satisfaction and eyed Alexander.

"Ever heard of anbo-jytsu?" he asked.

The boy shook his head. In fact, he hadn't heard of it. And more to the point, he had no idea what it had to do with his combat program.

The Klingon named Majjas sat in his heavy, carved chair against the far wall of his central hall, his white hair glistening in the light from several tall windows. He smiled benificently.

"This is quite a day," said Majjas. "Not only do I have the pleasure of meeting the Emperor Kahless and renewing my acquaintance with the sons of Mogh, though that would be honor enough. I am fortunate to have beneath my roof the esteemed Arbiter of Succession."

Picard smiled back. It wasn't just the slightly ironic twist the Klingon put on the word "esteemed" that elicited the human's admiration. It was the fact that Majjas had not waited for his wife to make introductions, but had glanced at each of his visitors in turn and identified them all without the slightest hesitation.

Not bad for a blind man, the captain thought. Especially one without a VISOR to rely on.

Apparently, Majjas had lost his sight several years ago in a weapons-room accident on a Klingon bird-of-prey. The scars that wove their way through the flesh around both his eyes bore mute testimony to that—though it was difficult to see the man's eyes themselves, slitted as they were and hidden beneath large, bushy white brows.

Kahless must have been surprised by Majjas's feat as well, because he grunted approvingly. "I see the stories about you are true," he remarked. "Majjas, son of Eragh, is as canny a warrior as ever served on a Klingon ship— and your blindness has not changed that."

Of course, Picard mused, the old man would have had warning of their visit. Kurn would have seen to that before he took them off Ogat in his private vessel. But still, to know each of them by their footsteps—or perhaps their scent—was certainly an accomplishment.

Majjas chuckled. "The Mogh family is coming up in the world," he jibed, "to be traveling in such distinguished company." Leaning closer to Kahless, he added: "For the record, I do not care in the least whether the scroll is authentic. I, for one, will always believe in the Kahless of legend. Now," he continued, leaning back in his chair, "what sort of impulse has brought you to my humble abode?"

No sooner had Majjas completed his question than a quintet of females emerged from a back room, carrying trays full of decantered drink and brazen goblets, and writhing gagh in bowls of supple, red *m'ressa* twigs.

The captain couldn't help noticing how beautiful they were. In a savage way, of course.

"My daughters," said the old man, his smile broadening—though from his tone of voice, it was clear even to Picard that Majjas would have liked a strong son to go with them.

As one of the trays was placed in front of him, the captain poured himself a goblet full of black Klingon wine—but declined when offered the gagh. He had eaten on the way here, after all.

Worf was the one who finally answered Majjas's question. "You have been a friend of my family for years," he told his host. "Since before Kuru and I were born."

"Since before your father was born," the old man interjected. "And a difficult birth it was."

Worf grinned. "I stand corrected, honored host. Since before our *father* was born." He paused. "I remember my father saying no one knows armaments like Majjas—regardless of whether they are daggers or disruptor cannons, phasers or photon torpedoes."

"Your father did not lie," the old man agreed. "That's what comes of serving on a Bird-of-Prey all one's life."

As Picard looked on, Worf's smile disappeared. "I am

glad to hear that," the lieutenant said. "We need such expertise on our side."

"Your *side?*" Majjas echoed. "Then am I to understand you're at odds with some other House?"

"With *someone,*" Kahless interjected. "Though it may be a great deal more than a simple conflict between Houses." He glanced meaningfully at the old man's wife, a slight woman with sharp features. "Perhaps this is something you alone may wish to hear, Majjas."

Their host shook his white-maned head. "My wife and my daughters—young as they are—are more than ornaments in this hall. You will not have occasion to regret your trust in them."

Kahless inclined his head, to show his compliance with Majjas's terms. If the old man couldn't see him, at least his wife could. Then the clone went on to describe all they'd learned—starting with his observations at Tolar'tu and ending with the bloodshed at the academy on Ogat.

By the time he was done, Majjas was scowling in his wispy, white beard. "You are dealing with cowards," he concluded, "and worse. But I see what you mean—this is more than a feud between Houses." The muscles in his temples worked, evidence of his determination to help. "What service may I perform for you, my friends?"

The captain watched as Worf opened the pouch on his belt and removed its contents, then placed them in their host's hands. Examining the metal fragments with his fingertips, Majjas harrumphed.

"Pieces of a bomb casing," he announced. "No doubt, from one of the firebombs your enemies set off at the academy. And what is it you wish to know about these pieces?"

"We were hoping," said Picard, "that you could provide us with some clue as to their manufacture. Preferably, something that might lead us to our enemies."

Our enemies, thought the captain. It was a phrase any ambassador in the Federation would have frowned on. However, it seemed eminently appropriate at the moment.

Majjas turned the shards over and over in his hands. "A clue, eh? I can tell you this—they're made of *mich'ara,* an alloy most often used in heating elements, since it conducts thermal energy so well. But for a time, it was *also* used in the making of explosive devices."

Picard nodded. Now they were getting somewhere. "For a time?" he prodded. "But no longer?"

"That is correct," said the old man. "The practice stopped when cheaper alloys were introduced, which could be applied to the same purpose."

Worf's eyes narrowed. "Then not *every* armory would provide our enemies with access to such a device."

"True," Majjas confirmed. "In fact, to my knowledge, there is only *one.* It is on Ter'jas Mor, not far from the city of Donar'ruq."

Worf smiled as warmly as the captain had ever seen him smile. "The House of Mogh is once more in your debt, my friend. If there were some way to repay you for your assistance . . ."

Their host shrugged. "You could take me with you," he suggested.

A silence fell . . . until Majjas began to laugh out loud in his beard. His daughters looked at one another with relief—the same sort of relief Picard himself was feeling.

"You may relax," the old Klingon assured them. "I

don't expect you to drag a blind man along. But if circumstances were different, it would be good to strike a blow again for the Empire." He sighed. "I tell you, I would have enjoyed that to the bottom of my heart."

"How long will you be staying here on B'aaj?" asked Majjas's wife, the epitome of Klingon gentility—though she must have already known the answer.

"I regret," Worf told her, "that we cannot remain here as your guests. Our mission is too urgent for us to delay."

"Except to finish your wine," the old man stipulated.

"Of course," Kahless replied. "It would be dishonorable to do otherwise." And with that, he drained his goblet.

Worf cleared his throat, causing Majjas to turn in his direction. "There is one other thing."

"And that is?" the old man inquired.

"I ask that you—and your family—refrain from mentioning you even glimpsed us. After all," said Mogh's elder son, "one never knows whom one can trust at times like these. And as far as our enemies are concerned, we are dead."

"Dead?" repeated Majjas. He laughed some more. "Some would say that is even *worse* than being blind."

Kahless stood and put his goblet down on a table made for such a purpose. "I am afraid," he said, "it is time to take our leave of you now. And if my companions are too polite to hurry out of your hall, I will bear the blame on my own shoulders."

But he hadn't offended their host, Picard observed. Far from it. Majjas's grin was so wide, it looked painful.

"Don't worry," the old man told them. "I am not

offended, Emperor. Rather, I am honored. Have a safe trip, my friends. It is a dark and dangerous road you have chosen."

"That it is," Kahless agreed. And without further conversation, he led the way out of Majjas's house— leaving Picard and the others no choice but to follow.

CHAPTER 20

The Heroic Age

For two days, Kahless drove his *s'tarahk* mercilessly, pausing only for the animal to munch on grass and groundnuts, and to water itself. Its rider, on the other hand, neither ate nor slept.

His mind had long ago settled into the rhythm of the beast's progress, avoiding anything so painful as a thought. Day turned into night, night became day, and he barely noticed.

But all the while, Morath was right behind him. He stopped when Kahless stopped and went on when Kahless went on. He didn't attempt to overtake him, or to speak with him again, only to haunt him from a distance.

At one point, just as twilight was throwing its cloak over the world, Kahless came to a fast-rushing stream. Seeing no way to go around it, he urged his *s'tarahk* to enter the water. But the beast wouldn't move.

It dropped to its haunches, then fell over on its side,

exhausted. And in the process, Kahless fell to the ground as well.

He looked back. Morath was sitting on his mount, saying nothing, making no move to come any closer. Only staring, with those dark, baleful eyes of his. But his stare was an accusation in itself.

Kahless grunted derisively. "Are you still here?" he asked.

Morath didn't answer. He simply got down off his *s'tarahk* and let the animal approach the stream. As it drank, Kahless grunted again.

"Have it your way," he said.

Kahless considered his mount again. The *s'tarahk* wasn't going anywhere in its depleted condition—not for a while. The outlaw was tired too. Taking his sleeping mat off the beast's back, he rolled into it and closed his eyes against the starlight.

It was possible that Morath would kill him while he was asleep. But Kahless didn't care. It would be as good a death as any other, and he wanted more desperately than ever to end his suffering.

Kahless woke with first light. The sun's rays were hot on his face and blinding to his eyes.

For a moment, staring at the *s'tarahk* grazing placidly beside him and the blanched hills all around, he didn't know where he was or how he had gotten there. For that moment, he knew peace. Then he remembered, and his load of misery crushed him all over again.

A shadow fell over him. Turning, he saw Morath standing there. As before, the younger man accused his comrade with his eyes.

"What is it you want from me?" asked Kahless.

Morath grunted. "I want you to pay for what you've done."

"Pay how?" asked the outlaw.

The other man was silent. It was as if he expected Kahless to know the answer. But Kahless knew nothing of the kind.

With an effort, he got up, his muscles sore from striving against Morath the day before, and limped over to his *s'tarahk*. The beast looked rested. That was good, because he didn't intend to pamper it.

There was a pit in his stomach, crying out to be filled. Kahless ignored it. Dead men didn't eat.

Getting back on his mount, the outlaw turned it north again. It wasn't as if he had a destination—just a direction. He would follow it until he could do so no longer.

But Morath wasn't done with him. Kahless could tell by the shadow the man cast as he mounted his *s'tarahk*, and by the scraping of the animal's claws on the hard, dry ground behind him. Morath followed him like a specter of death, unflinching in his purpose—whatever it was.

Not that it made any difference to Kahless. He was too scoured out inside to play his friend's games, too empty of what made a Klingon a Klingon. Nothing mattered, Morath least of all.

For a total of six days and six nights, Kahless led Morath high into the hills. Twice, they were drenched to the bone by spring sleet storms, which came without warning and disappeared just as suddenly. Neither of them cared much about the discomfort.

On some days, they wrestled as they had that first time, consumed with hatred and resentment for one another; on others, they simply followed the track on their poor, tired beasts. With time, however, their wrestling matches became shorter and farther between.

After all, their only sustenance was the water they came across in streams running down from the highlands. Neither of them ate a thing. They left to their mounts the few edible plants that grew along the path.

There was no conversation either, not even as prelude to their strivings with one another. Neither of them seemed to find a value anymore in speech. On occasion, Kahless saw Morath speaking to himself. But the outlaw wasn't much of a lip-reader, never having seen the need for it, so he couldn't discern the sense of the other warrior's mutterings.

Finally, on the morning of the twelfth day, in the shadow of a great rock alongside a windy mountain trail, Kahless woke with the knowledge that he could tolerate Morath's presence no longer. One way or the other, he had to be rid of the man.

Turning, Kahless eyed his comrade, who had more than once saved his life. When he spoke it was with a voice that sounded strange and foreign to him, a voice like the sighing of the wind in a stand of river reeds.

"I will go no further, Morath. I cannot stand the thought of looking back and seeing you following me. We'll wrestle again, eh? But this time, only one of us will walk away."

Morath shook his head. "No, Kahless." His voice was thin and harsh as well. "If you want to grapple, fine. But I have no more intention of killing you than I do of being killed myself."

Days ago, Kahless would have been moved to anger. Now, the remark only annoyed him, the way a mud gnat might annoy a *minn'hor* calf.

"Then I'll take my own life," he told Morath. "That will do just as well." He looked around. "All I need is a sharp rock . . . or a heavy one. . . ."

"No," said the younger man. "I won't allow it." As obstinate as ever, he placed himself in his companion's way.

Kahless eyed him. As far as he could tell, Morath meant it. Besides, there weren't any rocks around that filled his need.

The outlaw sighed. "What do you want of me?" he asked, not for the first time. He was surprised to hear a pleading quality in his voice, a weariness that went down to his very soul. "You mentioned a price, Morath. I'll pay it—I'll pay anything, if you'll only tell me what it is."

Morath's lips pulled back over his teeth, making him look more like a predator than ever. "Pay with your life then."

Kahless tilted his head, to look at the man. "Are you insane? I offered to end my life with my own hands. Or if it's vengeance you want—"

The younger man shook his head. "No, not vengeance," he insisted. "There's been altogether too much slaughter already. What I ask for is not a death, Kahless—but a *life.*"

Only then did the outlaw begin to understand. To pay for what he'd done, he would have to dedicate his life to those who had perished. He would have to become what Vathraq and the others thought he was.

A rebel. A man devoted to overthrowing the tyrant Molor.

At first, he balked at the idea. The tyrant was too powerful. No one could tear him down, least of all a pack of untrained outlaws, led by a man who had lost his stomach for fighting.

On the other hand, what was the worst that could happen? He would die. And right now, he welcomed death like a brother.

"A life," Morath repeated. It was more of a question than anything else.

The wind blew. The sun beat down. One of the *s'tarahkmey* grumbled and scraped the ground with its claws, looking for food.

At last, Kahless nodded. "Fine. Whatever you say."

"Then get on your *s'tarahk,*" said the younger man, his voice flat and without emotion, "and be the renegade you let others believe you to be."

Kahless straightened at the harshness of the retort. "Not yet," he said.

Morath looked at him. No doubt, he expected to have to argue some more. But it wouldn't be necessary.

"First," said Kahless, "I need something to eat."

Approaching a patch of groundnuts on shaky legs, he knelt and began to wolf them down. After he had taken a couple of mouthfuls, Morath joined him. They ate more like *targs* than men.

Then, their bellies full for the first time in many days, they mounted their beasts and turned back toward Vathraq's village.

At night, when Kahless was unrolling his sleeping mat, Morath began to speak. He was not a man given to long utterances, but this time he eyed the stars and spoke at length.

"My father," he told Kahless, "was a strange man. He

was raised as a devotee of the old gods. It was to them he cried out for help when my mother was giving birth to me.

"The gods, he said, promised him their assistance. Nonetheless, my mother died. My father lashed out at his deities, calling them deceivers—and smashed all the little statues of them that stood around the house. Thereafter, he hated deceit above all else.

"Somehow, I thrived. But my father neither took another mate, nor did he conceive another child. There were only the two of us, and he raised me with an iron hand.

"When I was five years old, he almost killed me for telling a small, inconsequential lie. Shortly thereafter, while I still bore the bruises of his beating, our house was set upon by reavers—cruel Klingons who obeyed no laws, self-imposed or otherwise.

"My father fought bravely—so bravely a chill still climbs my spine when I think about it. I remember being surprised that this was the same man who had beaten me so, protecting his son and his hearth with such feverish intensity.

"And I?" Morath grunted bitterly. "I ran away and hid in the woods, afraid to fight at my father's side—caught in the grip of wild, unreasoning terror. In the end, the reavers proved too much for Ondagh, son of Bogra. They killed him and took everything we had of value.

"Only when they were gone did I come out of hiding and see what they had done to my father. I knew that I should have fallen at his side, but I had not—and nothing could ever change that. Unable to bear my burden, I tried to run away again—this time, from my father's ghost.

"For a long time, I wandered the wide world, looking for a way to rid myself of my guilt. One day, after many years had passed, I came upon a still, serene lake and bent to drink from it.

"Then I recoiled—for it was my father's reflection I saw in the tranquil waters. And I realized I had been given a second chance. I would be Ondagh—not as he was, but as he could have been. I would brook no deceit, neither from man nor god. And I would never run away from anything again."

Having said his piece, Morath unrolled his own mat and laid down on it. In a moment or two he was asleep.

Kahless looked at his friend for a long time, beginning to understand why Morath did the things he did. Then, at last, he too fell asleep.

Kahless and Morath came in sight of Vathraq's keep twelve days after their departure. To the outlaw's surprise, his men were still waiting for him, still eyeing the horizon.

By then, of course, they had burned all the corpses, as much to deny the *kraw'zamey* a meal as to discourage the spread of disease. Unfortunately, that made it worse for Kahless. The mangled shapes of death held less terror for him than their empty aftermath.

The outlaw himself said nothing about the time he was gone. Morath didn't say much either. But he did mention how sore he was from wrestling with Kahless, and pretty soon the others picked up on it.

Before long, the story became amplified. The outlaw

and his friend had wrestled in the hills for twelve days and twelve nights, it was said, through heat and storm and all manner of hardship. Of course, no one could figure out why they would want to do that.

Nor did Morath disabuse them of the notion. Even for him, apparently, it was close enough to the truth.

CHAPTER **21**

The Modern Age

Picard breathed in the cold air and observed the contingent of Klingons on the next plateau, perhaps a hundred meters below him and his companions.

Their dark hair was drawn back and tied into ponytails, in the manner of Worf's. In the flat, gray light of predawn, their white *mok'bara* garb looked strangely serene against the coarse, black rock and the omnipresent tufts of hardy, red *en'chula* grass.

Of course, the Klingons themselves were anything but serene. Focused, yes. Entranced, perhaps. But serene? Even in the practice of so demanding a discipline, Klingon serenity was a contradiction in terms.

Anyone who doubted that had only to witness what the captain was witnessing—the ferocity with which these practitioners assailed one another, launching kick after deadly kick and blow after crushing blow, and following each with a guttural shout of exultation. Fortunately for them, none of these assaults found their targets—for as skilled as they were at attacks, they were just as skilled at avoiding them.

It was a mesmerizing spectacle, the captain mused. Like a spider of many parts weaving a continuous, flashing web. Or a particularly vicious species of bird writhing in a torturous form of flight, the reasons for which were lost in its genetic past.

Picard had seen Worf teach the *mok'bara* exercises to a dedicated few on the *Enterprise,* Beverly and Deanna among them. However, those maneuvers were to these as a jog in the woods was to the Academy marathon. Neither Beverly nor Deanna would have lasted more than a few brief seconds in so violent and rigorous a ritual.

"I am amused," Kahless hissed.

He was careful not to speak so loudly that he'd draw the attention of the martial artists below—though with all the bellowing going on down there, such care seemed rather unnecessary.

"In my day, there was no such thing as this. . . ." He turned to Worf. "What did you call it?"

The lieutenant scowled. *"Mok'bara,"* he replied.

"This *Mok'baaara,"* Kahless finished, butchering the word as if on purpose. He shook his head. "In my era, life itself contained all the exercise one would ever need. And if one still craved action at the end of the day, there was always the requisite afterdinner brawl."

Worf harrumphed. Clearly, thought Picard, his officer didn't appreciate the clone's disparagements.

"The ritual provides more than exercise," the lieutenant explained. "It helps one to set aside distractions—to concentrate on the advancement of one's spirit."

Kahless clapped him affectionately on the back. "I

don't mean to offend anyone, Worf—and certainly not my closest companions. If you want to perform panto-mimes in your night clothes, I have no objections."

Kurn looked at the clone. "With all due respect, Kahless, I can see why you were never revered as a diplomat."

"To *Gre'thor* with diplomats," Kahless spat—*Gre'thor* being the Klingon equivalent of Hell.

After some of his experiences with diplomatic envoys, the captain was inclined to agree. But, not for the first time since he'd embarked on this mission, he held his tongue.

Abruptly, he noticed the first brazen rays of the sun sneaking over the cliffs to his right. He turned to Worf, who'd mentioned earlier that the ritual would end when dawn touched the plateau.

"Lieutenant?" said Picard, by way of a reminder.

Worf glanced at the cliffs and nodded. "We should start down now."

Without further ceremony, he retreated from the edge of their rocky plateau and made his way across it toward a steep, winding path. By following this path, the captain knew, they would end up exactly where they wanted to be—and with any luck, see just whom they wished to see.

Their descent took them around a natural column of crags and boulders, one of many that seemed to punctu-ate the landscape. Though Picard's interests leaned more toward archaeology than geology, he resolved to learn someday what sort of forces created these structures.

As the sky continued to lighten above them, they came to the end of the path and gathered in a hollow. By peering through a cleft in the rocks, they could see the slope just below the *mok'bara* practitioners' plateau. To be sure, it was a gentler way down than the one they'd just taken—but more importantly, it narrowed to a point right near the cleft.

They'd barely arrived when the martial artists began to descend. It was remarkable how calm they seemed, after the effort they'd put into their ritual just a few moments earlier.

The Klingons were conversing quietly, nodding, even smiling at one another. It seemed to the captain they'd come from a sewing bee instead of a potentially lethal combat.

"Which one is Godar?" Kahless asked softly.

"He is the last of them," Kurn replied. "As always. You see him? The tall, wizened-looking one with the simple chin-beard?"

"Ah, that one," said Kahless, craning his head to get a better angle. "And you believe he can be trusted?"

Worf's brother grunted. "I believe so, yes."

"You seem to trust a great many people," the clone commented.

"Like you," Kurn told him, "I have no choice."

In moments, most of the *mok'bara* practitioners had passed the cleft on their way down from the plateau. None of them seemed to notice Picard and his companions. But after what had happened in Tolar'tu, that was little assurance in the captain's eyes.

As Kurn had indicated, Godar was the last of them. He too appeared unaware of the quartet that had traveled so far to speak with him. That is, until Kurn croaked his name.

At first, the man seemed confused as to who might have called him. Then he happened to glance in the direction of their hiding place.

Under similar circumstances, Picard thought, he himself might have cried out in surprise—or bolted, fearing an ambush. But Godar did neither of these things. Still invigorated by his exercises, he simply altered his stance a bit, ready to take on whatever awaited him.

"Who is it?" he rasped, darting a sideways look at his fellow practitioners, who seemed not to have missed him—at least not yet. "Speak quickly—and give me a reason not to warn the others."

"It's me," Worf's brother whispered. "It's Kurn, son of Mogh."

Immediately, Godar's expression changed. He became more curious than wary. "Come forward, so I can see it is really you," he demanded.

Worf's brother complied with Godar's wishes. As the hollow filled with sunlight, the man saw the truth of the matter—and grinned.

"Kurn," he said. "You Miravian slime devil!"

Reaching in, he grasped Kurn's arm in a handclasp reserved for brothers and close allies. "What in the name of *Fek'lhr* are you doing on Ter'jas Mor?" He squinted. "And who the blazes is in there with you?"

Kurn moved aside, so the older man could get a better look into the hollow. "You will find," he explained, "that I travel in unusual company."

As Godar spotted Worf and then Picard, his elderly brow creased with curiosity. And when he realized that Kahless was with them, the crease became a deep, dark furrow in the center of his forehead.

"Unusual company indeed," the man murmured. He turned back to Kurn. "And how does this involve *me*, son of Mogh?"

As he did at Majjas's house, Worf's brother explained

what was going on. However, he left out Majjas's name, referring to the blind man simply as "an expert in armaments."

The *mok'bara* practitioner nodded. "And since I was once the master of the defense armory on this world, you believe I can tell you who might have stolen the bomb."

Worf shrugged. "If anyone knows the people who worked there, it would be you. If you were pressed to come up with a name . . ."

Godar didn't respond right away. Finally, after what seemed like a long time, he came up with not one name but two—and a bit of information to back up his suspicions.

"Mind you," he told them, "I don't know for a fact that they're guilty. I'm only guessing."

Kurn snorted. "A guess from Godar, son of Gudag, is better than a certainty from anyone else. I thank you, my friend—and I trust you will keep the matter of our survival a secret."

The *mok'bara* practitioner laughed softly. "I haven't lived *this* long by betraying my friends, Kurn. Your secret is safe with me." He gazed downslope again. "But if I don't hurry, my companions will wonder what kept me so long. Follow the path of honor, Son of Mogh."

And with that, he was gone. Picard looked at Kurn. "I assume we'll be paying our bombing suspects a visit."

Kurn nodded. "You assume correctly."

"Then what are we waiting for?" asked Kahless.

"We're not," Worf's brother replied.

Pulling up his sleeve to expose the remote control band on his forearm, he tapped in the necessary information. Then he activated the link to his vessel's transporter system.

The captain felt a brief thrill, something like a low-voltage electrical current, running through him—the earmark of Klingon transporter technology. A moment later, he was back on Kurn's ship—though with what they knew now, he was certain he wouldn't stay there very long.

CHAPTER 22

The Heroic Age

Kahless looked at all those who had assembled in the village of T'chariv, along the edge of the northern forests. His own men were only a small part of the crowd that huddled under a gray sky, surrounded by low wooden houses and a flimsy-looking barricade.

Last of all, the outlaw glanced at Edronh, the man he had fought over the *minn'hor* herd nearly a year ago. Edronh nodded, and Kahless looked back at the funeral pyre that stood behind him.

Torch in hand, he approached the pyre, with its burden of half a dozen corpses. The wind whistled in his ears, whispering things he didn't want to hear or know about.

Touching his torch to the kindling beneath the wooden platform, he waited until the fire caught. Then he watched as logs were placed on the burning branches, feeding the flames until they enveloped the bodies above.

Finally, assured that all was as it should be, he withdrew to stand by Edronh.

As the fire danced around the pyre, Kahless looked deep into the outlaw's eyes. He saw the sort of agony there that he himself had known. The kind of torment only the loss of a loved one may bring.

He wanted desperately to look away. But he couldn't, not ever again. He could ignore the wind, but not what he saw in a man like Edronh.

If he was to lead a rebellion as so many wished him to, he would have to understand their pain. He would have to distill it, like bloodwine. And he would have to give all of Molor's people a taste, so they would know what they were fighting for.

Out of the corner of his eye, he could see Morath staring at him, silently keeping him to his promise. But Kahless no longer fomented rebellion for Morath's sake alone.

Now he did it for himself as well—and for Kellein. He had discovered it was the only thing that made his heart stop hurting for her, the only balm that worked for him.

Had he been the one to die instead of Kellein, she would have made the rest of her life a tribute to him. She would have turned her sorrow and her anger into something useful—and deadly.

Could he do any less?

"Rannuf," Edronh whispered, the flames reflected in his eyes as they picked at his child's bones. His wife moved closer to him, to give comfort and to take some. "My son," he said, "my strong, brave son."

Kahless nodded as a bone popped and sparks flew, rising like a swarm of fiery insects among the twists of smoke. "Rannuf," he echoed.

Edronh turned to him. "You knew him, my friend. He laid his sword before you, that day in the woods. You saw his courage, his manliness."

I saw how young he was, Kahless thought. How excessive in his eagerness. But he didn't mention that.

"Rannuf was a warrior," he said. "He died defending his people against the depravities of Molor."

That much was true. The tyrant must have gotten wind of the things Edronh was saying about him. And though Edronh and his men were outlaws, every outlaw had kin somewhere. Once Molor had determined where that somewhere was, the rest was simple.

He had sent his soldiers to T'chariv with fire and sword, just as he had once sent Kahless himself. Unfortunately for Rannuf, he had been home at the time, visiting his mother and his younger brother. Seeing what the tyrant's men intended, he had met them blow for blow.

But the soldiers were more numerous than the village's defenders and had killed them to a man—then lopped off their heads for good measure. The only good fortune was that the soldiers had spared the village itself, their point having been made.

Do not think to defy your lord Molor, they had said— if not with their tongues, then with their sharp-edged swords. After all, no one can hope to stand against him.

In the last half-year, that message had been carved like a bloodeagle from one end of the tyrant's domain to the other. Vathraq's village had only been the beginning. Nor would T'chariv be the end.

Kahless looked at Edronh. "It would be a shame," he said, "if Rannuf were to go unavenged."

The other man bit his lip. Clearly, he wasn't as enthusiastic about revolution as he had been.

Until now, Edronh had thought himself too far north to feel Molor's sting. To his everlasting regret, he had learned that was not so. Having seen Rannuf's mangled body, having lifted it in pieces onto the pyre, he had become wary.

But if he was to have a hope of toppling the tyrant, Kahless needed men like Edronh. Men who could not only fight, but spread word of their struggle to others.

"I had a lover," he told Edronh, plumbing the depths of his own sorrow. "We were betrothed before you and I met. But before I could return to her, Molor crushed her village and everyone in it."

The other man looked at him. "The tyrant is everywhere."

Kahless grunted. "Because we allow him to be everywhere. Because we sit in our own separate hideaways and wait for him to bring us misery."

Edronh's eyes narrowed. "What are you saying?"

"Only this," said Kahless. "That it is not enough to speak of rebellion, as we have done in the past. It is time we let our swords do our speaking for us. Together, as one army, we can show Molor what misery truly is. And in time, we can destroy him as surely as he destroyed Rannuf."

Edronh seemed to be mulling it over. After a while, he spoke in a voice thick with emotion.

"I have only one other son, my friend. I could not bear to lose him as I lost Rannuf."

Kahless eyed him sternly. Perhaps it was not enough to distill the pain of Molor's victims. Perhaps he needed something more.

And instinctively, he seemed to know what that something would be.

"Then you will lose more than your sons," he told Edronh. "You will lose everything."

Edonh shook his head. "Everything?" he echoed.

"Everything that matters," the outlaw explained. "The day we met, Edronh—you remember it?"

The other man said he did. "As if it were yesterday."

"You spoke to me of honor that day—the honor a warrior may accord another warrior, whom he has come to respect. But there is another kind of honor, my friend. It is the kind a man must seek in himself—a love of virtue he must not abandon, no matter the consequences—or else admit to the world he is less than a man."

Edronh's features hardened, as if he had been challenged. "I am a man, Kahless. I have never been anything less."

"Then fight," the outlaw spat. "Fight for your honor, your dignity. Fight to make this land free of Molor's tyranny."

Edronh grunted. "Brave words, Kahless. But I fear to take part in a halfhearted venture—one which would spur Molor to even greater atrocities."

The outlaw nodded. "I understand. And I swear to you, we will finish what we start, or I am not the son of Kanjis. I will not lay down my sword until the tyrant is dead—or *I* am."

Edronh measured the size of Kahless's conviction—and found it sufficient. He clapped his friend on the shoulder.

"I will not lay down my sword either, then," he promised. "From this day on, I fight at your side. And so do all those who ride with me."

Kahless smiled. "I want more than that, Edronh. I want

you and your men to go out as messengers—to speak with everyone you know, every hearth you can find. Tell them I am gathering an army to march against Molor in the tyrant's own stronghold. Tell them I am doing this for the sake of their honor." His smile widened. "And tell them they will never have a chance like this again."

Edronh smiled too, though the flames of the funeral pyre turned his eyes to molten gold. "I will do it. You have my word."

Kahless could almost hear the pounding of the black-smith's hammer as he forged the first link in his chain of rebellion. But it was only one link, he had to remind himself. He would need an entire chain before he could challenge the likes of Molor.

Feeling someone's stare on the back of his neck, he turned. Morath was looking at him. The younger man seemed pleased.

Kahless nodded at him. It had begun.

CHAPTER 23

The Modern Age

Unlike his captain, Riker had never been to the Klingon
Homeworld. But he was familiar enough with Worf's
holodeck programs to know which cavern he was standing in.

It was called DIS jajlo', literally "dawn cave." He
didn't know how it had gotten that name, since the shaft
of light that came from above was only visible in midday.

At least, that was true of the real DIS jajlo', back on
Q'onoS. In this program, for all he knew, the shaft of light
never moved.

Right now, nothing else was moving either. With a
single command, he had frozen Alexander's Klingon
adversary in place. And the boy himself was so focused
on the first officer, he might as well have been frozen too.

Well, thought Riker, I seemed to have piqued his
interest. Now it's time to follow through.

"Anbo-jytsu," he said, "is a martial art form back on

Earth—a one-on-one confrontation, much like the one you're involved in now." He raised his chin to indicate the Klingon warrior. "Of course, there are some differences. In anbo-jytsu, you wear a padded suit and your weapon is a stick three meters long. On one end of the stick, there's a proximity detector. You need that because you're wearing a blindfold the whole time you're at it."

Alexander looked at him. "A blindfold?" he echoed.

"Right—you can't see. That makes it pretty important to have a good sense of balance. And to be able to anticipate your enemy's moves. Here, let me show you what I mean."

Again, the first officer looked to the stalactite-riddled ceiling of the cavern. "Computer, I need a blindfold."

A band of white cloth materialized in Riker's hand. Grasping it, he approached the Klingon warrior. Then the first officer tied the blindfold around his head, covering his eyes, and raised his *bat'telh* in front of him.

"Computer," he called, "resume program."

Riker heard the rustling that meant the warrior had come back to life. Taking a step back, he felt for a stalagmite with his heel—and found one. That told him how far backward he could go.

A moment later, he heard the derisive grunt that signified the Klingon's recognition of what he was facing. Clearly, he didn't expect a man who couldn't see to put up much of a fight. Under normal circumstances, he'd probably have been right.

But the first officer had been honing his skills at anbo-jytsu since he was eight years old. He no longer needed a proximity detector to sense an attack coming, or to know what to do about it. And even though he had a *bat'telh* instead of a three-meter-long staff in his hand, a two-handed weapon was pretty much a two-handed weapon.

Listening carefully, Riker heard a sharp intake of breath. Bracing himself, he allowed his instincts to take over. Without actually thinking about it, the first officer found himself moving to block a blow from the warrior's right hand.

Careful to remain balanced, attentive not only to what he heard but also to what he smelled and felt in the movements of the air, Riker parried a second attack from the same quarter. And a third.

Apparently, the Klingon was going to keep trying the same thing, over and over again. Either he had some idea that the human was more vulnerable there or the warrior was himself limited. Say, by a wound he'd sustained before Riker arrived.

There was only one way to find out. Before his opponent could strike again, the first officer shifted the *bat'telh* in his hands and swung hard at the Klingon's left side. He heard a cry of apprehension, then felt his blade connect with something solid. It made a *chukt* as it sliced through leather body armor and maybe flesh as well.

The warrior cried out, then made a shuffling sound. A moment later, Riker heard him grunt as he hit the ground. Then there was a clatter, as of something metal.

"Freeze program," he said.

Removing his blindfold, the human surveyed his handiwork. The Klingon was on his back, clutching his left arm. His face was a mask of pain, his *bat'telh* lying at the base of a stalagmite.

Riker turned to Alexander, who was looking at him with a new respect. The first officer smiled. "I guess you get the picture."

The boy nodded. "But how did you—?"

"Practice," Riker told him. "Want to give it a shot? I'll be your sparring partner."

"Okay," said Alexander.

Coming around behind him, the first officer placed the blindfold across the boy's eyes and tied it. Then he stepped in front of him with his *bat'telh*.

"Here we go. Keep your feet wide apart for balance. With all these stalagmites around, it's easy to trip. Now, listen as hard as you can, and tell me what I'm doing."

Taking care not to make too much noise, Riker moved to his right. At first, the boy seemed confused. Then he turned in the right direction.

"That's good," said the first officer. "You've got sharp ears."

This time, he moved to the left. Again, Alexander hesitated for a second. Then he seemed to find Riker's position.

The first officer didn't say anything right away. He wanted to see if the boy wavered in his conviction. But Alexander continued to stare in the same direction.

"Excellent," the first officer noted. "Keep trusting your senses and you'll be fine. Now, the toughest test of all."

Moving to his right again, he shifted his *bat'telh* from one hand to the other, making enough noise to give the boy a fighting chance. Then he raised the weapon high and brought it down slowly toward Alexander's shoulder.

The boy reacted in plenty of time, but held his *bat'telh* in position to stop a thrust, not a downward stroke. Only at the last second did he realize his mistake and bring his blade up over his head—just in time to ward off the attack.

Riker was impressed. Alexander was doing things it

took him years to learn. But then, the boy was part Klingon. He had a warrior's instincts imprinted in his genes.

Alexander grinned. "I did it!" he cried.

"You sure did," said the first officer. "You can take off your blindfold now."

Still grinning, the boy did as he was told. He got a kick out of seeing Riker just where he expected to see him.

But a moment later, his joy faded. Apparently, he had remembered whatever it was he had on his mind.

"Something wrong?" asked the first officer.

Alexander sighed. "You know there is. Otherwise, Counselor Troi wouldn't have sent you to talk to me."

Riker had to smile. "It was that obvious, was it?"

The boy nodded. Placing his back against a stalagmite, he slid down the side of it and came to a stop when he reached the ground.

The first officer sat, too. "So? Do you want to get it out in the open, or do I just mind my own business?"

Alexander pretended to inspect his *bat'telh*. "We can talk," he said.

"Is it about the scrolls?" Riker asked. "The ones that suggest Kahless isn't all he's cracked up to be?"

The boy looked up at him. "You know I was reading them?" Then he must have realized how easy it would have been for the first officer to determine that. "Of course you do. You're in charge of the ship. You've got access to everything."

"Well?" the first officer prodded. "Is that it? You're disillusioned by what you read?"

He fully expected Alexander to nod his head. Instead, the boy shook it slowly from side to side.

"Don't tell my father, but I don't care how many days

Kahless wrestled his brother, or how hard it must have been to plow his father's fields with his *bat'telh,* or how terrible a tyrant Molor was." He shrugged. "They're terrific stories, sure, and I love to listen to them—but they're just stories."

Alexander went back to inspecting his weapon. There was a discomfort in his features that Riker hated to see there.

"To me," the boy went on, "being a Klingon isn't about being like Kahless. I hardly know Kahless. It's about being like my father."

The first officer smiled. Funny thing about sons, he thought. No matter how different they may be from their fathers, they always want to idolize them.

But he still didn't understand why Alexander was upset. "I don't get it," he said. "If what you read in the scrolls didn't bother you—"

"It *did.*" Alexander's brow creased. "But not because *I* was disappointed. It bothered me because I know how my father feels about those stories. I don't want *him* to be disappointed."

Riker grunted. Obviously, the boy had zeroed in on the truth.

First, he had seen Worf receive a subspace packet. Then his father had taken off on a secret mission in the Empire. Coincidence, maybe. But coincidences were seldom what they seemed.

Alexander couldn't have discovered any of the details of the venture, of course—couldn't have guessed that the captain and Worf were investigating a conspiracy to overthrow Gowron and throw the quadrant into disarray.

But he seemed to understand the significance of the scroll. He had sensed that what was at stake was nothing less than the Klingon faith. And he knew how very much that faith meant to his father.

"You're a very clever young man," the first officer told his young companion.

The boy looked at him, his brow still heavy with concern. "Thanks." He got up. "I think I've had enough training for today."

Riker got up too. "Same here." He looked at the ceiling of the cavern. "Computer, end program."

A moment later, the cavern and everything in it—the wounded warrior, the blindfolds and the *bat'telhmey*—gave way to the stark reality of the black-and-yellow hologrid. As they headed for the door, it opened for them.

The first officer wanted to tell Alexander that everything would be all right. He wanted to assure him that Worf would come back with his faith intact. But he couldn't.

This wasn't a folktale. This was the real world. Here, nothing was certain. One had to take one's chances and hope for the best.

As they exited from the holodeck into the corridor outside, Riker put his hand on the boy's shoulder. Alexander looked up and managed a smile, as if he shared the first officer's thoughts.

"It's all right," he said. "I'll be okay. Really."

Riker stopped. As he watched, wishing he could have done more, the boy headed for his quarters.

CHAPTER 24

The Heroic Age

Kahless whirled on his *s'tarahk* and cut at his adversary with his sword. With a speed born of self-preservation, the soldier parried the blow with a resounding clang, then launched an attack of his own.

But Kahless's first cut had only laid the groundwork for his second. Ducking to avoid his enemy's response, he struck hard at the man's flank.

The soldier couldn't react in time. Kahless's sword bit deep between two ribs, eliciting a scream. Then, while the man was at a disadvantage, the rebel sat up again and delivered the deathstroke.

As the soldier fell from his mount, his throat laid open, Kahless turned and surveyed the barren hillside he had chosen. No one else was coming for him. Satisfied that he was safe for the moment, he surveyed the changing terrain of the battle.

It was his first full-scale clash with Molor's forces—a

clash designed to test the mettle and dedication of his ragtag army. So far, it seemed to him, the battle was more or less even. To their credit, the rebels were holding their own.

Still, they could be overrun if some pivotal event went against them. The same with the tyrant's army. That was the way of such conflicts—Kahless knew that from his service to Molor during the border wars.

He was determined that if the battle turned, it would do so in the rebels' favor. That meant he could not simply wait and hope—he had to make something happen on his own. And he knew just what that something might be.

Cut off a serpent's head. Had that not been the tyrant's own advice to him in the border wars?

Seeking out the warlord in charge of Molor's forces, he found the man directing a charge against the rebels' flank. Kahless smiled to himself. He couldn't see who the warlord was for the hair that obscured his face, but it didn't matter. He would bring the man down or die in the attempt.

Spurring his *s'tarahk* with his heels, he sliced his way through the ranks of the enemy. When he was close enough, he bellowed a challenge—one that could be heard even over the din of battle. As he'd hoped, the warlord turned to him.

And Kahless realized then whom he'd challenged. The man's name was Yatron. And like Starad, he was Molor's son.

The rebel clenched his teeth. He had already earned the tyrant's hatred many times over, hadn't he? What difference did it make if he gave Molor one more reason to despise him?

"Kahless!" bellowed Yatron, consumed with rage.

He seemed to recognize his brother's killer. And judging by the expression on his face, Yatron had no intention of adding to his father's miseries. Digging his heels into the flanks of his *s'tarahk,* he charged at Kahless, his sword whirling dangerously above his head.

Raising his own blade, Kahless charged too. They met in an empty space, each trying to skewer the other with the force of his attack. But somehow both of them escaped untouched, their only injuries the numbness in their sword arms.

Yatron whirled and hacked at the rebel's head, but Kahless was ready for him. Turning the weapon away, he stabbed at the warlord's chest. Fortunately for Yatron, he was quick enough to catch the stroke and deflect it.

For a long time, they exchanged brutal blows, neither of them giving an inch. Kahless was gouged and cut and battered, but none of his wounds were enough to slow him down.

It was the same for Molor's son. As many times as the rebel tried to slice him or run him through, Yatron always eluded the worst of it—and came back for more.

Kahless's sword became too heavy to swing. His throat grew raw with the dust he raised. And still he fought on.

Finally, he saw an opening—a hole in the web of steel Yatron wove about himself—and took advantage of it. Reaching back for whatever strength he had left, the rebel brought his blade around in a great and terrible arc.

When he was done, Yatron lay in the dirt, clutching at his entrails. Exhausted as he was, Kahless didn't let him lie there that way for long. As he'd shown mercy to one of Molor's sons, he now showed mercy to the other.

Done, he thought. The serpent's head is off.

The rebel paused for a moment, chest pounding, sweat

streaming down both sides of his neck. It was a moment too long.

Out of the corner of his eye, he saw something bearing down on him. Too late, he turned and brought his sword up. He had time to glimpse a flash of teeth and a pair of murderous eyes before he felt a sword bury itself in his side.

With a sucking sound, it came out again. Kahless bit back a cry of agony and clutched at the neck of his *s'tarahk*, trying desperately to steady himself. He could feel his strength ebbing, feel his side growing cold and wet with blood.

His attacker spun about and came back at him to finish the job. Somehow, despite his agony, Kahless found the strength to lash out backhanded.

He was lucky. The edge of his blade caught his enemy in the forehead, sending him twisting down to the ground.

The outlaw had no time to congratulate himself. He was losing his grip—not only on the reins, but on his senses. The battle churned and tossed about him like an angry sea, disorienting him until he didn't know up from down.

Kahless was weak from loss of blood, and it was getting worse. If he was to achieve victory today, he would have to hurry. Hanging on as best he could, he raised his sword with a trembling arm.

"Their warlord is dead!" he thundered, though the ground seemed to reach up at him. "Without him, they are no better than we are!"

His words seemed to have the desired effect. With cry upon cry, his warriors surged against Molor's forces like a ponderous surf, a force that would not be denied.

The outlaws shoved the tyrant's men back. And again, and further still. And moments later, Molor's army broke like a dam trying to hold back a flood.

Kahless yelled at his men, urging them on. But he himself didn't have the strength to dig his heels in and follow. His hands and feet had become cold as ice, his vision had grown black around the edges.

Finally, mercifully, the ground rushed up at him. He had no choice but to give in to the darkness.

CHAPTER **25**

The Modern Age

The installation that included Ter'jas Mor's defense armory was so big and stark and gray, Picard had trouble believing even a Klingon would have found it esthetically pleasing. But then, it was built more for security than esthetics.

And certainly, under normal circumstances, the place's state-of-the-art security systems would have kept intruders from getting in. But these were not normal circumstances—and Kurn, with his thorough knowledge of Defense Force design methods and codes, was hardly the average intruder.

Kahless grunted. "I never thought the day would come when Kahless the Unforgettable wore a mask like a lowly sneak thief." Reaching underneath his hood, he scratched some part of his face to relieve an itch.

"I sympathize," said the captain.

He, too, felt funny wearing a mask—and he doubted

that Worf and Kurn liked it any better. Among Klingons, as in many other cultures, masks were badges of dishonorable intent.

However, it was important that they not reveal themselves here in the heart of a Defense Force installation. Hence the additional precautions, which included concealing themselves in the shadows until their prey entered their trap.

Picard had barely completed his thought when he heard footfalls approaching from the far end of the alley. Exchanging looks with Worf, he pressed his back that much harder against the wall that concealed them.

As their objective came closer, the captain all but stopped breathing. It was important that this be as quick and silent as they could make it. If anyone else heard what was going on, all their hard work might go for nothing.

Luck was with them. The Klingon armory worker didn't have the slightest inkling they were about. Without a care in the world, he approached his door and tapped in the security code on the well-worn padd beside it.

It wasn't until the door began to slide aside that he heard even the slightest sound. And turned. And opened his mouth to cry out.

But by then, it was too late. Grasping the man by the back of his neck, Kahless pushed hard—sending him hurtling into his abode, where he sprawled on the hard, smooth floor.

Twisting about to see who had attacked him, the Klingon might have had ideas about getting up or sounding an alarm—but it was too late for that as well. Worf was already standing over him, the disruptor in his hand pointed directly at the center of the Klingon's forehead. And at this range, it was highly unlikely he would miss.

Of course, as far as Picard could tell, Worf had no intention of using the weapon, except as a bluff. But the object of their attentions didn't know that.

Picard touched a wall padd beside the door and the metal panel slid closed. That left the four of them alone with their newfound friend.

"What . . . what is it you want from me?" the Klingon grated.

He was a lean man with a head that somehow seemed too large for his body. Though his skin was dark, his eyes were large and blue, and his only real facial hair was a tuft of beard in the center of his chin.

Kahless knelt beside the armory worker and grabbed a fistful of his tunic. When he spoke, his voice dripped with deadly intent. What's more, the captain thought, the clone wasn't just pretending—he *meant* it.

"What do we want?" Kahless echoed. "We want to know what possessed you to steal a bomb from the place where you're employed."

The man shook his head vigorously. "Whoever you are, you're mistaken. I stole no bomb."

Kahless leaned closer, his eyes smoldering through the slits in his mask. "Do not lie to me, *p'tahk*. I hate liars more than anything. Now tell me—why did you take the bomb? Do you get some sort of perverse satisfaction from destroying innocent children?"

"I know nothing of this," their host complained. "You must be thinking of someone else."

Kahless tilted his head as he studied the worker. "Perhaps you are right. Perhaps we have the wrong man."

Abruptly, he struck the Klingon across the face with his

free hand. The captain winced beneath his mask and the worker flung his hands up to protect himself from a second blow.

But it was unnecessary. Kahless had made his point.

"Perhaps that is so, Adjur, son of Restagh. Perhaps we have made a mistake. But," the clone growled, "I do not think so. I think we have *precisely* the man we are looking for."

"We know you stole the bomb," said Worf, a voice of reason in comparison to Kahless. "Tell us who else was involved. Your accomplices, your contacts in the Defense Force, everything. Or you will not live long enough to regret the blood you've shed."

The Klingon looked from one masked and hooded face to the next, his blue eyes full of fear. By now, he must have known how slim his chances of survival were—unless he cooperated.

There was still the chance that he was telling the truth, of course, and was completely innocent of the charges against him—but Picard doubted it. He'd been a captain long enough to know when someone had the stench of treachery about him—and this one stunk to high Heaven.

"All right," Adjur relented. "I'll talk." His eyes narrowed. "But first, you must tell me what you meant about the children."

Was it possible he didn't know? Certainly, his question seemed sincere enough. Or was he simply building a case for his ignorance?

Kurn spat. "The bomb was used to destroy an academy. Some of the victims weren't tall enough to cut your throat."

That got a reaction from the Klingon—an expression of shame and disgust. "I did not know," he swore heatedly. "If I had, I would never have gotten involved with them."

"With who?" asked Kahless.

Adjur scowled. "The one who came to me was a Klingon named Muuda. He's a merchant of some sort."

"Tell me more," the clone advised him.

Adjur's scowl deepened. "Muuda said he represented a conspiracy to overthrow Gowron, and to replace him with someone else. But he never said who the other conspirators were or who they proposed as council leader."

"And you didn't care enough to ask?" Worf prodded.

The armory worker shrugged. "What difference would it have made to me? Besides, Muuda was willing to offer me latinum in exchange for my cooperation. One in my position does not often get such an offer."

"Who else accepted this offer?" asked Kahless.

Adjur went silent. "No one," he said.

Based on Godar's comments, they suspected otherwise. This was their chance to have the suspicion corroborated.

"A lie," snarled the clone, tightening his grasp on the Klingon's tunic. "Tell me the truth, son of Restagh, or I'll see to it you never walk the same way again."

Adjur swallowed. "His name is Najuk, son of Noj. We made the deal with Muuda together. Najuk got one bomb and I got another."

Picard nodded. Godar had been correct. Besides, he recalled seeing two separate explosions at the academy.

Kahless pulled the armory worker's face closer to his

own. "Listen carefully," he rasped. "I should turn you in for what you've done—but I won't, if you continue to help me. I want to know how to find this Muuda."

Adjur saw he had little choice in the matter. "That goes for all of you?" he asked. "You won't turn me in?"

"All of us," Worf confirmed.

That was good enough for Adjur. "He lives on Kerret'raa, just north of the city of Ra'jahn. He once described the place to me."

"Anything else we should know?" asked Kurn.

The armory worker thought for a moment. "Yes. You'll know Muuda at a glance because he has only one arm. He lost the other in a battle with the Romulans twenty years ago."

Kahless made a sound of disgust as he thrust Adjur away from him. "A real patriot, this Muuda. Good. Then we won't have to twist off his other arm to get some information out of him."

The armory worker must have thought his ordeal was over. But as the clone turned away from him, Kurn pinned Adjur hard against the wall. Behind his mask, the governor seemed to be smiling.

"If I were you," he said, "I would pack up and run. *Tonight.* Otherwise, you will be *kraw'za* food before you know it."

The Klingon looked confused. "But I told you what you wanted to know. You said you wouldn't turn me in."

"And we won't," Kurn assured him. "But that doesn't mean we won't tell the families of those who were killed."

Adjur paled. His eyes grew larger than ever. "You wouldn't," he moaned.

Worf's brother didn't answer. He just released the armory worker as if he were some diseased animal. Then he tapped the appropriate keys on his wrist controller.

The next thing the captain knew, they were back on Kurn's ship, and its master was setting the controls for Kerret'raa.

CHAPTER 26

The Heroic Age

Like a man who had discovered how to see for the first time, Kahless opened his eyes. He was standing in a courtyard.

The stones beneath his booted feet were small and gray, deftly cut and fitted together. The walls around him were gray as well, and taller than he had ever imagined walls could be. Even the barriers around Molor's fortress at Qa'yarin seemed small and frail-looking by comparison.

The doors to the keep here were made made of heavy wood, and bound between sheets of tough, black iron. As Kahless watched, they opened for him. A din of music and laughter poured out, making the courtyard ring. Curious, he ventured inside.

There was no one in the anteroom to ask him his name or his business there, no one to stop him. Glad of it, he hurried on into the feast hall.

It was huge and imposing, with beams and poles and rafters made of rich, red *teqal'ya* wood and a flock of exotic birds roosting in the recesses of its high vaulted ceiling. The place was ringed with benches, on which sat a veritable host of armed men. And in the center of the hall, two warriors in leather armor clashed and clattered and raised a terrible commotion with their swords, though neither seemed to sustain any wounds.

Kahless shook his head in wonder. Whose hall was this? How had he gotten here? And who were these warriors?

Suddenly, he noticed that someone was standing next to him. Expecting a threat, he whirled.

But it wasn't a threat. A cry stifled in Kahless's throat. Reaching out, he touched the side of Kellein's face with infinite gentleness.

"How . . . ?" he stumbled, drinking in the sight of her.

Kellein grasped his hand and placed it against her breast. He could feel her *jinaq* amulet.

"Do not ask how," she told him. "Nor when, nor where, nor why. Only trust that I am who I seem I am, and that we have a pitifully short time to be together."

He drew her closer. "Kellein . . . I wish I . . . if only . . ."

She shook her head. "You did not fail me, Kahless, son of Kanjis. I was meant to perish along with the rest of Vathraq's people. There is nothing you could have done about it."

He couldn't accept that. "But if I had turned down your father's invitation, if I had kept riding—"

"The same thing would have happened," Kellein insisted, "albeit it in a different way. We were meant to find this place."

Kahless looked around and realized where he was. He swallowed hard. Until now, it had only been a legend to him, a tale told to children around the fire. Now it was wonderfully, painfully real.

"Enough of me," his betrothed said. "I need to speak of you, Kahless. Soon, you will leave this place, because you do not belong here. And when you return to the world, there is something you must do."

He looked around at the warriors seated on the benches, and he began to see among them faces that he recognized—faces of men who fought beside him on the frontier. And also, the faces of those who had fought against him.

Finally, he turned to Kellein again. Her hair was black as a *kraw'za's* wing and her eyes were green as the sea. She looked every bit as strong and defiant as the day he saw her in the river.

"I don't want to go anywhere," he told her. "I want to stay."

Her eyes flashed. "No, Kahless. You *must* go back. You have come a long way toward tearing down the tyrant Molor, but there is yet much to do."

"Molor means nothing to me," he declared. "The rebellion means nothing, except for my promise to Morath. I would give it all up in a moment to have you with me again."

Even before Kellein spoke, he knew the truth of the matter. "It is not possible," she said. "At least, not now. You have a destiny to take hold of—and in their hearts, all who follow you know that. But to succeed in your quest, you will need a sword."

Kahless shrugged. "There are plenty of swords in the world."

MICHAEL JAN FRIEDMAN

She grasped his arm. "No. This one is different. It will be a friend to you in battle. It will make you unbeatable."

Kahless wanted to laugh, to tell her that a sword was no better than the warrior who wielded it. But he could see his Kellein was not in a joking mood.

"Listen carefully," she told him.

Kellein gave him directions on how to make the sword. First, he had to take a lock of his hair and dip it in the hot blood of the Kri'stak Volcano. Then he had to cool the thing in the waters of Lake Lusor. Finally, he had to twist it just so.

"Only then," she said, "will you have the kind of weapon you need to overthrow the tyrant." She squeezed his hand harder than ever. "Only then will you achieve a victory unequaled in the history of the world."

Kahless moved his fingers into the softness of her hair. He didn't want to be talking with her about swords and tyrants. He wanted to tell her how much he ached for her still, how he would never forget what she meant to him.

But before he could utter a word, Kellein faded like smoke on the wind. And before he knew it, he held nothing in his hands but empty air.

He would have bellowed then like a wounded *minn'hor*, making the rafters ring with his agony, except someone had leaped off one of the benches and was approaching him. Someone he knew all too well.

It was Starad, Molor's son. And he was whole again, unscathed.

The warrior had a sword in his hand, and it seemed he was looking for trouble. But something told Kahless that he could not be harmed here. After all, Kellein had said he had a destiny to seize elsewhere.

"Kahless?" Starad laughed, brash as ever. "Is it really you?"

The rebel held his ground. "You can see it is."

Molor's son stopped in front of him and sneered. "I know what you're up to, Kahless. But you're just a *yolok* worm beneath Molor's boot. Oh, maybe you'll win a battle or two, but in the long run you can't hope to accomplish anything." He leaned closer to the rebel, grinning with his long, sharp teeth. "Why not give yourself up and save everyone some trouble?"

Kahless could feel his own lips pulling back. "You were a fool when you were alive, Starad. I never thought to seek your counsel then, so why would I heed it now?"

Molor's son raised his sword before his face. Catching the light, the blade glinted murderously.

"Ignore me if you want," he rasped, "but you will not be able to ignore my father's power. When the deathblow falls and your wretched rebellion falls along with it, you will remember me." His eyes slitted with barely contained fury. "You will remember Starad."

Kahless cursed him. "You think I wanted this?" he hissed. "You think I wanted to be hunted like an animal? To see my mate lying dead on her father's ground? To be deprived of comfort everywhere I turn?"

Starad opened his mouth to reply—but nothing came out. And a moment later, he had faded to smoke, just like Kellein before him.

Kahless felt a hand on his arm. He turned and found himself face to face with Rannuf, Edronh's son. The boy was just as he had been in the forest that snowy day, ruddy-cheeked and full of life.

"Rannuf," he said, his anger abating. In its place, he

223

felt only heavy-hearted remorse. "I am sorry you had to die. Believe me, I wish it were otherwise."

Rannuf shook his head. "You misunderstand, Lord Kahless. I have not come to exact an apology from you, or to blame you for my death. I have come to warn you about impending treachery."

"What treachery?" the rebel asked.

"It is my father," Rannuf explained. "Edronh plans to sell you out to Molor's forces. He grows weary of losing his family and his possessions—weary of the bloodshed. The only way it will end, he believes, is when the tyrant has your head."

"No," said Kahless. He shook his head. "That is not possible. Edronh has never shown me anything but loyalty."

The youth smiled grimly. "Molor might have said that about *you* once, my lord. Men change."

Kahless frowned. He couldn't ignore Rannuf's advice—not under the circumstances. It was said the dead had knowledge that was denied the living.

"All right," he replied. "What does your father intend to—?"

He never finished his question. Like the others, Rannuf wavered and blew away on a puff of air.

Kahless turned to the center of the hall, where the two warriors were still raising a terrible noise. The multitude of spectators egged them on from their seats. Up above, strange birds flew from one rafter to the next.

Kellein had said he didn't belong here. It seemed to him that she was right—that he wasn't meant to leave the world of the living quite yet. But how was he supposed to get back?

What offering did he have to make, and to whom? There was no sign of the serpent said to guard this place and keep it inviolate, or of the ancient ones who had challenged it. . . .

Just as he thought that, the hall itself began to quake and come apart, as if under the influence of a powerful wind. Oblivious to it, the warriors on the benches continued to cheer for one fighter or the other, and the birds continued to fly. But Kahless could see the hall shiver and dissipate, and its occupants along with it.

Finally, he himself began to lose his shape, to twist in the wind and drift away. He cried out . . .

. . . and found himself sitting upright in a tent, the air cold on his skin. His heart was pumping like a bellows and his eyes stung with sweat that had pooled in the hollows of their sockets.

Kahless wasn't alone, either. Morath was sitting in a corner, alongside Porus and Shurin, and a heavyset man he didn't recognize at first. Then he remembered. The man's name was Badich. He had professed to be a healer when he joined them.

"Kahless is awake!" snapped Shurin.

Morath got to his feet and came closer. "He looks better, too. I think the fever has broken."

"What did I tell you?" asked Badich, getting to his feet as well, albeit with a good deal more difficulty. "It was the poultice I made him. There's nothing it can't cure."

"How long have I been here?" asked Kahless.

"Two days," said Porus. "Your wounds became infected. You were so feverish, we thought we had lost you. How do you feel?"

225

Kahless didn't answer him. He just grabbed his tunic and slipped it on. It wasn't easy, considering he hurt in a dozen places, all of which were dressed and bandaged.

"What are you doing?" asked Morath.

Kahless found his belt and cinched it around his waist. Then, with an effort, he pulled his boots on.

"Where's Edronh?" he wanted to know.

The others looked at one another. Judging by their expressions, his question was a surprise to them.

"Edronh?" echoed Shurin. "What difference does it make?"

"It makes a difference," Kahless insisted. "Where is he?"

Porus shrugged. "With his men, I suppose."

Kahless grunted. "Let us see if that is so."

Doing his best to forget how much he still ached, he emerged from the tent. It was dusk. The fires of his followers stretched for a distance all around him.

"Edronh and his men are *that* way," said Morath. He pointed in the direction where the sky was lightest and the stars already dwindling. "They're guarding our front against the enemy."

"Show me," Kahless ordered.

Morath led him and the others to the place where Edronh was supposed to be encamped. Neither the north-lander nor his warriors were anywhere to be seen, nor had their fires been tended lately.

"Maybe we were wrong," said Porus. "Maybe they bedded down somewhere else."

Kahless sniffed the wind. Nothing yet. But soon, there would be plenty.

"You were not wrong," he told Porus. "They were

supposed to be here and they are not. They are off betraying us instead."

Morath looked at him, his brow wrinkled with concern. "How do you know that?" he demanded.

"I heard it in a dream," Kahless replied. "Now listen closely. We have to move before Molor takes Edronh's treachery and skewers us on it." He turned to Porus. "Stay here with a hundred warriors. Pretend to sleep, but keep your blades at hand."

"And what of the rest of us?" asked Shurin.

Kahless clapped him on the shoulder. "The rest of us will slip away quietly and take up positions along the enemy's flank."

"But the enemy is not in the field," Badich protested. "He *has* no flank."

"Not yet," Kahless agreed. "But he will soon enough."

CHAPTER 27

The Modern Age

As Picard and his comrades materialized on the perimeter of Muuda's estate, the first thing that struck the captain was the heavy-handed showiness of the place. It was not a tribute to elegance by any standard, Klingon or otherwise.

All around the low-lying *m'ressa*-wood structure, there were ornate fountains of polished marble and overgrown *tran'nuc* trees and elaborate stone paths leading through seas of ruby-red fireblossoms.

And statues. Lots of statues.

Ironically, the largest of them depicted Kahless's epic struggle with the tyrant Molor. In this particular piece, they were locked in hand-to-hand combat, their *bat'telhs* broken and lying in pieces at their feet. Both were bleeding from a dozen wounds, eyes locked, muscles straining in a life-or-death battle that would decide the fate of a civilization.

The clone had apparently noticed the statue as well. "Nice likeness," he grunted matter-of-factly from beneath his cowl. But he said nothing more on the subject.

Of course, if the scroll were to be believed, Kahless's encounter with Molor had been of a different nature. But if the clone wasn't inclined to comment, Picard wouldn't either.

There was no evidence of a security system on the grounds or around the house. Apparently, Muuda had spent all his *darsekmey* on his esthetic, unable to imagine that his deeds would come back to haunt him.

But haunt him they would, and with a vengeance. Picard and his allies would see to that.

Proceeding along one of the wildly meandering stone paths, the four of them made their way to a window in the back. Worf peered inside, then turned to face the others.

"There are warriors inside. Females as well," he said, his mask muffling his voice. "But they all appear to be asleep, some with bottles of Warnog in their hands."

Kurn grunted. "Drunk. Muuda must have thrown a party with his latest infusion of blood money."

Kahless nodded. "The same sort of blood money he used to buy this estate and furnish it with heroic images. I say we burn it down and him with it—give him a taste of what he did to those children."

"*After* we've dragged some information out of him," Kurn noted.

"Yes," said the clone. "Afterward, of course."

The captain looked at them with some alarm. But Worf made a gesture of dismissal, indicating it was only talk. The Klingons wouldn't incinerate these people any sooner than Picard would.

It wouldn't be honorable. And to some Klingons, honor was still an issue.

"Come on," said the lieutenant.

He moved to the next window and looked through it. This time, the captain saw Worf's lip curl in disgust. When he turned to them again, he didn't report out loud as before. He just tilted his head to indicate Muuda was inside.

Kahless didn't hesitate. Taking out his *d'k tahg,* he turned it pommel-first and smashed the window glass. Then he vaulted through the aperture, oblivious to the shards that still stuck to the frame.

In rapid-fire succession, the others followed. As Picard leaped through the ruined window, he saw a one-armed Klingon lying in a bath of faceted obsidian, surrounded by three levels of steps. Despite the noisiness of their entrance, Muuda was still unconscious.

But then, Warnog had that effect. Warriors had been known to sleep for days after a particularly generous dose of the beverage.

Not so the two females who had shared Muuda's bath. Eyes wide, they slithered out of the water and ran for the door, naked as the day they were born. But Kurn blocked their way, his drawn dagger enough of a threat to stop them in their tracks.

They hissed at him. "Let us go," one of them insisted, showing her teeth. "We have done nothing wrong."

"Get back," the governor instructed, obviously not in a mood to argue the point.

Worf grabbed a couple of robes hanging on a wall rack and threw them at the females. "Clothe yourselves," he told them. "Then find a corner and be still. Cooperate and we'll leave you unharmed."

Ultimately, the females had little choice. Catching the robes in midair, they put them on and relegated themselves to a corner of the room. But even then, they were far from docile-looking.

Having dealt with Lursa and B'Etor of the House of Duras, the captain knew how big a mistake it would be to underestimate the "gentler" Klingon sex. He resolved to keep an eye on the females until they were done with their business here.

Advancing to the bath, Kahless walked up the steps and reached for Muuda's hair, which lay spread about his shoulders. Grabbing a lock in his fist, the clone tugged without mercy.

Crying out, Muuda brought a bottle out of the water with his good hand. Out of instinct, he tried to strike Kahless with it. But the clone batted it away. A moment later, it shattered on the floor, leaving an amber-colored pool on the stone.

"Muuudaa," growled Kahless, drawing the name out, making it plain it left a bad taste in his mouth.

The Klingon in the bath looked up at him through bloodshot eyes, still half in an alcoholic stupor. But he wasn't so drunk he didn't know what kind of danger he was in.

"Who . . . who are you?" he stammered.

The clone took out his dagger and laid its point against Muuda's cheek. "I will ask the questions here," he said.

Realizing this was no dream, the Klingon swallowed. "Yes," he agreed. "You will ask the questions."

"You bought two bombs from a pair of armory workers on Ter'jas Mor," Kahless told him. "Bombs intended for use in an academy on Ogat. But you didn't see them planted yourself. You were merely a go-between—a middleman. Who was it you bought the bombs for?"

Muuda swallowed again, even harder than before. Obviously, he was thinking of what would happen to him if his employers discovered he had identified them. But he also had to be thinking about the more immediate danger—the masked intruders in his bath chamber.

Noting Muuda's indecision, the clone flicked the point of his dagger, breaking the skin of the Klingon's cheek. He winced as a droplet of lavender blood emerged.

"I asked you a question," Kahless hissed. "I expect an answer."

Muuda glared at him. "All right," he said, slurring his words. "I'll tell you. Just let me up. It is cold in here."

The clone shook his head. "Not a chance, *p'tahk*. You will have plenty of time to warm yourself when we are done here. Now who was it?"

Seeing his ploy wouldn't work, the Klingon acquiesced. He told them not only who was involved in the plot, but the role each of the conspirators had assumed in it.

It was just as Kahless had been telling them all along. These people were some of the most highly placed officers in the Klingon Defense Force. And there was one name that was not associated with the Defense Force, but was nonetheless more important than all the others.

"All well and good," said Worf. "But what proof do we have that this *ko'tal* is telling the truth?"

The merchant licked his lips. "There is a way to prove it," he replied. And he informed them of it.

When Muuda was done, the clone took his knife back and sheathed it. "That is more like it," he said. "Now we leave you to your newfound wealth and your companions. But trust me, coward, when I say you will not have long to enjoy them. The innocents you killed will not soon be forgotten."

Picard saw the look in Muuda's eyes. The Klingon believed it. No doubt, it would take the pleasure out of his revels, knowing how short-lived they would be. At least, the captain wanted to think so.

With a jerk of his shaggy head, the clone advised them it was time to withdraw. The warriors in the house might come out of their drunken sleep at any moment, and it would be tempting fate to stay and lock horns with them.

Instead, Kahless slipped out of the window, and the others followed. Before Muuda and his females could sound the alarm, Picard saw the glimmer in the air that signified their transport.

CHAPTER 28

The Heroic Age

Kahless and his men had barely settled in when Molor's army began to move, charging headlong without the least bit of caution. After all, the enemy's warchiefs expected the rebels to be helpless and exposed. Thanks to the warning Kahless had received, they were neither.

He waited only until Molor's soldiers had moved past them and were on the verge of the rebel camp. Then, with guile and fury and righteous indignation, he attacked. The tyrant's men never knew what hit them.

The outlaws cut through them like a scythe, harvesting death, irrigating the ground with the blood of their adversaries. Kahless searched for Edronh across the battlefield, but never found him. It wasn't until later that he realized why. Apparently, Morath had found him first and showed him the error of his ways.

In the end, Kahless routed Molor's men, sending away half the number that had come after him. It was his second great victory in three days. More importantly, it showed his followers they could go nose-to-nose with the best-trained army in the world.

When the combat was over, and Kahless was surveying the field with Morath at his side, he remembered another bit of advice he had gotten in his dream. Unfortunately, he could not take it literally.

A lock of hair was not a good think to make a weapon of, no matter how cleverly it was twisted. Nor was the crater of an active volcano any place for a man who still clung to sanity.

Still, Kellein's directions made a kind of sense if one looked at them the right way. A sword like that would be more than a means of killing one's adversaries. It could become a symbol.

Of self-reliance. Of freedom. And ultimately, of victory.

"I need a metalsmith," Kahless said out loud.

Morath looked at him. "Right now?" he said.

"Right now," the rebel confirmed. "And so he will have something to work with, I will need twenty swords plucked from the hands of the enemy's corpses. And of course, whatever he needs to make a smithy."

His friend grunted. "Did you hear about this in your dream as well?"

Kahless nodded. "As a matter of fact, I did."

As it happened, there were several metalsmiths among the rebel forces. The best one was Toragh, a man with short, gnarly legs, a torso like a tree trunk, and biceps each the size of a grown man's head.

"You want what?" asked Toragh, after Morath and Porus had brought him to Kahless's tent.

A second time, the rebel chieftain showed the metalsmith what he wanted, carving the same shape into the soft dirt. "Like so," he said. "With a grip here in the center, and an arc here, and cutting edges all around."

The metalsmith looked at him as if he were crazy. "I have been at this for twenty years, and I have never heard of anything like this. How did you come up with it?"

"Do not ask," Morath advised him.

"Where I got the idea is not important," Kahless added. "What is important, metalsmith, is whether or not you can make it for me."

Toragh stroked his chin as he considered the design in the dirt. Finally, he nodded. "I can make it, all right. But it will not be easy. A weapon like this one will require a steady hand at the bellows, or the balance will be off—and balance is everything."

"I will work the bellows myself if I have to," Kahless replied. "Rest assured, you will have everything you need."

Toragh eyed him. "And you're certain this will help us to tear down the tyrant?" He seemed skeptical.

Kahless laughed. "As certain as the bile in Molor's belly."

CHAPTER **29**

The Modern Age

Propelled by only a fraction of its impulse power, Kurn's craft drifted ever closer to the subspace relay station that hung in space dead ahead. Picard had seen plenty of such stations before, but never one operated by the Klingon Defense Force.

The difference was pronounced, to say the least. Though the station's sole function was to transmit data from one place to another, its architecture was so severe as to look almost ominous. The captain wouldn't have been surprised if it turned out to be better armed than some starships.

It wasn't long before they got a response from the station. A lean, long-faced Klingon with a thin mustache appeared on the monitor screen set into Kurn's console. His garb suggested that he was in command of the facility.

"Who are you and what do you want?" the Klingon

grated. His eyes, one dark brown and the other a sea green, demanded an answer.

In any other culture, Picard knew, this would have been a sign of disrespect, perhaps even a challenge. However, Klingons did not waste time with amenities. They simply said what was on their minds.

Still, Kurn put on a show of anger. As he had explained minutes earlier, the best way to deal with a bureaucrat was to seem even more annoyed than he was.

"I am Kurn, son of Mogh," he grated. "Governor of Ogat and member of the High Council."

The station commander's eyes narrowed. "I have heard of Kurn. But for all I know, you could be a slug on the bottom of Kurn's boot."

Worf's brother made a sound deep in his throat. "Then look for yourself. Bring up my file image and compare it to what you see."

The station commander wasn't about to take anyone at his word. Barking an order to an offscreen lackey, he glared at Kurn—as if trying to decide what to do with him if he *wasn't* the council member.

A few moments later, the same lackey whispered in the station commander's ear. A look of confusion passed over the Klingon's face, like the shadow of a cloud on a sunny day.

"You do indeed appear to be Kurn," he said finally. "But according to our information, Kurn is supposed to be dead."

Fortunately, Worf's brother was prepared for this. Tossing his shaggy head back, he laughed out loud. "Dead?" he roared. Abruptly, he leaned forward, so that his face was only a couple of inches from the monitor. "Tell me, son of a *targ*—do I *look* dead to *you?*"

The station commander swallowed. "No," he conceded, "you do not."

"Then lower your shields," said Kurn, pressing his advantage, "and prepare for our arrival."

The Klingon on the relay station hesitated—but only for a moment. Then, looking as if he'd just eaten something distasteful, he turned and barked an order over his shoulder.

"Our shields have been lowered," he reported. "You may beam aboard the station whenever you please."

That was Picard's cue. Still wearing the cloak he had used on Ter'jas Mor, he picked up the hood and brought it down over his face. After all, it would arouse instant suspicion if a human were to beam aboard alongside Kurn.

Since Kahless and Worf might also have been recognized, they donned their hoods as well. Only Kurn went bareheaded.

Picard and his lieutenant set their disruptors on stun. However, their companions, Klingons through and through, did nothing of the sort.

Worf's brother then reached for the remote transporter controls set into his armband. He tapped out the proper sequence and glanced at the captain—as if to make certain he was ready for what would follow.

Picard was ready, all right. The next thing he knew, he was standing on what appeared to be the relay station's main deck, almost face-to-face with the Klingon he'd seen on the monitor.

Kurn interposed himself between them, so the station commander wouldn't be tempted to try to peer inside the hood. Of course, that didn't stop the other Klingons present.

Each of them looked up from his duties and wondered at the newcomers. The captain noted that the Klingons were all armed—not that that was a surprise. And he was certain *their* disruptors weren't set on stun.

"I want to download secured transmission records," Worf's brother announced. "My ship's computer is ready and waiting. All I need is your help to get past the security codes."

The station commander glanced at Picard, Worf, and finally Kahless. Then he turned back to Kurn.

"You travel in mysterious company," the Klingon observed.

"My choice of companions is not your concern," Kurn snapped. And then, to throw out a bone: "A man in my position finds the best bodyguards he can, Klingon or otherwise. Now, the help I asked for?"

The station commander frowned. Obviously, this wasn't going to be as easy as they had hoped.

"You have not yet stated your reasons for coming here," he maintained. "It's one thing to allow you entry, considering your position with the Defense Force. But to circumvent the security codes, I would require clearance from the homeworld. I have not received any such clearance."

Kurn grunted. "And if I told you I was here on Council business? And that the Council does not wish its dealings to be known beyond these bulkheads?"

The station commander thrust out his beardless chin. "In that case, I would *still* require some form of—"

Kurn didn't allow him to finish his statement. Instead, he backhanded the Klingon across the mouth with a closed fist, sending him staggering into a bulkhead. When the station commander looked at him again, there was hate in his eyes and lavender blood running down his chin.

But by then, Worf's brother was aiming his disruptor pistol at the Klingon's forehead—just as his companions were pointing theirs at the various other personnel on the station.

Kurn took a step closer to the station commander, keeping his weapon level. The look in his eyes said he wouldn't think twice about using it. In fact, he might relish the experience.

"Thank your ancestors I am a merciful man," Kurn bellowed. "But I will not ask you again." He tilted his head to indicate the communications console at one end of the room. "Do it—or you will wish you had."

Suddenly, Picard heard a shout from somewhere behind him. He whirled just in time to see yet another Klingon emerge from behind a sliding door—a Klingon with a weapon in his hand. He must have been working in a storage area when Kurn's group arrived.

And now, he had returned to the main deck—only to see his comrades held at disruptor-point. Under the circumstances, the man's reaction was understandable. The captain sympathized.

But that didn't mean he was going to stand there and present an easy target for the Klingon's disruptor fire. Ducking to his right, he watched the disruption beam pass him and strike a bulkhead, where it disintegrated a good part of the thing before its destructive energies wore themselves out.

That could have been me, Picard told himself. At the same time, he returned his adversary's blast—crumpling the Klingon where he stood.

It might have ended then and there. However, their

comrade's entrance gave the stationkeepers the chance they'd been looking for. Or so it seemed to the captain, as the place turned into a chaotic mess of hurtling bodies and flailing limbs, not to mention the occasional errant disruptor beam.

"Watch out!" cried a familiar deep voice.

Before Picard could determine what he had to watch for, he saw Worf rush past him—in order to meet another Klingon head on. The human winced at the bone-jarring sound of their clash, and was only slightly relieved when he saw his officer had come out on top.

A disruptor beam sizzled by his ear. Turning, Picard aimed at the source of it and let fly with a beam of his own.

It hit a stationkeeper's hand and knocked the pistol out of it. And before he could recover, Kahless slammed his fist into the Klingon's jaw, sending him sprawling.

But before the captain could seek out another target, he felt something strike him in the back of the head. There was a moment or two that seemed very long, much too long, and then the floor rose up to meet him with a sickening impact.

Tasting blood, Picard turned his head to see what was going on. Something descended on him—something big and dark and powerful-looking. He was about to lash out at it with the heel of his foot when he realized it was Worf.

"Captain," said his tactical officer, evincing obvious relief. "When I saw you go down, I was afraid they had—"

Picard waved away the suggestion. "The point is, they didn't," he said. With Worf's help, he got to his feet and surveyed the place.

About half the stationkeepers were unconscious. The

rest of them were gone without a trace. Fortunately, the station commander was among those who still remained.

With Kahless's help, Kurn dragged the Klingon over to the main console and placed the commander's hand on the appropriate padd—the customary Defense Force security bypass. Abruptly, the console lit up with a pattern of green and orange lights.

"*Qapla*'," said Kahless, smiling.

"*Qapla*' indeed," agreed Kurn, as he set out to download the transmission records. It only took a minute or so, once they had access to the system. Had it been a Federation system, it wouldn't even have taken that long.

"Your computer has the information?" the clone asked.

Worf's brother nodded. "The transmission is complete."

"Good," said Kahless.

Lifting his disruptor pistol, he trained it on the console and fired. The thing was consumed in a matter of seconds.

"Now," he declared, "these burden beasts will be unable to call for help when they come to."

In fact, the "burden beasts" in question were already stirring. Picard looked at Kurn, who nodded once and worked the controls on his armband.

The captain drew his next breath on Kurn's ship. Kahless snorted, a sound of triumph. Worf eased himself into the pilot's seat and brought the ship about as his brother went to the sensor panel.

Picard joined Kurn. "No sign of any transmission, I trust?"

Without looking up, Kurn shook his head. "None. And to my knowledge, there are no backup systems. Klingons are not enamored of redundancies."

Except when it comes to parts of your anatomy, the captain thought, remembering how Worf's biological redundancies had enabled him to walk again after his back had been broken. But as with so much else, he didn't say it out loud.

"Wait," said Kurn. "There *is* a transmission."

Kahless came over to see it with his own eyes. "I do not understand," he said. "I destroyed the communications panel. You all saw it."

"It is not coming *from* the station," Worf's brother explained. "It is being sent there from somewhere *else.*"

The emperor snorted. "That's more like it. What does it say?"

Kurn brought it up on his monitor. Of course, Picard couldn't read Klingon very well. He had to wait for the others to provide a translation.

But after only a few moments, he could tell that the news was not good. Suddenly, Kahless blurted a curse and turned from the console.

The captain looked to Kurn. "What is it?" he asked.

"It is about the scroll," Worf's brother told him. He glanced at the emperor. "It was tested for authenticity— and it passed. Apparently, even the clerics of Boreth are now satisfied the thing is authentic."

CHAPTER 30

The Heroic Age

In the center of Tolar'tu, Kahless held Shurin's battered body in his arms and roared at the gathering storm. Rain fell in heavy, warm drops, mixing with Shurin's blood and marking the dirt at the rebel's feet.

"This was my friend," Kahless cried. "Shurin, who never knew his father or mother, who lost an eye fighting Molor's wars. Yet he saw more clearly than most men, for he was among the first to turn against the tyrant."

With a sudden heave of his powerful arms, the outlaw raised Shurin's loose-limbed corpse to the heavens. More importantly, he made it visible to the vast mob gathered before him—an assemblage of rebels that packed the square from wall to wall and squeezed into the narrow streets all around.

Nor was he the only one with a dead man in his hands. There were hundreds of others clasped by friends and kin, grim evidence of the efficiency of Molor's soldiers and the sharpness of their swords.

But for every rebel that fell, two of the tyrant's men had gone down as well. For every one of Kahless's outlaws, two of Molor's soldiers. And in the end, that had been enough to save Tolar'tu from destruction.

Not all of it, unfortunately. Not the outer precincts, where the enemy had smashed and burned and gutted at their warlord's command. But thanks to the courage of these rabble and riffraff, this square and the buildings around it had gone unscathed.

"What will I tell this man of courage," Kahless raged, "when I see him on the far side of Death? What will I say took place after he left us? What tale will I bear him?"

There were responses from the crowd, guttural demands of vengeance and promises of devotion. He couldn't make out the exact words for the echoes. But he could see the expressions on the rebels' faces, and by those alone he knew he was reaching them.

Strange, the outlaw thought. He had always been able to reach them this way, hadn't he? He had just never paused to reflect on it. Kahless raised Shurin's body a little higher.

"Will I tell him his comrades came as far as Tolar'tu, then faltered? That at the last, they spit the bit and allowed his death to come to nothing? Or will I tell him we persevered, and went on to Qa'yarin, and trampled the serpent there under our heel?"

This time the answer was so deafening, so powerful, Kahless thought the buildings around him might crumble after all. It was like being in the center of a storm, the likes of which the world had not known since its beginnings—a tempest made of men's voices and clashing swords and a yearning so fierce no enemy could stand against it.

Truth to tell, Shurin had broken his neck falling off his *s'tarahk* in the midst of the battle. Kahless himself had seen the beast stumble and throw the man to the ground, and he had seen Shurin lie still as other beasts came and trampled him.

It might not have been that way if the man hadn't had too much bloodwine the night before. Or if he had slept more instead of rolling gaming bones halfway to morning.

But that was not the picture the outlaw wished to paint—and since he had been the only witness to Shurin's death, he could paint it as he liked. The one-eyed man would be an asset in death as he was in life. A hero if necessary, a martyr if possible. Shurin himself would have laughed at the notion, but he was no longer alive to have a say in the matter.

Lowering Shurin's corpse, he laid it on the ground. Then he stood again and waited for just the right moment.

"Wait!" Kahless shouted suddenly, as the cheers began to die down. "Stop! What in the name of our ancestors are we doing?"

The throng grew quiet, peering at him through faces caked with dirt and blood. *What sort of question is that?* they must have wondered.

"Are we insane?" the outlaw asked. "Just because we have triumphed in a few small skirmishes, does that make us think we can win a war? Molor is no petty despot, cowering in his keep. He is the master of all he sees, power incarnate, the hand that clutches the throat of the world entire!"

There were protests, some of them heartwarmingly

savage. But Kahless had more to say. As it happened, a lot more.

"And who are we to dare this?" he bellowed. "Not soldiers, not warriors, only old men and children who have become skilled at pretending. We have learned to fool ourselves. We have learned to believe we can tear down the mightiest tree in the forest, when all we have in our hands are our fathers' rusted *d'k tahgmey!*"

"No!" cried a thousand voices.

"Lies!" thundered a thousand more.

"We are warriors!" they rumbled. "Warriors!"

"For that matter," Kahless roared, "why should we fight at all? For honor? For dignity? We have none of these things—and we deserve none! We are outlaws and worse, less than the dirt beneath the tyrant's feet!"

"More lies!" came the thundrous reply.

"We are Klingons!" they stormed.

"Molor will fall!"

"For honor!"

"For freedom!"

And on and on, one shout building on another, until they were all one cry of rage and purpose, one savage chorus with but a single idea burning in their minds—to tear down the one who had brought them so much misery. To pry Molor loose from his empire and grind his bones to dust.

And as if in support, the skies answered them, crashing and lightning and pelting them with rain. But the rebels didn't budge. They stood there, their hearts raised as high as their voices, and let the water from the heavens run over them and cleanse them.

Kahless smiled, but only to himself. They had needed their spirits bolstered after such a hard fought and bloody battle. And with the power he had discovered in himself, he had done what was necessary.

Molor might beat them yet. He might show them the depth of their foolishness at Qa'yarin. But it would not happen because the rebels' courage had not been fanned to a fever pitch. If they failed, it would not be because Kahless had not done his part.

And who knew? Perhaps in ages to come, warriors would sing of the battle at Tolar'tu, and the speech a rebel had made there. Not that it mattered to Kahless if he was remembered or not.

He glanced at Morath, who was in the first rank of onlookers. The younger man remained calm and inscrutable as ever, as the rain matted his hair and streamed down his face.

Morath was truly the backbone of this rebellion. Kahless might have been its voice, its heart, but it was his friend who made it stand straight and tall and proud.

Well done, Morath told him, if only with his eyes. *You have put the fire in them. You have spurred them as no one else could.*

Had he been aware of the way Kahless had ennobled Shurin's clumsiness, he would not doubt have disapproved. But he did not know, and the outlaw had no intention of telling him.

In his own way, he had kept his vow, made in the depths of weariness and madness in the hills north of Vathraq's village. And he would continue to abide by it a little longer, until either he died or Molor did.

Then, either way, his work would be done. If the outlaw succeeded, Morath could have Molor's empire, to do with as he wished. And if Kahless fell short, Morath could make of that what he wanted as well.

Feeling a hand on his shoulder, he turned. It was Porus, who had suffered a cut to his brow during the battle. Rain was already dripping from his chin and the end of his nose.

"Enough," he said. "The troops are gnashing their teeth in anticipation of Qa'yarin. Right now, we have to dispose of poor Shurin."

Kahless nodded. "You're right. I will see to it."

Porus waved away the suggestion. "I can do it. You have done the work of a thousand men this evening."

The outlaw shrugged. "If you say so."

Still standing there in the center of the square, he watched as Porus began organizing the construction of a funeral pyre. Of course, they would need a great many of them. Tolar'tu had never seen so much blood.

Nor had An'quat before it. Or Serra'nob. Or any of the other places where they had clashed with Molor's forces.

As Morath joined him, Kahless grunted. "Once the rain stops, there will be a fire that will be seen for a hundred miles around."

"And bodies enough to keep it going for a day and a night," Morath added. "But that is the price of victory. Of freedom. Of honor. Nor will it compare to the flames that will rage outside the tyrant's citadel."

The outlaw nodded. "One way or the other."

CHAPTER 31

The Modern Age

On the bridge of Kurn's vessel, Kahless found a seat and lowered himself into it. He looked drained. Lifeless. Crushed by the reality he had hoped so fervently to deny.

Picard sighed and went to the emperor's side. What could he say? "Are you all right?" he asked at last.

Kahless was on his feet suddenly, his anger twisting his features as he thrust them like a weapon into the captain's face. "What do *you* think?" he roared.

Picard said nothing, but stood his ground. After a moment, the clone lumbered past him and stared out an observation port.

"Am I all right?" Kahless repeated, every word as sharp as a dagger. He shook his head. "I am far from all right. The conspirators were correct all along, Captain. Kahless was a fraud—and therefore, so am I."

His fists clenched at his sides and trembled in white-

251

knuckled rage. Then the emperor's right hand reached up, tore at something near his neck and cast it on the deck beside him.

It was the *jinaq* amulet—the one the historical Kahless had received from his lover as a sign of their betrothal. Picard looked at Worf's brother and saw the expression of worry on his face.

If the clone was modeled after someone who never existed, Kurn seemed to say, what chance did they have? Was Gowron's reign not doomed, no matter what they did to preserve it?

And if all they had believed in until now was a fraud, a mockery, should they even try?

It was Worf who finally provided the answer. Getting up from his pilot's seat, he approached Kahless. For a moment, he simply regarded the emperor, as if weighing what to do next. Then he knelt, retrieved the amulet, and stood up again.

"I believe this is yours," he said, holding the thing out in the palm of his hand.

Kahless turned to him and growled: "Leave me be, Worf."

"I will not leave you be," the lieutenant told him, "until you return this to the place of honor where it belongs."

Apparently, that was not what the emperor wished to hear. With a bellow of rage and pain, Kahless lashed out and struck Worf across the face with the back of his hand. As the cabin echoed with the sharp, explosive sound of the blow, Worf took a couple of steps back.

But he didn't fall, as the clone might have expected. Instead, he came forward like a wild *targ*, grabbed

Kahless by the front of his robe, and pinned him against the nearest bulkhead.

"Are you out of your mind?" the emperor bellowed, his eyes bulging with outrage. "I have *killed* men for far less!"

"Then kill *me*," Worf advised him, showing no fear. "But not before I have had my say."

Opening his hand, he showed Kahless the amulet. The emperor bared his teeth at the sight of it, then turned his face away.

"Get it away from me!" he cried.

He tried to wriggle free from Worf's grasp. But the lieutenant, quite a powerful individual in his own right, would not let him go.

"Not so long ago," Worf snarled, "you told me the *original* Kahless left us a powerful legacy. A way of thinking and acting that makes us all Klingon. If his words hold wisdom—if the philosophy they put forth is an honorable one—does it really matter what Kahless himself was like?"

The lieutenant thrust the amulet at the clone, who snatched it away from him. Then Worf released him and took a step back. But Kahless didn't strike the lieutenant again, nor did he turn his back. He went on listening to what Worf had to say.

"What is important," the lieutenant went on, in an even yet forceful tone, "is that we follow his teachings. For, at least in this case, the words are more important than the man."

The clone stood there for a moment, the *jinaq* amulet in his hand, the muscles in his jaws working furiously. It looked to Picard as if he were chewing something tough, something difficult to swallow—and perhaps he was.

Worf had thrown his own words back in his face—the same words Kahless had uttered on the *Enterprise*. Like it or not, the clone couldn't dismiss them out of hand. He had to consider them.

"What about the people?" Kahless asked at last. "They will shun me. They will call me a fraud—and a liar."

"Perhaps a few of them," said Worf. "But not all. Not the headmaster of the academy we visited, or blind Majjas. They and all the other Klingons who want a Kahless—who *need* a Kahless—will make the leap of faith, just as they did when they found out you were a clone."

"I wish I could believe you," Kahless told him.

"You must," Worf replied. "Our people care less about the scroll's authenticity than they do about what Kahless taught them. Only give them time and you will see I am right."

For what seemed like a long while, the clone was silent, the *jinaq* amulet resting in his large, open hand. Picard wondered if Worf's little pep talk had worked . . . or if Kahless was as resigned to failure as before. A moment later, he received his answer.

Closing his fingers around the amulet, the emperor held it against his chest. The glint of purpose returned to his eyes. Raising his chin, he looked at his companions.

"Very well," he agreed. "We started this together. We will see it through together. And in the end," he went on, a smile playing at the corners of his mouth, "let our enemies beware."

CHAPTER 32

The Heroic Age

Molor's citadel bulked up huge, dark, and foreboding against the gray, brooding sky. Its battlements bristled with a thousand archers, and there were a thousand more within its gates.

Still, the road that led to this pass had been no less formidable and Kahless had traveled it without faltering. With luck, he and his men would not falter now either.

"The tyrant is within our grasp," said Morath. His *s'tarahk* pawed and snuffled the ground.

The outlaw turned to him and snorted. "Or we are within his. It all depends on your perspective."

Kahless was whole again, recovered from the wounds he had suffered at Tolar'tu. In fact, he had never felt stronger in his life. Constant strife had a way of hardening a man.

Looking back over his shoulder, the outlaw surveyed the ranks of his followers, who were nearly as numerous as Molor's soldiers and twice as eager. A mighty siege engine constructed of sturdy black *skannu* trees rose up in the midst of them—a fifty-foot tall monster with a battering ram slung from its crossbar and a platform big enough for a hundred archers.

Such devices had been used in the past, when a great many lords vied for supremacy on the continent. But never had one so large and sturdy been built. Then again, no one had ever tried to take a fortress like this one.

It had been difficult to haul the towering *skannu* trees out of the steep valleys south of here, but they had had no other option. If they were to break the tyrant's power, they would need the proper tools.

At least, that had been Morath's contention. And Kahless had come to see the wisdom in it—just as he now saw the wisdom in most everything his friend said or did.

The outlaw had accomplished everything Morath had required of him. He had forged a rebellion out of countless tiny uprisings and dissatisfactions, and with it had shaken the foundations of Molor's supremacy. But without the younger man's part in it, the rebellion would never have lasted this long or come this far.

Kahless was just the point of a dagger, the razor edge. Morath was the one who cut and thrust with it.

Porus rode up to them, his face dirty with the dust of the road. Squinting, he scanned Molor's defenses.

"Too bad we all could not have lived to see this," he rumbled. Then he turned to his leader. "When do we attack?"

Kahless frowned. If it were the tyrant sitting outside these gates and someone else were within, the assault would already have begun.

"Now," he replied.

Gesturing, he ordered his men to bring up the siege engine. With a collective grunt, they put their backs into it.

As the engine rumbled forward on massive wooden wheels, the outlaw glanced at the faces of the tyrant's archers. Even from this distance, he could see the apprehension there, the realization that they were not as safe within their walls as they had imagined.

He laughed a hollow laugh. Vathraq's walls hadn't kept Molor from murdering Kellein. Why shouldn't he return the favor?

But the engine alone would not carry them to victory. At another signal, his most agile warriors climbed the monstrous timbers of the thing, their bows slung over their backs.

When they reached the platform, they took up their positions and knelt. Of course, Molor's archers would have an advantage over them, firing down from a greater height. But Kahless's archers were not charged with tearing down the gates. They were only there to provide cover fire, so those below could do their job.

Faster and faster the engine rolled, heading for the great, iron-bound doors to the tyrant's citadel. Kahless himself rode beside it, raising his *bat'telh* to the heavens and bellowing a challenge to the enemy.

The sense of it did not matter, only the sound itself. Hearing it, each of his warriors took up the cry, until it drowned out the rumble of the engine's wheels with its thunder and echoed back at them from Molor's walls.

The outlaw ignored the arrows that rained down on them, taking the mounted and those on foot alike. His place was in the lead, no matter the danger. Anything less would have been a breach of his promise to Morath.

He would sooner have died than breach that promise. And just in case he came to feel differently at some point, Morath was right beside him to remind him of it.

As they approached the gates, Kahless clenched his teeth with determination. Rocks, not just arrows, were pelting the ground all around him. Warriors died in agony and were flung from their screaming *s'tarahkmey*.

But this was just a taste of the carnage to come. Just the merest hint of the blood that would be spilled this day.

As if to underscore the thought, the outlaw wheeled on his *s'tarahk* and uttered a new command. Heeding it, the archers on the siege engine braced themselves—and those on the ground gave it one last push. Despite its terrible weight, the thing surged forward.

It couldn't go far on its own, Kahless knew. But it didn't have to. Molor's iron-bound gates were only a couple of yards away.

With a earsplitting groan, the engine's front wheels slammed into the gates. A second later, the immense battering ram swung forward. Unlike the engine itself, nothing had stopped its progress yet.

Then that changed. The ram struck the gates, sending up a whipcrack of thunder. The outlaw's bones shuddered with the impact.

"Again!" he cried.

As his archers provided cover, his ground forces drew the ram back and then drove it forward again. The gates creaked miserably, like a mighty animal in awful pain. But they didn't yield. At least, not yet.

A second time, the ram was drawn back and thrust forward. And a third. But it was only with the fourth blow that the mighty gates began to cave inward. The rebels bellowed, drawing courage from it.

The fifth stroke sounded like rocks breaking; it caved the gates in even more. And the sixth burst them open at last, giving the invaders access to what was inside.

Like *yolok* worms reaching for an especially luscious piece of fruit, Kahless and his warriors swarmed around and through the siege engine. After all, the thing had done its job. The rest was up to the strength of their arms and the hatred in their Klingon hearts.

The courtyard was packed tight with defenders. But they wielded long, heavy swords and axes, the kind warriors had used for hundreds of years. They were not made for infighting.

The rebels' *bat'telhmey* were a different story entirely. Lighter, more versatile, they represented a huge advantage in close quarters. And Kahless had equipped fifty of his best fighters with them.

Cutting and slashing, the outlaw led the way into the citadel, with Morath barely a step behind. Nor did Kahless's warriors disappoint him. Battering and thrusting, they followed him inch by bloody inch.

The fighting was intense, unlike anything the outlaw had seen before. But his *bat'telh* served him well. Like a hunting bird, it swooped and swooped again, each time plucking a life from the enemy's midst.

Blood spilled until it was everywhere, making the ground slick beneath their feet. Warriors fell on both sides, slumped on top of one another, glutting the confines of the courtyard with their empty shells.

And still the two sides battled, matching blow with clanging blow, war cry with earsplitting war cry, neither side willing to yield. Kahless's men fought for freedom from the tyrant, Molor's men because they feared his wrath. But in the end, both sides suffered their share of casualties.

Nor did the outlaw wade through the struggle unscathed. By the time he came within reach of the tyrant's keep, he was bleeding from a dozen wounds. But he was only vaguely aware of them, his heart pounding too hard for his head to keep up with it.

A year earlier, he would never have imagined this—would never have believed it possible. Yet here he was, a mighty force behind him, knocking on the tyrant's door. With a vicious uppercut, he dispatched one defender, then skewered another one on his point. A backhanded blow sent a third warrior to the afterlife.

Suddenly, the inner gate was naked before him. Lowering his shoulder, he slammed into it with all his strength. It didn't budge. And the siege engine wasn't narrow enough to make it into the courtyard.

But there was more than one way to skin a serpent. Raising his *bat'telh* as high as he could, he sent up a cry for help. And before he knew it, a dozen rebels had appeared to add their strength to his.

Morath, of course, was the first to lean into the gate with his friend. Digging in with their heels, the others did the same. Then they pushed as hard as they could, grunting with the effort.

At first, there was no more progress than when Kahless had tried it himself. But a few seconds later, the outlaw heard the shriek of bending iron.

"Harder!" he roared. "We are almost in!"

They drew deeper, finding strength they did not know they had, and used all of it against the gate. There was another shriek of twisting metal, and all of a sudden the thing surrendered to them.

Flinging the gate wide, Kahless took in the sight of Molor's torchlit anteroom. It was full of tall, powerful warriors, who grinned at him with eyes full of venom and mouths full of sharpened teeth.

The tyrant's personal guard, two dozen strong. The most devastating fighters the world had ever known. Or so it was said.

Kahless tightened his grip on his *bat'telh*. One way or the other, he repeated to himself, remembering the words he had spoken at Tolar'tu. One way or the other.

Then, as a handful of his men clustered about him, he raised his weapon high and charged into the midst of the enemy.

CHAPTER 33

The Modern Age

The house was an impressive one, broad and angular as it bulked up against the faintly pink underbelly of the sky. It dwarfed the other buildings in this wealthy and less-travelled part of Navrath.

Still, Lomakh was no longer quite so awed by it as he had once been. After all, he had visited the place several times in the last year, on the occasion of one splendid feast or another. Its owner—a wealthy and prominent member of the high council—was quite fond of extravagant celebrations.

And not just feasts. He liked to sponsor local festivals and opera performances as well. But he most enjoyed inviting people to his home.

During one such revelry, the council member had shown Lomakh his family armory—and invited the Defense Force officer to join a young but burgeoning conspiracy. Of course, the wealthy one had done his research. He knew Lomakh was disaffected with Gowron's reign and bold enough to do something about it.

Lomakh had hesitated—but only for a second or two. Then he had pledged himself to their common cause.

He was still pledged to it now, heart and hand. And though some small matters had not gone as smoothly as he would have liked, larger matters had more than made up for them.

In the end, the conspirators' victory seemed assured. The Empire was still reeling over the confirmation of the scroll's authenticity, the clone and his comrades had been destroyed in the explosions on Ogat, and Gowron was too stupid to believe in the threat right before his eyes.

By the time he gave the rumors of conspiracy any credence, it would be too late for the council leader and all his supporters. Gowron would be gone, and another raised in his place. And the alliance with the Federation would be a grim and distasteful memory.

Most important of all, Lomakh would be a man held in the highest esteem by Gowron's successor. Such a man could have most anything his heart desired—power, latinum, vengeance against old enemies.

Yes, the officer mused. Things were going very well indeed.

Such were Lomakh's thoughts as he approached the house's sturdy, *qava*-wood gates and the sensor rods on either side of them. Pulling the cowl of his cloak aside for a moment, he glanced over his shoulder to make sure no one had followed him through the streets. Apparently, no one had.

Satisfied, he moved forward to stand between the sensor rods and waited. He didn't have to wait long. In a matter of moments, the house guards had emerged from between the gates—a quartet of them, each one bigger and more hostile-looking than the one before him.

Familiar with their routine, Lomakh opened his cloak to show them the extent of his armaments. Removing his disruptor from his belt, he turned it over to the biggest of them. He kept his *d'k tahg,* however. It would have been a breach of propriety to strip a Klingon of *all* his weapons.

Satisfied, the guards escorted him through the gates and into the courtyard. On the far side of it, there was another set of gates, a bit smaller but otherwise identical to the first. There were sensor rods there too, in case the first set malfunctioned.

Lomakh passed between them without incident. As two of the guards opened the gates, he entered a pentagon-shaped anteroom. Just past it was the stronghold's central hall.

It wasn't quite as big as the High Council chamber and its ceiling certainly wasn't as high, but it was just as majestic and well appointed. And the high seat at its far end was, if anything, even larger and more formidable than Gowron's.

The one who occupied that seat was formidable too, the hairlessness of his large head accentuating the darkness of his brows. Right now, his face illuminated by the flames from freestanding braziers placed at intervals, the council member looked as hard and unyielding as stone.

At first, Lomakh believed his host was the only one who awaited him. Then, as he came closer, he realized there were other figures there.

Four of them, to be exact, all but obscured by the shadows outside the circle of torchlight. What's more, Lomakh recognized them.

Tichar. Goradh. Olmai. Kardem.

All high-ranking officers in the Klingon Defense Force. All, like Lomakh himself, key participants in the conspiracy. They turned at his approach, their eyes narrowing beneath the ridges of their foreheads.

What was going on? they seemed to ask. Lomakh wanted to know himself. He looked to their host for an answer.

Unarrh, son of Unagroth, looked back at him from his high seat. He leaned forward, so that the lines in his squarish face were accentuated and his eye sockets were swallowed in shadow. Only his irises were visible as pinpricks of reflected firelight.

"Lomakh," Unarrh rumbled. "Finally. Now tell me quickly, before my patience runs out—why did you call us here?"

"Yes," added Olmai, "tell us. I thought we had agreed not to meet in large numbers until the rebellion was well under way."

"I thought the same," spat Goradh.

"And I as well," added Tichar.

Lomakh shook his head. Clearly, he had missed something. Or *someone* had.

"I did not call anyone," he protested.

"What?" The council member's brows converged over the bridge of his nose. "Then why are you here?" he asked.

Lomakh indicated one of the other conspirators with a tilt of his head. "I received a message from Kardem, summoning me. Though I must admit, it seemed strange to me at the time."

Unarrh's eyes narrowed. He looked from one of his fellow conspirators to another. "Someone is lying," he said.

The Defense Force officers glanced at one another, hoping someone would step forward and tender an explanation. No one did.

The council member's eyes opened wide. He cursed lavishly beneath his breath. "This must be some kind of trap," Unarrh decided. "The best thing for us to do is—"

He was interrupted by a commotion in the corridor outside. A moment later, one of Unarrh's house guards came hurtling into the hall. Then another. Both sprawled on the floor, unconscious, bleeding from the head and face.

The other guards, Lomakh observed, were nowhere to be seen. He could only conclude they had been neutralized as well.

Immediately, his hand went to his belt, where it expected to find his disruptor pistol. But of course, it was no longer there, so he had to settle for the ceremonial knife concealed in the back of his tunic.

Unarrh shot to his feet like a rearing *s'tarahk*. "What is the meaning of this?" he roared.

An instant later, the intruders entered the hall. First, a group of three, one of whom seemed vaguely familiar even in darkness. Then another group, cloaked and cowled like the conspirators themselves.

"Who are you?" Unarrh demanded. "By what right do you impose yourselves on my house?"

By way of an answer, a member of the first group stepped forward into the light from the braziers. Instantly, his features became recognizable. They were, after all, those of the honorable Gowron—son of M'rel and leader of the Klingon High Council.

Unarrh's eyes took on an even harder cast. His voice

was taut, commanding, as he addressed the council leader.

"I trust there is some meaning in this *somewhere*, Gowron. Because if there is not, you will regret barging in on me like this."

The council leader scowled. "I assure you, Unarrh, I did not come here simply to annoy you." He jerked his chin at the four who still stood in the darkness, their faces concealed by their hoods. "It was they who persuaded me. They claimed they had something to tell me—but would not reveal it except in your presence."

Unarrh turned his gaze on the quartet. "And who are *they?*" he rasped.

All four of them pulled back their cowls. Then they joined Gowron in the circle of illumination.

Lomakh's mouth went dry as he saw who had come calling on him. "Kahless . . ." he gasped.

The clone grinned fiercely. "Yes, Kahless, back from the dead. I seem to specialize in that, don't I?"

Lomakh looked at the others, their faces revealed now as well. His mouth twisted with hatred and frustration.

The sons of Mogh, Worf and Kurn. And the human, the damned Arbiter of Succession—Picard of the Federation.

All alive. And from the look of things, undeterred in their pursuit of the conspirators. Lomakh grunted softly, wondering what would come next and how to play it.

"What interesting companions you have," Unarrh commented, glaring at Gowron and choosing to ignore the others.

Kahless chuckled, indicating the Defense Force officers with a sweep of his arm. "I might say the same of you," he countered.

Unarrh's lips curled back, exposing his teeth. With obvious reluctance, he turned his gaze on the clone.

"I will not tolerate your presence here much longer," he snarled. "If you have something to say, say it."

Lomakh grunted. Unarrh must have known their conspiracy had been discovered. He was simply playing for time, trying to find out how much Kahless knew before making his move.

Or did the council member truly believe he could talk his way out of this? Lomakh tightened his grip on the dagger in his tunic—aware of the possibility that Unarrh's plans for saving himself might not include the preservation of his allies.

In the meantime, the clone had been digging in his belt pouch for something. He extracted it now and held it up to the light.

It was a computer chip—the kind used here on the homeworld, and therefore compatible with systems of Klingon manufacture. Lomakh tried to anticipate how it might incriminate them—and couldn't.

But he didn't have to wait long to find out.

"This chip," Kahless hissed, "contains information downloaded from a Klingon subspace relay station—one my comrades and I had occasion to visit recently." He smiled at Worf, who stood beside him.

"On the main communications band," the clone continued, "there is nothing more than the usual subspace chatter. But on a frequency normally left unused by the Defense Force, there is something more. . . ."

Lomakh knew what that something was, even before Kahless finished his thought. After all, he had taken part in it—in the early stages of the conspiracy, before Unarrh decided to clamp down on security.

". . . a record of several conversations," Kahless went on, "in which certain Defense Force officers repeatedly conspire to tear down the honorable Gowron. And the name Unarrh always seems to figure prominently in these discussions." The clone scanned the officers assembled, clearly enjoying himself. "It occurs to me all of those who took part in this conspiracy are now present in this hall." His smile broadened as he turned to Gowron. "A great convenience, if you ask me."

The council leader didn't say anything. But Lomakh wasn't blind. He could see Gowron's interest in the chip.

Worf took another step toward Unarrh and lifted his arm to point at the council member. "All along, you have claimed to be a supporter of Kahless and his orthodoxy. Yet you were nothing of the kind."

The hall rang and echoed with his accusation. Unarrh's eyes grew wide, but he said nothing in his defense.

"In truth," Kurn added, "you were the guiding force behind the rebellion all along—even before the scroll was made public."

Kahless handed the computer chip to Gowron. The council leader hefted the thing in his hand, then turned again to Unarrh.

"Bring me a playback device," he told his host.

"Unless you fear what is on it," Worf suggested, relentless in his pursuit of the truth.

Unarrh laughed an ugly laugh. "I fear nothing and no one." As he glowered at Worf, his eyes seem to burn in the firelight. "Especially a *p'tahk* who was discommendated for his family's treachery."

Worf was incensed. "Duras was the *p'tahk,* not I. And who are you to speak of treachery?" he thundered. "You, who would have torn the council apart without a second thought—though it was Gowron who raised you to your office in the first place?"

Unarrh turned a dark and dangerous shade of red. Reaching behind him, he produced a disruptor pistol—one even Lomakh hadn't known about. Apparently, the council member had anticipated some sort of trouble.

Before anyone could move, Unarrh took aim at one of Gowron's guards and pressed the trigger. A blue beam shot out and consumed the warrior in a swirl of rampant energies. Then the council member aimed and fired again, and Gowron's other retainer died in agony.

Lomakh had seen enough. Unarrh seemed to have decided he had run out of options—and was taking his best shot at survival.

Unfortunately, even if he destroyed all his enemies, he would have to explain his actions to the council. And they would not look kindly on his killing Gowron and Kurn—apparently without provocation.

More than likely, Unarrh would have to throw them a bone—a Defense Force officer or two, to punish as they saw fit. And Lomakh had no desire to be sacrificed in such a manner.

Let Unarrh fend for himself, he thought. I will be elsewhere, making new allies, before he can point a finger at me.

With a hiss of metal on molded leather, he drew his dagger and made a break for it. Nor were his fellow officers far behind.

CHAPTER 34

The Heroic Age

In Molor's anteroom, Kahless swung his *bat'telh* and struck down one of Molor's guards. Beside him, Morath disemboweled another.

For a time, the tyrant's retainers had held their own, even against greater odds. Perhaps twenty of the rebels lay stacked about them, blood running from twice as many wounds.

But now there were only a dozen defenders left, and none of them were grinning as eagerly as before. A couple barely had the strength to stay on their feet. Slowly but surely, the tide was turning against them.

"They're faltering!" Kahless cried. "It won't be much longer now!"

Still, every second they delayed him was like the sting of a *pherza* wasp. He wanted desperately to reach their master and see an end to this.

Blinking sweat from his eyes, Kahless hacked at another of Molor's warriors. The man stumbled backward, barely managing to deflect the blow in time. In another moment, he would come back with one of his own.

But in the meantime, the outlaw had a clear path to his goal—a long, straight hallway that led deeper into the bowels of the citadel. With a burst of speed, he seized the opportunity.

And Morath was right behind him. As always.

"Kahless!" he cried.

The outlaw turned, barely breaking stride. "What is it?"

"We should go back and finish them," Morath protested.

"No," said Kahless, firm in his resolve. "If you want to end this, I'll show you a quicker way."

Morath hesitated. But in the end, he came running after his friend. "All right," he said for emphasis. "Show me."

The outlaw pledged inwardly to do his best. Pelting down the long, echoing hallway, he tried to remember the layout of the place. After all, he had only been here a couple of times, and both seemed impossibly long ago.

At the end of the hallway, there was a choice of turnings. The corridor to Kahless's left was decorated with heroic tapestries and ancient weapons. The one to his right held a series of black-iron pedestals, each one host to something dark and hairy.

A head, the outlaw recalled. A *stuffed* head.

Turning to the right, he broke into a run again. As before, Morath followed on his heels.

"What are these?" his friend asked, referring to the heads.

"The tyrant's enemies," Kahless told him. "Though from what I've heard, they plague him no longer."

Unexpectedly, he drew courage from the sight. It was as if every shriveled, staring face was shouting encouragement to him, every hollow mouth crying out silently for vengeance.

These were his brothers, the outlaw told himself, his kinsmen in spirit. He would do what he could to see all their demands fulfilled—for if he did not, he would almost certainly join them.

The corridor ended in the beginnings of a circular stairwell, one narrow and smoothed by age. Hunching over, Kahless took the steep, uneven steps as quickly as he could.

"Where are you going?" asked Morath.

The outlaw stopped long enough to look at him. "You want Molor, don't you?"

The warrior's brow knotted. "How do you know he's up there?"

Kahless grunted. "I was one of his warchiefs, remember?"

"But you've never seen him defend against a siege," Morath protested. "He could be anywhere."

Kahless didn't answer. He just started up the stairs again. After all, he knew the tyrant as well as any man.

Besides, he had been gambling and winning battle after battle for months now. Why stop?

Halfway up the steps, he heard something. Barely a sound—more like the absence of one. Slowing down ever so slightly, he braced himself.

Suddenly, a spear came thrusting down at him. Though he was prepared, it was no easy task to batter it aside with his *bat'telh*—or to keep from staggering under the weight of the warrior who came after it.

Still, the outlaw managed to keep his footing, and to grab his adversary's wrist before the man's hand could find Kahless's throat. Then, off-balance as he was, smashed his *bat'telh* into the guard's face.

There was no cry, no bellow of pain. Just a gurgle, and the man collapsed on him. Pressing his back against the wall, the outlaw allowed the corpse to fall past him, end over end. Farther below, Morath did the same.

It was not the last obstacle Kahless would face on his way up the steps. He had to dispatch two more warriors, each more fierce than the one before, in order to reach his destination. But reach it he did.

And all the while, Morath pursued him, ready to take his place if he was cut down. Fortunately for both of them, it was not necessary.

Reaching the top of the stair, Kahless emerged onto a dark, windowless landing. At the opposite end, he saw a door.

If he was right, Molor would be behind it. And some guards as well? he wondered. Or had he dispatched them all already?

Morath came up beside him. For a moment, both of them listened—and heard nothing. Shrugging, the younger man pointed to the door. Kahless nodded and took its handle in his hand. And pushed.

It wouldn't move. It had been bolted from the inside.

Clenching his teeth, the outlaw slashed the door with his *bat'telh*—once, twice, three times, until it was a splintered ruin. Then, with a single kick, he caved in the remains.

As Kahless had suspected, Molor was inside.

The tyrant was plotting his next move at his *m'ressa*-wood table. His large and imposing frame was hunkered over a map of his citadel, casting a monstrous shadow in the light of a single brazier.

The outlaw had looked forward to the expression on the tyrant's face when he saw his warchief coming back to haunt him—to exact revenge for Kellein, and for Rannuf, and for all the other innocents Molor had trampled in his hunger for power.

But what Kahless saw was not what he had expected. Halfway into the room, the outlaw stopped dead in his tracks, stunned as badly as if someone had bludgeoned him in the head.

"Blood of my ancestors," he breathed.

Molor looked up at him, his eyes sunken into his round, bony head like tiny, black dung beetles. The tyrant's skin was intricately webbed as if with extreme old age and riddled with an army of open purple sores. His once-powerful body was hollowed out and emaciated, his limbs little more than long, brittle twigs.

"Greetings," he rattled, his voice like a serpent slithering through coarse sand. "I see you've found me, Kahless."

Molor said the outlaw's name as if it fascinated him, as if it were the very first time he'd had occasion to say it out loud. His mouth quirked in a grotesque grandfatherly smile, revealing a mottled tongue and rounded, worm-eaten teeth.

A moment later, Morath came into the room behind his friend. Glancing at him, Kahless saw the horror on the younger man's face—the loathing that mirrored Kahless's own.

"As I expected," the tyrant hissed gleefully, "your shadow is right behind you."

Molor wheezed as he spoke, the tendons in his neck standing out with the effort it cost him. Spittle collected in the corners of his mouth.

"What happened to him?" asked Morath, seemingly unable to take his eyes off the tyrant.

"What happened?" echoed Molor, his voice cracking. "I'll tell you. I fell victim to the plague that's been killing all the *minn'hormey.*"

He tossed his head back and made a shrill, harsh sound that Kahless barely recognized as laughter. Threads of saliva stretched across the tyrant's maw. Then, with a palsied, carbuncle-infested hand, he closed his mouth and wiped the drool from his shriveled chin.

"Funny," he said, "isn't it? My physicians tell me the disease afflicts one Klingon in a thousand. And of all the wretched specimens on this wretched continent, whom should it bring down but the most powerful man on Qo'noS?"

Molor started to laugh again, but went into a coughing fit instead. He had to prop himself up on the table for support. When he was done, he looked up at his enemy again.

"I hope you are not disappointed," he rasped. "I would give you a fight even now, Kahless, but it would not be much of a match. You are such a strong and sturdy man still, and I . . ." The tyrant's face twisted with revulsion, with hatred for the reedy thing he had become. "I do not believe I would stand up to a stiff wind."

The outlaw shook his head. He had come here thirsting for vengeance with all his heart. But he knew now he couldn't slake that thirst. As long as he lived, he could *never* slake it.

He would get no satisfaction from killing a plague victim, no matter what Molor had done. But he couldn't let the *p'tahk* live, either. The tyrant had to pay for his crimes somehow.

With that in mind, Kahless used his left hand to remove his dagger from the sheath on his leg. With a toss, he placed it on the table in front of his enemy. It clattered for a moment, then lay still.

"What are you doing?" asked Morath.

"I am giving him a chance to take his own life," the outlaw answered, "before my warriors tear him limb from limb. It was more than he did for Kellein and her people. And it is certainly more than he deserves. But nonetheless, there it is."

Molor picked up the *d'k tagh* with a trembling hand. And with difficulty, he opened it, so that all three blades clicked into place.

"You're right," he told Kahless, as he inspected the weapon. "This is considerably more than I deserve. However—"

Suddenly, the tyrant's eyes came alive. He drew back the dagger with an ease that belied his appearance and balanced it gracefully in his hand.

"—it is precisely what *you* deserve, son of Kanjis!"

In that moment, the outlaw realized how badly he'd been duped. He saw all he had worked for—all his friends had given their lives for—about to vanish in a blaze of stupidity.

Before he could move, Molor brought the knife forward and released it. But something flashed in front of

Kahless—and with a dull thud, took the blade meant for him.

Openmouthed, the outlaw stared at his friend Morath. The *d'k tahg* was protruding from the center of the warrior's chest. Clutching at it, Morath tried to pull it out, to no avail. Then, blood spilling from the corner of his mouth, he sank to his knees.

Kahless was swept up in a maelstrom of blind, choking fury. He turned to Molor, the object of his hatred now more than ever.

The tyrant was drawing a sword from a scabbard hidden underneath his *m'ressa*-wood table. With spindly wrists and skeletal fingers, Molor raised the weapon. And brought it back. And with a cry like an angry bird, braced himself for his enemy's attack.

But it did the tyrant no good. For the outlaw was already moving forward. Tossing the heavy table aside with his left hand, he brought his *bat'telh* into play with his right.

First, Kahless smashed the sword out of Molor's hand. Then, putting all his strength behind the blow, he swung his blade at the other man's neck. With a bellow—not of triumph, but of pain and rage—he watched the tyrant's head topple from his shoulders.

As Molor's skull clattered to the floor, followed by a splash of blood, the outlaw turned to Morath. His friend was sitting on his haunches, still trying to draw the *d'k tahg* from his chest. With Kahless watching, Morath toppled to one side and lay gasping on the floor.

Tossing his *bat'telh* aside, the outlaw fell to his knees and lifted his friend up in his arms. Kahless wanted to tell him there was hope he might outlive his wound, but he knew better. And so did Morath.

"This is wrong," the outlaw railed. "You cannot die now, damn you. Not when we have *won.*"

"Your promise to me," Morath began, his voice already fading. "It is not yet . . . not yet done. . . ."

Kahless shook his head, his sweat-soaked hair whipping at his face. "No," he snarled, like a *s'tarahk* struggling against its reins. "I told you I would tear the tyrant down. And I have done that."

"A life," Morath reminded him, his mouth bubbling with blood. "You said you would pay with your *life.* The people . . . they still need you. . . ."

The outlaw's teeth ground in anger. But his friend was dying, having taken the dagger meant for Kahless.

How could he deny Morath this last request? How could he think of himself after all the man had done for him?

"A life," he echoed, hating even the sound of the word. His lip curling, he swallowed back the bile that rose in his throat. "As I promised you in the wilderness, a *life.*"

Morath managed a thin, pale smile. "I will speak well of you to your ancestors . . . Kahless, son of Kanjis. . . ."

Then, with a shudder, his body became an empty husk.

The outlaw stared at the flesh that had once been Morath. He couldn't believe his friend was dead—and he, Kahless, was still alive. If anything, he had expected it to be the other way around.

Abruptly, all his exertions and his wounds tried to drag him down at once. He bowed his head under the terrible weight of them.

How could it have happened this way? he asked. How?

He was supposed to have gotten rid of all his burdens. Now he had undertaken more of them than ever. No longer merely a rebel hungry for vengeance, he would become a thrice-cursed king.

With a grimace of disgust, Kahless found the strength to get to his feet. Picking up Morath's body, he slung it over his shoulder. Then he righted Molor's *m'ressa* table and lowered the body onto it.

Grasping his *d'k tahg* by its handle, he tugged it free of his friend's chest. Then he tucked it into his belt, still slick with Morath's blood.

Finally, he turned back to Morath's body—to the eyes that still stared at him, refusing to release him from his vow. Kahless scowled. *Even in death,* he thought. *Even in death.*

He took a deep, shuddering breath. When warriors sang of this day, they would not forget the son of Ondagh. This, he swore with all his being.

And Kahless would remember too. Morath the warrior and the liberator, who was a better man than Kahless by far. Morath his pursuer and his tormentor, who was more a brother to him than a friend.

Unexpectedly, a wellspring of grief rose up in him, and he raised his voice in a harsh yell—just as he had raised it over the body of Kellein those long months ago. He yelled until he was hoarse with yelling, imagining that his noise was speeding Morath's soul to the afterlife.

Not that Kahless believed in such things. But Morath did. For his friend's sake, the outlaw would give in just this once.

There was just one more thing to do while he was up here. Better to do it quickly, Kahless thought, before any more blood was shed.

Molor's head was lying in a corner of the room, soiled

with a mixture of gore and dust. Picking it up by the strands of hair still left on the tyrant's chin, he pulled aside a curtain to reveal another winding stair—a much shorter one, which led up to a high balcony.

One by one, he ascended the stone steps. The last time the outlaw had negotiated them, he hadn't been an outlaw at all, but chief among Molor's warlords. The tyrant had wished to show him what it was like to hold the world in the palm of one's hand.

Those days were long gone. Now it was *Molor* he held in his hand, and the world would have to find somewhere else to reside.

As Kahless emerged into the wind and sky, he saw the battle still raging below him on the battlements and in the courtyard. He could hear the strident clamor of sword on sword, the bitter cries of the dying, the urgent shouts of the living.

"Hear me!" he bellowed at the top of his lungs.

Not everyone turned to him at once. But some did. And as they pointed at him, amazed by the sight, so did others. In place after place, adversaries stepped back from one another, curious as to how the outlaw had reached Molor's balcony—and what that might mean to them.

Kahless filled his lungs. The wind whipping savagely at his hair, he cried out again.

"The tyrant Molor is dead! There is nothing left to fight for, you hear me? Nothing!"

And then, to substantiate his claim, he lifted Molor's head so all could see. For a second or two, he let it hang there, a portent of change.

Then, drawing his arm back, he hurled it out over the heart of the battle like a strange and terrible missile. It turned end over end, rolling high and far across the sky, until gravity made its claim at last and the thing plummeted to earth.

"There," the outlaw said, in a voice only he could hear. "That should put an end to it."

On shaky and uncertain legs, he came down from the balcony. Out of the wind, into the quiet and the shadows.

Now, he thought, came the hard part.

CHAPTER 35

The Modern Age

Worf was closer than anyone else to Unarrh's high seat. When the council member started firing his disruptor at Gowron's men, the lieutenant knew he had only two choices.

He could retreat and flee Unarrh's hall—perhaps the safer route. Or he could go forward and try to wrest the disruptor from Unarrh's grasp.

In his years with Starfleet, the Klingon had learned there was no shame in retreating. Often, it was the wiser course. But in his heart, he was a warrior, and a warrior always preferred to attack.

Besides, it was a good day to die. And the rightness of his cause made it an even better day.

Lowering his head, he put aside any thought of danger to himself and charged the high seat. Just before he reached Unarrh, he caught a glimpse of his enemy's weapon, its barrel swinging in his direction.

Even as Worf hurled himself at the council member, he was blinded by the blue flash of disruptor fire. But a moment later, he felt the reassuring impact of bone and muscle as he collided with Unarrh.

Apparently, he thought, the blast had missed him. He was not dead—at least, not yet.

Then his momentum carried both him and Unarrh backward, toppling the man's chair in the process. They landed heavily on the stone floor, Worf's left hand gripping the council member's powerful wrist.

Unarrh tried to roll on top of him, to pin the lieutenant with his considerably greater weight—but Worf was too quick for him. Using a *mok'bara* technique he had demonstrated on the *Enterprise* only a week ago, he brought his right hand around his adversary's head and grabbed Unarrh by his left ear. Then he pulled as hard as he could.

Screaming for mercy, Unarrh rolled onto his back to lessen the pain. Taking advantage of the council member's discomfort, Worf smashed Unarrh's weapon hand against the floor. The impact was enough to dislodge the disruptor and send it skittering over the stones.

But Unarrh wasn't done yet. Far from it. Continuing to roll, he drove his elbow into Worf's ribs, knocking the wind out of the security officer—and forcing him to release Unarrh's ear. And once free, the council member lunged for his weapon again.

Still on his back, Worf grabbed Unarrh by his calf and kept him from reaching his goal. Then, flipping onto his stomach, he got to his knees to improve his leverage.

But Unarrh lashed out with his heel, hitting the Starfleet officer in the shoulder. The shock forced Worf to release him again—but the lieutenant wouldn't be denied. Leaping on Unarrh's back, he grabbed the back of the council member's hairless head as best he could.

With all his might, he drove Unarrh's chin into the stone floor. Not once, but three times. Finally, after the third blow, Unarrh went limp.

Just in case it was some kind of trick, Worf launched himself over his adversary and grabbed the disruptor. But it wasn't a trick after all. Unarrh remained right where he was, clearly unconscious.

The lieutenant snarled—all the victory celebration he would allow himself. Then he looked to his comrades.

Picard saw Worf topple Unarrh as Lomakh and his friends drew their daggers. Trusting to his lieutenant's fighting skills, he drew his own *d'k tahg* and blocked the entrance to the hall.

Unfortunately, there were other ways out—and the conspirators took one of them when they bolted. Seeing the way to the front door guarded, they fled the other way, deeper into Unarrh's mansion.

Even then, as it turned out, their path wasn't exactly clear. Kurn and Kahless managed to tackle two of the conspirators from behind. And a moment later, Gowron flung his knife into a third.

Two were still on their feet, however. As they disappeared, the captain raced after them. Crossing the hall, he saw Kurn tumble end-over-end with his adversary. But the clone was more expedient, slamming his opponent headfirst into a wall.

When the conspirator slumped to the floor unconscious, Kahless looked up and saw Picard. There were no words exchanged between them, but the clone seemed to understand two of the traitors were unaccounted for. Without hesitation, he joined the captain in his pursuit.

As they darted out of the hall into a curving corridor, Picard caught sight of their objectives. One was Lomakh, the conspirator they had spied on in Tolar'tu. The other was an even taller and stronger-looking Klingon named Tichar.

No doubt, Kahless would have been perfectly willing to take on both of the plotters by himself. Fortunately, that wouldn't be necessary. The clone may have begun this fight all on his own, but it wouldn't end that way. He had help now.

Meanwhile, Lomakh and Tichar led them through one winding passageway after the other, their heels clattering on the stone floors. But they couldn't shake their pursuers. Kahless was like a bulldog, refusing to let go. And though the captain was no longer the youth who had won the Academy marathon, he was hardly a laggard either.

Of course, their chase couldn't go on forever, Picard told himself. Sooner or later, Lomakh and his comrade had to hit a dead end of some sort. Then they would have no choice but to turn and fight.

Events quickly proved him right. Racing down a short, straight hallway, the captain got the impression of a large, dim room beyond. As he and the clone entered it, they saw it had no other exit.

Lomakh and Tichar were trapped inside. But that didn't mean they intended to go down without a struggle.

As luck would have it, they had stumbled onto an armory of sorts. There were bladed weapons of all shapes and sizes adorning the far wall, along with a variety of other, more arcane devices. Unarrh, it seemed, was a collector of such things.

First Lomakh reached for a *bat'telh,* then Tichar did the same. Grinning, they advanced on Picard and his companion, shifting their weapons in their hands as if looking forward to what would come next.

"Bad luck," Kahless muttered.

"It seems that way," the captain agreed.

He gauged his chances of getting past the conspirators to obtain a *bat'telh* of his own. The odds weren't very good at the moment. Gritting his teeth, he weighed his other options.

He and Kahless could give ground, perhaps go back the way they came. But if they went back far enough, Lomakh and Tichar might find a way out of Unarrh's complex. And once they did that, they would have a chance to escape.

Picard knew he couldn't live with himself if these two got away. He recalled the faces he saw in the ruins of the academy on Ogat—the faces of the innocent children who died at the hands of the conspirators.

No one should be able to do that with impunity, he thought. Lomakh and Tichar would have to pay for their crimes. And if they had some other outcome in mind, they would have to go through the captain in order to obtain it.

"Out of our way!" growled Lomakh.

"Not a chance in Hell," Kahless shot back.

"You'd rather die?" asked Tichar.

The clone's eyes narrowed. "There are worse things, *p'tahk!*"

Kahless' lips pulled back past his teeth in a feral grin.

He rolled his *d'k tahg* in his hand. Clearly, he had come too far and fought too hard not to see this through to its conclusion.

Picard had to admire his courage and his persistence. Perhaps this was not the Kahless of legend, but the clone had the heart of a hero.

The conspirators seemed to think so, too. The captain could see it in their eyes, in the way they hunkered down for battle. Despite their advantage in the way they were armed, they knew this would not be easy for them.

For a moment, there was only the echo of advancing footfalls on the floor, and the glint of firelight on their blades, and the pounding of Picard's heart in his chest. Then Kahless sprang forward like a maddened bull and the combat was joined.

The armory clattered with the clash of metal on metal as the powerful Tichar met the clone's attack with his *bat'telh*. At the same time, the captain saw Lomakh come shuffling toward him sideways, bringing his weapon up and back for a killing blow.

Picard didn't waste any time. Darting in close, he ducked and heard the whistle of the blade as it passed harmlessly over his head. Then he stabbed at the conspirator with his *d'k tahg*, hoping to find a space between the Klingon's ribs.

It didn't work out as he'd hoped. Not only did Lomakh ward off his blow, he struck the captain in the mouth with the heel of his hand. Staggering backward with the force of the blow, Picard tasted blood. As he tried desperately to steady himself, he felt something hard smack him in the back—and realized it was the wall.

The conspirator's eyes gleamed as he saw his chance. With a flip of his wrists, he swung his *bat'telh* a second time. But Picard regained control in time to roll to one side, removing himself from harm's way.

The *bat'telh* struck the wall where he had been, giving rise to a spray of hot sparks. Enraged, Lomakh turned to his adversary and went for him again, thrusting with the point of his blade.

But this time, the captain had a better plan. After all, he had studied fencing as a youth, and his instructor had emphasized the importance of distance. Peddling backward suddenly, his dagger held low, he managed to keep his chin just beyond the leading edge of Lomakh's *bat'telh*.

As the conspirator came on, trying to extend his reach, Picard maintained his margin of safety. Then, without warning, he drove Lomakh's blade aside with a vicious backhand slash. His adversary lurched forward, unable to regain his balance, much less protect himself.

Taking advantage of the opening, the captain grabbed the front of Lomakh's tunic with his free hand and dropped into a backward roll. Halfway through the maneuver, he planted his heel in the Klingon's chest and allowed Lomakh's momentum to do the rest.

As Picard completed his roll, he saw the Klingon sprawl, a tangle of body and limbs and razor-sharp *bat'telh*. Lomakh bellowed with pain before he came to a stop. A moment later, the captain saw what had caused the warrior so much discomfort.

The *bat'telh* had imbedded itself in Lomakh's tunic, cutting through flesh as well as leather. With a guttural curse, the Klingon tore the blade free and staggered to his feet.

"For that," he spat, "your death will be slow and painful!"

Picard smiled grimly, caught up in the interplay of bravado. "This may surprise you," he said, "but I have heard that before."

Again, Lomakh charged him. And again, the captain let him think he was on the verge of achieving his goal. Then, at the last possible moment, Picard turned sideways, flung up his arms, and let the conspirator's *bat'telh* shoot past him.

As Lomakh followed through, the human brought the hilt of his dagger down on the base of the Klingon's skull. With a grunt of pain, his adversary fell to his knees. His weapon slipped from insensible hands. And before he could recover, Picard's knee was in the small of the Klingon's back.

Driving Lomakh down with all his weight, the captain gripped the conspirator's hair with his left hand and pulled. Then, with his right hand, he placed the edge of his blade against Lomakh's eminently exposed throat.

"Bljeghbe'chugh vaj blHegh!" Picard growled. "Surrender or die!"

The conspirator tried to twist his head free, but the captain only increased the pressure of dagger against flesh. He repeated the order, this time in the short form. *"Jegh!"*

Lomakh groaned, awash with shame—but not so much he would die to rid himself of it. *"Yap,"* he rasped. "Enough."

Careful not to let his guard drop, Picard looked up—in time to see Kahless dodge a sweeping attack from Tichar. As the human watched, the clone struck back—once, twice, and again, battering down the conspirator's defenses. Tichar looked a little clumsier and a little more fatigued with each blow leveled against him.

But then, Kahless was wearing down too. Sweat streamed down either side of his face and his barrel chest was heaving for air. Besides that, there was a nasty cut on his forehead just below his hairline, and the blood from it was seeping into his eyes.

Finally, the clone seemed to find an opening, a gap in his opponent's defenses. Taking advantage of it, he darted in for the kill—and Tichar was too weary to stop him in time. With a savage *thukt*, Kahless's *bat'telh* buried itself deep in the conspirator's belly, just below the sternum.

The clone snarled as he drove his point upward, lifting his enemy off the ground despite his bulk. Picard winced as he watched Tichar scream in agony. Finally, Kahless let the conspirator down.

Tichar sank to his knees, mortally wounded. Applying his boot to the conspirator's chest, the clone pulled his blade free and let Tichar sprawl backward. Then Kahless turned to the captain and grinned through his own gore, more like an animal than a sentient being.

But then, thought Picard, that was and always had been the nature of the Klingon dichotomy. Canny intelligence mingled with the most relentlessly violent impulses. A dream of greatness floundering in a sea of blood.

Unable to contain his exuberance, the clone bellowed in triumph. He sounded like a storm, like a force of nature. The walls echoed with it and the rafters seemed to quiver.

This was joy pure and unbridled, an emotion as honest as it was repugnant to the human sensibility. It was Kahless's answer to those who questioned his authenticity, his challenge to those who would stand against him.

Here I am, he seemed to say. *Neither legend nor fraud,*

but a Klingon in all my earthly glory. Strive to be like me if you dare.

Ultimately, that was his appeal—and his greatness. Kahless was the Klingon Everyman, a mirror in which every last son of Qo'noS might find the noblest parts of himself.

The captain was so taken with the passion of the clone's display, he almost didn't see Tichar sit up, mortal wound and all. And even when he saw it, all he could do was cry out.

"Kahless!" he roared.

But it was too late. With his last reserve of strength, the conspirator hurled his *bat'telh* at the clone. As it whirled end over end, Kahless saw the look in the human's eyes and turned.

He had no time to ward the *bat'telh* off—not completely. All he could do was bring his own weapon up and hope for the best.

Unfortunately, the clone's action didn't slow the blade down one iota. The *bat'telh* punctured his tunic in the center of his chest. Staggered, he sank to one knee.

His face a mask of pain, Kahless gripped the *bat'telh* with both hands and tugged it free. Then, with a curse, he flung it from him. The blade scraped along the floor.

"My god," whispered Picard.

Was it possible the Klingon had come all this way just to perish in the end? Could Fate be so cruel?

He saw Kahless find him with his eyes. For a moment, they stared at one another, neither one knowing what to expect. Then the clone's teeth pulled back in a grin again, and he howled louder than ever.

The captain stared openmouthed. He didn't understand. He had seen the point of the *bat'telh* bury itself in Kahless's chest.

But as the Klingon approached him, caught up suddenly in the throes of laughter, he made the answer clear. Reaching into his leather tunic, he pulled out the betrothal amulet he wore—the one modeled after that of the original Kahless.

It was badly dented. In fact, the closer Picard looked, the more it seemed to him the thing had taken the brunt of a *bat'telh* thrust.

"Apparently," the clone boomed, "there is something to be said for tradition after all!"

Before the armory stopped ringing with his words, reinforcements arrived in the form of Worf, Kurn, and Gowron. And several of Gowron's guards, whom he had left outside at first, were there to back them up.

Relieved, the captain released Lomakh and got to his feet. At last, he told himself, it was *over*.

CHAPTER **36**

The Heroic Age

Emperor Kahless looked out the window. There were endless crowds gathered on either side of the road that led from his citadel—once Molor's citadel—to the eastern provinces. Though he hadn't shown himself yet, they were cheering and pumping their swords in the air.

The old warchief sighed. He had intended for only his closest friends and servants to know that he was leaving. Somehow, the word had leaked out.

"It wasn't me," said Anag.

Kahless turned to look at his chief councilor. Anag was a lean, dark-skinned man with a big, full beard. He was also Kahless's handpicked choice of successor.

"*What* wasn't you?" Kahless asked, confused by the declaration.

"It wasn't me who told the people of your departure," the younger man explained.

The emperor grunted. "Oh. That." He shrugged. "And

if it *were* you, Anag? Would I have boiled you in *en'tach* oil for your transgression?" He laughed. "There hasn't been a secret kept in these halls since I took the tyrant's life. Why should my leaving be any exception?"

Anag frowned. "You are . . . certain about this?"

Kahless nodded. "I am certain. Let us not have this conversation again, all right? I am an old man. I need to leave under my own power, and I will not have the chance to do that much longer."

He went over to his bed, where he had left his traveler's pack—a cracked leather relic of his days as an outlaw. There were still a few things he wanted to add to it.

Anag shook his head. "I still don't see the need for it. If you died in your bed, what difference would it make?"

The emperor looked at him. "You are right."

His councilor seemed surprised. "About your staying, you mean?"

"No," said Kahless. "About your not understanding."

Morath would have understood. Hell, he would have come up with the idea in the first place.

After all, it had only been a few decades since Kahless overthrew Molor and united the Klingon people. But in that time, he had seen his deeds magnified into the stuff of legend. If he could make a myth of his passing as well, it would only strengthen his legacy.

And a true legacy it was. With the tyrant overthrown, he had given the Klingons a set of laws by which they could conduct themselves honorably. Naturally, the basis for those laws was the principles Morath had lived by.

Keep your promises to one another. Deal openly and fairly, even with your enemies. Fight a battle to its end, giving no quarter. And when it is necessary to die, die bravely.

His people had embraced these precepts as a man dying of thirst might embrace a skin full of water. What's more, they had been quick to give Kahless credit for them. But he had insisted that Morath be known as the source of their wisdom—thereby fulfilling the vow he had made to his friend more than thirty years earlier.

Kahless had also set free the provinces that used to pay Molor tribute, inviting them instead to join his confederacy of free states. As he could have predicted, the provinces swore allegiance to him—and instead of tribute, they now paid taxes.

The same situation, of course, but a different appearance. Over the years, Kahless had learned to play his role well.

Morath would no doubt have been proud of all his friend had accomplished—if not of Kahless himself. After all, the emperor took no pride in what he had done for his people. His only motivation had been to please Morath's ghost—to keep his word to the man.

To remind himself of that promise, he had kept the dagger that killed Morath—still black with Morath's blood—in a glass case in his throne room. People had tried to confuse its significance, to say it was Kahless's blood on the thing—but again, he had insisted on the truth.

It was Morath's blood. *Morath's.* And it was important to him that they remembered that.

After all, Morath had been a man of honor. And Kahless himself was just a fraud in honor's clothing—a fake, playing the part of the beloved emperor—even if he was the only one who knew it. Fortunately, he would not have to maintain the pretense much longer.

"What is that?" asked Anag.

Kahless looked at the scroll in his hand—the last thing he meant to pack. He chuckled. "Nothing, really. Just a collection of maps to guide me in my travels."

It was a lot more than a collection of maps. It was an account of his life—not the one shrouded in legend, but a true story with all its blemishes. He believed it would be of value someday, when myths were no longer quite so necessary, and Klingons had learned to embrace truth.

His councilor sighed. "There's nothing I can say, then, to talk you out of this? Nothing I can do to make you stay?"

Kahless put his hand on Anag's shoulder. "You are a wise man," he said, "and an honorable one. But you talk entirely too much. Now come, son of Porus, walk me downstairs."

With that, he hefted his pack and made his way to the ground floor. Anag followed a step behind him, saying nothing, no doubt still puzzling over his emperor's motives.

Kahless wished he could have stayed and seen how Anag ruled. He wished he could have been assured of a smooth succession, and prosperity for his people, and the survival of Morath's laws.

But there were no assurances in life. He had learned that long ago. Men might keep promises, but Fate bound itself to no one.

The emperor reached the foot of the stairs, crossed the anteroom, and made his way out into the courtyard. The gates were open. Beyond them, he could see the multitude that had gathered on either side of the road.

Some of the faces closest to him were familiar ones.

They were his retainers, those charged with seeing to his safety. No doubt, the news of his leaving had been more confusing to them than to anyone.

For a single, astonishing moment, he thought he caught a glimpse of Kellein in the crowd. She seemed to be waving to him, standing tall and beautiful in the fading light.

His heart leaped in his chest. How was it possible . . . ?

Then he realized his eyes were playing tricks on him, and his heart sank again. But then, that happened when one got old.

Putting one foot before the other, he walked out through the gates, leaving Anag behind. Nor did he look back.

On one side and then the other, people pushed out from the crowd to speak to him. To appeal to him with their eyes. To pose the same question in different forms, over and over again.

"Master, where are you going?" asked one of his retainers.

He smiled, exposing teeth that were still sharp and strong. "To a place called *Sto-Vo-Kor*," he answered. "Where no one lacks sustenance or bends his knee to anyone else. Where in every hall, the clash of swords rings from the rafters. And where men hold honor above all else."

In truth, he didn't know where he was going, or how long he would survive. But it didn't matter. Like an old *rach'tor* who couldn't hunt anymore, he knew it was simply his time to go.

"Where is this *Sto-Vo-Kor?*" asked a woman.

Kahless thought for a moment. Then he pointed to the

evening sky, where the stars were just making their presence felt.

"There," he said.

Then he pounded the center of his chest with his fist. The impact made a satisfying sound.

"And here," he said.

Last of all, he pointed to his temple. He left his finger there for a moment.

"And here," he told his people. "That is where you will find *Sto-Vo-Kor.*"

Inwardly, he chuckled. Such a cryptic answer. If he was lucky, they would puzzle over it for a hundred years to come.

There were other questions, other pleas for him to stay, other blessings heaped on him. But he didn't stop to respond to them. He just walked east from the citadel, taking strength from their clamor.

Vorcha-doh-baghk! they cried. *Vorcha-doh-baghk, Kahless!*

All hail! All hail Kahless!

It was easy for him to go. They *made* it easy. With their adulation to lighten the pack on his back, Kahless the Unforgettable carved his name into Klingon history.

At least for a while, he thought. No one knew better than Kahless that nothing lasts forever.

CHAPTER **37**

The Modern Age

Night had fallen in the city of Navrath, but the pinkish cast had remained in the sky. In the courtyard of what had been Unarrh's house until just a few moments ago, Picard and his three companions watched Gowron hold their computer chip up to the light of a coal-filled brazier.

It was strange to see a symbol of modern technology in such a stark and primitive-looking place, under such a primal, foreboding sky. But somehow, the smile that reshaped Gowron's face seemed even stranger.

The council leader did not often display a sanguine expression. It spoke volumes that he did so now.

"Empty?" Gowron echoed, eyeing Worf.

The lieutenant nodded. "Empty." he confirmed.

"Completely," Kurn added for emphasis.

"Though no emptier than Unarrh's head," Kahless laughed—wincing at the pain his quip brought on, but determined to ignore it.

Gowron's eyes narrowed as he tried to puzzle it out. "But you *did* visit the relay station, did you not?"

"That we did," the captain agreed. "And we downloaded the accumulated data, just as we described. However, the computer files were damaged in the melee. The parts we were interested in were wiped out, obliterated—though we didn't discover that until it was too late."

The council leader grunted—a sign of admiration, apparently. "Then it was all a deception. You had no incriminating evidence at all."

"However," Worf remarked, "Unarrh and the others didn't know that—so they provided the evidence themselves."

"Indeed," Gowron commented. He looked at the chip again. "And this is your only copy of what you downloaded?"

"It is," the lieutenant confirmed.

"Good," said the council leader. Dropping the chip in the dirt at his feet, he ground it beneath the heel of his boot. "Defense Force data is still Defense Force data. It is not," he remarked pointedly, "for public consumption."

Gowron might have dismissed them at that point. But he didn't. Apparently, he wasn't done with them yet.

"Needless to say," he remarked, "there is still a great deal of work to be done before we can identify the rest of the conspiracy—some of which may be closer to home than I would like."

"Needless to say," the clone echoed.

"However," said Gowron, "I want you to know you have my gratitude for what you have done. My gratitude and that of the Empire."

Picard grunted softly. Gratitude wasn't something one associated with the council leader either.

Kahless elbowed Worf in the ribs. "Tell our esteemed companion the Empire is quite welcome. However, its council leader could have ended this a long time ago, simply by heeding its emperor's concerns."

Gowron gazed at Kahless. But if he was angry, he didn't show it. In fact, the captain thought he saw a hint of admiration for Kahless there, no matter how well the council leader tried to conceal it.

"Perhaps," said Gowron. "Perhaps."

"Well," Picard interjected, "Lieutenant Worf and I would love to stay and chat. Unfortunately, we have other duties—that's the way of Starfleet. And Governor Kurn has been good enough to offer us a ride to the Neutral Zone." He eyed the most powerful Klingon in the Empire. "I'm glad everything worked out, Gowron."

The council leader inclined his head ever so slightly—a sign of respect. "No more glad than I am, Picard."

With that, Gowron crossed the courtyard and exited through the gate in the wall. The captain watched him go, knowing the man still had his share of battles to fight. One could not sit where he sat without looking over one's shoulder now and then.

Picard just hoped the pressures surrounding Gowron would never turn him against the Federation. The last thing he wanted was to cross blades with the son of M'rel.

For a moment, the courtyard was silent except for a rising wind. Then Kahless spat on the ground.

"He has the tongue of a serpent," said the clone. "If I were you in the Federation, I'd be wary of Gowron's gratitude—almost as wary as I would be of his enmity."

The captain silently noted the similarity between the Klingon's views and his own. "I will remember that," he promised.

"On the other hand," said Kahless, "you have nothing to fear from *my* gratitude. And I am grateful indeed." He turned to Worf, to Kurn, and back to Picard. "It was because of you three I was able to rescue the Empire— not to mention the ethos of honor that is its foundation. My namesake would have been proud of you."

"I think I speak for all of us," the captain replied, "when I say we were happy to be of service."

The clone eyed Worf. "I am indebted to you in particular, son of Mogh."

The lieutenant looked at him. "Me?" he echoed.

"Yes. It was you who made me see the truth—that it is not the myths that bolster belief in Kahless, but rather the idea of Kahless that bolsters belief in the myths."

Picard smiled. It was an interesting observation, all right. His security officer had developed a knack lately for coming up with the right insight at the right time.

Kahless clapped Worf on the shoulder. "I hope the majority of our people will end up hanging on to their beliefs, despite the scandals inscribed in that damned scroll."

"I believe they will," the lieutenant told him.

Now that he had time to think about it, the captain believed so, too. If he had learned one thing in all his years in the center seat, it was that a person's faith was often stronger than the most concrete scientific fact.

In time, he mused, this entire affair might become a historical footnote, nothing more. And while the name of Olahg would be forgotten, the name of Kahless would be revered for ages to come.

After all, he wasn't called Kahless the *Unforgettable* for nothing.

EPILOGUE

As Worf entered his quarters, he didn't ask for any illumination. It was the middle of the night, according to the ship's computer, and Alexander would be asleep in the next room.

The lieutenant smiled to himself. It was good to be back on the *Enterprise*. As much as he yearned sometimes to immerse himself in his Klingon heritage, it was here he felt most at home.

This was where his friends were. This was where his sense of duty called the loudest and was most resoundingly answered. Even Kahless had been able to appreciate that.

After all, a Klingon could be a Klingon anywhere—even all by himself, if necessary. Nor was it necessary to be raised as one to *be* one.

Being Klingon was a path one either chose or disdained, a way of looking at things with the heart as much as the mind. It was not always a clear path or an easy one, but it was always there if one looked hard enough for it.

Suddenly, he heard an intake of breath at the far end of the room. At the entrance to Alexander's quarters, a shadow moved.

"Lights!" said a voice, before Worf could make the same request.

A moment later, the lieutenant saw his son standing there in his bedclothes, squinty-eyed with sleep. But when the boy realized who had come in, a smile spread from one side of his face to the other.

"Father!" he cried.

Alexander crossed the room in a leap. Before Worf knew it he was holding the boy to his chest, slender but strong arms wrapped around his neck. The lieutenant grinned as if he were a child as well.

"Alexander," he replied.

Worf said nothing more than that, just the boy's name. But it carried all the depths and shades of emotion clamoring inside him.

"I was worried about you," Alexander confessed.

The lieutenant nodded. "I knew you would be."

Leaning away from him, the boy looked at him. "Did everything go all right? Is the homeworld okay now?"

"Yes," Worf assured him. "The homeworld is fine."

For now, he thought. As for as long as Kahless and Kurn and others like them refused to let their guards down.

Alexander's eyes narrowed. "And what about you, Father? Are *you* okay?"

The Klingon was surprised by the question. "As you can see," he began, "I am in good health."

The boy shook his head. "No, I mean *inside.* Are you okay with what it said in the scrolls?"

Worf's first impulse was to scold his son for accessing what he had intended to be private property. Then he remembered that he hadn't left any instructions to that effect, or taken any precautions against Alexander's prying.

Based on such evidence, Deanna would have said he *wanted* the boy to see the scrolls. Subconsciously, at least. And he wasn't absolutely certain she wouldn't have been right.

"Yes," he answered, putting the lecture aside for another time. "I have accepted what it said in the scrolls. I am . . . okay."

Alexander smiled. "Good. I hate it when you're unhappy."

Worf eyed the boy. "Right now, it would make me happy to see you in bed. It is late and you have school tomorrow."

His son frowned. "Okay. But can you sit with me a while? Just a few minutes maybe, until I fall asleep?"

It was not the sort of request a Klingon child made to his parent. But then, the boy was only *three-quarters* Klingon.

"Actually," the lieutenant said, "I was about to suggest that myself."

As he returned Alexander to his room, Worf basked in the glow of his progeny. That was a part of being a Klingon too.

A very *important* part.

Look for STAR TREK Fiction from Pocket Books

Star Trek®: The Original Series

Star Trek: The Next Generation®

Star Trek: Deep Space Nine®

Star Trek: Voyager®

Flashback • Diane Carey

**It is the Day of Reckoning
It is the Day of Judgment
It is . . .**

STAR TREK

THE DAY OF HONOR

**A Four-Part Klingon Saga
That Spans the Generations**

**Coming Fall '97
from Pocket Books**

STAR TREK
THE DAY OF HONOR

A Four-Part Klingon Saga

Coming Fall '97
from Pocket Books

Following the overwhelmingly popular **STAR TREK: INVASION!** series (over 1,000,000 copies in print), next spring Pocket Books will present **STAR TREK: THE DAY OF HONOR,** a four-part series centered around the most important Klingon holiday.

To a true Klingon warrior, no occasion is more sacred than **The Day of Honor,** the day when he must reflect on his own honor and that of his enemies. But honor always exacts its price.

The story begins in *Star Trek: The Next Generation:* **ANCIENT BLOOD** by Diane Carey (creator of **STAR TREK: INVASION!**), continues in *Star Trek: Deep Space Nine:* **ARMAGEDDON SKY** by L. A. Graf and *Star Trek: Voyager:* **HER KLINGON SOUL** by Michael Jan Friedman, and concludes in *Star Trek: The Original Series:* **TREATY'S LAW** by Dean Wesley Smith and Kristine Kathryn Rusch, which tells the story of the founding of The Day of Honor.

STAR TREK
THE DAY OF HONOR

<u>**ON SALE IN MID-AUGUST**</u>

THE DAY OF HONOR

Book One of Four

ANCIENT BLOOD

by

Diane Carey

Worf finds his honor tested when he goes undercover to infiltrate a planetary criminal network. How can he root out the corruption on New Delphi without resorting to deceit and treachery himself? Worf's dilemma is shared by his son, Alexander, who is searching for the true meaning of honor in the human side of his heritage. Along with his son, Worf must confront deadly danger that threatens far more than just his life.

STAR TREK
THE DAY OF HONOR

<u>**ON SALE IN MID-AUGUST**</u>

THE DAY OF HONOR

Book Two of Four

ARMAGEDDON SKY

by

L. A. Graf

A hunded years ago he was Commander Kor of the Klingon Empire, and one of the founders of The Day of Honor. Now, having thrown away the Sword of Kahless, he is nothing but a harmless old man—or is he? While Dax and Bashir fight to save a colony of Klingons banished to Cardassian territory for their loyalty to Worf's family, Worf and Kor must face the hard choices that their honor has led them into.

STAR TREK
THE DAY OF HONOR

ON SALE IN MID-SEPTEMBER

STAR TREK
VOYAGER

THE DAY OF HONOR

Book Three of Four

HER KLINGON SOUL

by

Michael Jan Friedman

Even light-years from the Klingon Empire, The Day of Honor is known. And sometimes honor is found in the most unlikely places.

Lieutenant B'Elanna Torres has never cared for The Day of Honor. The holiday is an unwelcome reminder of the Klingon heritage she has tried to repress. But when Torres and Ensign Harry Kim are captured by alien slavers and forced to mine deadly radioactive ore, B'Elanna will need all her strength and cunning to survive—and her honor as well.

STAR TREK
THE DAY OF HONOR

<u>ON SALE IN MID-SEPTEMBER</u>

STAR TREK®

THE DAY OF HONOR

Book Four of Four

TREATY'S LAW
by
Dean Wesley Smith and
Kristine Kathryn Rusch

By the time of *Star Trek: The Next Generation*, The Day of Honor is celebrated throughout the Klingon Empire. But every tradition has its starting place.

Signi Beta is an M-Class planet ideal for farming. The terms of the Organian peace treaty have given the planet to the Klingon Empire. Captain Kirk is not happy to lose this world to Commander Kor, his frequent enemy. But when a mysterious fleet attacks both the Klingons and the *Enterprise*, Kirk and Kor must rely on each other's honor—or neither of them will live through the day.